ORION
LOST

ORION LOST

ALASTAIR CHISHOLM

nosy crow

To Rose and Amelie, who are the masters of their own ships.
And to Catherine, for everything.
A.C.

First published in the UK in 2020 by Nosy Crow Ltd
The Crow's Nest, 14 Baden Place
Crosby Row, London, SE1 1YW, UK

Nosy Crow and associated logos are trademarks and/or registered
trademarks of Nosy Crow Ltd

Text © Alastair Chisholm, 2020
Cover illustration © Dan Mumford, 2020

The right of Alastair Chisholm to be identified as the author of this
work has been asserted by him in accordance with the Copyright,
Designs and Patents Act, 1988

Printed and bound in Great Britain by Clays Ltd, Elcograf S.p.A.
Typeset by Tiger Media

Papers used by Nosy Crow are made from wood grown in sustainable
forests.

ISBN: 978 1 78800 592 0

www.nosycrow.com

Author's note

In this book you will meet an alien species, called the *Videshi*. Some of you may know that this is a real word – in Hindi, *Videshi* (विदेशी) means *foreign*, or *foreigner*, or *stranger*.

This book takes place in the future, and when I was imagining the world of the future, I thought that India would probably become a prominent power, perhaps even the leading spacefaring nation – the captains and commanders of space exploration. I imagined that it might be an Indian crew who met the first alien ship. What would they call this alien? I thought they might call it *stranger*. *Foreigner*. *Alien*. And they would report it back to the people of Earth, who would use their word ... *Videshi*.

Prologue

There was a ship, in space, lost.

It was a large, old, mining transport, designed for long-haul trips to small moons and asteroids. The enormous squat engines and hydrogen scoop underneath gave cheap and steady propulsion, but not much acceleration. The command module was small, but its cargo section was huge, taking up most of the ship.

It was broadcasting a radio signal: —*Earth ship* Orion, *four months out of Earth and heading for Eos Five. Our location is Sector 278. Coordinates 549 dash 2 by 902 dash 8 as of*—

An experienced miner might notice odd things about the ship. It had been patched and refitted, and its life support systems – gravity, oxygen, food processing – extended to cope with a much larger crew. Extra equipment was fastened round the hull, designed for planet exploration. Rovers, diggers, habitats, all with landing gear but no launch rockets of their own. They could land but they'd never take off again.

Not a mining transport any more then, but a colony ship, taking a group of brave new-worlders off to some distant settlement, and then staying to help them set up.

—*currently adrift*, said the message, *and we have no propulsion, although our Jump drive is functioning.*

Four large power generators bulged out near the base, but two of them were cold and dark and only a few of the ship's outer lights were working. It was turning gently, and as it turned, it revealed an enormous scorched rupture near one of the engines.

We have experienced severe damage to the ship.

A ship in deep space hardly ever sent out a distress signal. What would be the point? Ships were like tiny motes of dust in the vast sky, so far apart that the chance of one coming across another by accident was effectively zero. Near Earth, or around the Solar System, sure, perhaps heading to one of the older and more established colonies, on a well-known route. But not out here. Here you could travel for six months and see no one, and no evidence that anyone else had ever existed. Here there were no friends.

Command has been compromised and we are unable to establish order. All command crew ranked able-bodied or higher are disabled and cannot resume control.

In fact, this far out – so far from Earth you could barely see its sun as a tiny flickering star – if you found anyone at all, it would be more likely to be Scrapers, pirates and thieves. Or worse still, the mysterious, alien Videshi: strange, half hidden, half understood, terrifying.

A ship in deep space hardly ever sent out a distress signal, because if you were helpless enough to send one, then you did not want to be found.

The message repeated: *This is a general Mayday from the Earth ship* Orion, *four months out of Earth…*

Something found them.

1

Beth

"I think I'm going to be sick," said Beth.

Her mum, strapped into her seat like the other passengers and crew of the shuttlecraft, looked up from her mission manual.

"No you're not," she said.

"No, really, I don't feel so good. It's the gravity, it's—"

"No, you're *not*." Beth's mum leaned across and gazed into her eyes. "I know it was pretty intense when we launched. And yes, zero gravity is strange, and a long time ago people *did* get sick, but not these days. You've had your pill, and you'll be fine. Trust me."

Beth nodded. She didn't feel fine. She felt as if her stomach was turning over and over, floating free and ready to jump in any direction. She tried to smile.

"OK … I guess. I feel a bit funny, though."

Her dad turned to her and grinned. "Me too. I think everyone's twitchy, don't you?"

Beth looked around.

The ship they were on – the *transport*, her mum called it – had about sixty seats, all full. Suitcases were strapped against the walls and ceiling to stop them flying around during launch, but a few of them had been unfastened since; they trailed tendrils of Velcro and bobbed slightly, like jellyfish. Most of the passengers were also strapped in, though some had undone their webbing after take-off.

Take-off... Wow. Beth had flown on planes and travelled on the Hoop, but she'd never felt anything like the launch, when the transport and everyone on it had hurled into the sky like a thrown pebble. She hadn't felt sick then; instead there had been a sensation that she was going to faint, that she was melting into the chair, that she was on the world's biggest, maddest roller coaster and *she couldn't get off*.

Then the odd awareness of reaching the top of the climb, and the weightlessness, and that moment just before you fall back down to Earth ... only there was no falling back. Instead they fell *forward*, very slightly, and Beth had watched in astonishment as one end of her strap had floated, gently, in front of her.

And then the seat-belts had unlocked and most of the children had scrabbled to free themselves, and the adults had pretended that it was all completely normal. But they'd been shaking and gaping as much as the kids.

That was two hours ago. After the launch, there had been the long slow drift towards the exit point, and the sight of Earth through a thick window, gradually shrinking. Gasps as the Moon came into sight – still small and far away, but perfectly clear. And after a while, the wonder and astonishment becoming slowly normal.

"We'll see the *Orion* soon," said her mum. "Look out for it, towards the left."

Beth peered through the porthole but couldn't see anything. She shrugged. It would show up on the screen soon enough – the portholes were just a luxury, only on this ship, command class. The other transports were sealed in and twice as full. Benefits of her mum's command position as a lieutenant. Beth smiled. Not quite as posh as the *first*-class cabin ahead, for the captain and senior officers, but even so. Pretty cool.

Her stomach was still bouncing and jumping around. She wondered if Dad was right, if everyone else was really feeling like this. The other children seemed fine. One girl, three rows down, was typing rapidly at a pad on her lap and staring at two screens that floated in front of her, held in place with some sort of thin elastic. Her hair was tied into dozens of thin black braids drifting around her head, fastened with pink butterfly clips; the screens bobbed and turned and the girl's head bobbed with them. *How is she OK?* wondered Beth.

The other girl felt her looking, glanced up and waved. Beth managed a pallid smile and moved her hand in a tiny 'hello' motion.

Beneath her, she felt a rumble and a momentary sense of weight to one side.

"Look," Mum said. "You can see her on the screen."

On the display panel, small but very clear, hung a tiny ship, small as an acorn and about the same shape, fat and round. As it came into focus, passengers looked up from their pads, stopped their conversations. Someone gave a small whoop and people laughed.

"Isn't she something?" said Mum. They stared at the little acorn.

"I dunno," drawled Dad. "Looks a bit small to me."

"Oh, she's not!" exclaimed Beth. "She's six hundred and seventy-two metres end to end and four hundred side to side, and – oh, shut up." Her father grinned and she rolled her eyes.

Mum said, "Ignore him. She's a good size. Plenty of storage, plenty of room for berths." She smirked. "Even enough for your space chickens, dear."

"Hah!" he snorted. "And space *pigs*, I'll have you know. And space wheat, and space courgettes, and a whole

7

space farm for that matter. And if you don't want to be eating flavoured yeast all the way to Eos Five then you'll be nice about them, and nice to the farmer."

Her mum sniffed. "Nothing wrong with transport rations; I've eaten them many times. And your two pigs aren't going to feed a thousand colonists. But don't you worry – we'll still let you have your little garden."

"You do know which way to point that old pile of junk, do you?" he asked. "Could be more than nine months. I've seen you trying to read a map before."

They glared at each other and then giggled.

"Shut *up*, you two," said Beth, going red. "Everyone's *looking*."

Mum waved a hand. "Let them." She shook her head. "Anyway, I won't be navigating. I'm purely third class, scraped in by my knuckles. I'll mostly be making the coffee."

Beth looked across at her. She couldn't imagine anyone ordering Lieutenant Carol McKay to make coffee. With a face apparently chiselled from stone, Beth's mum had grey eyes that looked like they were staring into a storm at sea, and white-blonde hair cropped into an army bob. She was born to lead a battalion into battle. Compared to her, Dad seemed like a cheerful bag of laundry.

The *Orion* was closer now, and Beth stared at the screen.

It *did* look like an acorn. And for the next nine months it would be their home. They would live in it, all bundled together, and it would carry them far, far away – so far it was impossible to imagine – to a tiny prick of light, and a tiny pebble around that light, and then…

"It's a new world out there," said Mum softly. "Ship life is awkward sometimes, but it's not so bad. And when we get to Eos Five … there's a future waiting for us. A chance to make our own decisions, create our own lives."

"I know," said Beth. "But what if something happens on the trip? What about the Scrapers? Or the Videshi…" She shuddered.

Beth's mum shook her head. "No. We're going well away from the common routes. And space is so … *big*. There's no chance of meeting anything, really. Trust me – the worst thing that might happen on this trip is boredom." She bumped heads gently with Beth. "I know you're nervous, but it will be fine. And when we get there it will be hard work. But it will be *ours*."

She grinned, and despite her worries, Beth grinned back. Yes. She could do this. Everything was going to be great. Yes.

Then she was sick.

2
Day One

Their cabin was small, and beautiful.

Beth had known roughly what to expect; she'd seen layout plans back on Earth and taken the virtual tour. It was like a caravan, or a ship's kitchen, hiding storage space in secret compartments and nooks. Every square metre of wall had cupboard doors. There was a sofa with drawers underneath and a large screen that folded away. Everything seemed to be made of wood, which was nice, even though she knew it wasn't real. A warm carpet felt soft underfoot as she walked in.

Walking... Thank *god*. When they'd finally docked with the *Orion*, after what seemed like hours of waiting (with the faint smell of sick and cleaning foam pervading the shuttle, and everyone pretending not to notice), Beth had felt the gentle pressure of gravity push her into her seat and had groaned with relief.

Dad had given her a hug. "That's it, love," he'd said.

10

"You made it. Normal gravity from now on, eh?"

She knew this wasn't quite true. The 'gravity' on board *Orion* was a force generated from the middle of the ship, like an apple core. If you went out to the edges you would feel it less, and as you climbed down inwards you would feel it more … until you reached the centre, and it simply disappeared.

Weirder still was that it always pulled towards the core, so people round the far side of the ship seemed 'upside down' compared to you. Normally you couldn't see them, but as you moved towards the front you would meet them in corridors that came together as the gravity faded away. The thought of it made Beth's stomach wobble again.

But here everything seemed normal. Her legs lifted her and moved her about, things stayed where you left them, and she walked into their new home and looked around.

The ceiling was low, but there was space to stand up. They had a tiny kitchen nook, enough to make tea or coffee or a snack; they would be eating from the ship canteens for the most part. Her parents had one small bedroom and Beth another, even smaller, just a narrow raised bed with cupboards and a tiny workspace underneath. The opposite wall was less than an arm's reach away; it was like living inside an egg. She loved it the moment she saw it.

She unpacked in ten minutes. A pile of clothes dumped into the cupboards, a precious few knick-knacks on a thin shelf. Her diary – an actual physical book, a real luxury and her one true indulgence – stowed safe with some pens under her pillow. A couple of posters on the ceiling, and she was done. She sat on the bed and looked around, happy.

Her mum knocked on the wall next to her door and leaned in. "Hey."

"Hey," said Beth, smiling.

"All unpacked? Everything neatly folded and put away?"

"Oh, sure."

"Uh-huh." Beth's mum looked sceptical. "Dad's gone to the farm to see how the animals are doing – want to join him?"

Beth shrugged. "Maybe later. Can I explore?"

Mum nodded. "If you head towards the front, you should be able to find the cafeteria. That's probably where everyone will be. If you get lost, ask the ship."

So Beth found herself outside the cabin, trying to remember whether the front of the ship was left or right. She picked left and wandered along, examining everything.

The corridors were squat and plain – no fake wood

here, just metal and cream paint that still smelled recent. Messages and indicators flickered by on display panels along the walls. The *Orion* was an old ship and even with the new paint the corridors felt aged.

There was a faint rumbling sound everywhere she went, perhaps from the generators. Sometimes the corridor sloped downwards, and occasionally she came to a split and picked directions at random. They always seemed to lead to more corridors; the ship felt *huge*.

Eventually she gave up.

"Ship," she said, and in front of her a head appeared: the face of Ship, the *Orion*'s central interface.

The head was a hologram, apparently floating. It was blue, and completely smooth and bald. The designers had shied away from making it look *too* human, because that sort of thing creeped people out. But its eyes were very lifelike.

"Hello, Beth." Ship's voice was calm and neutral, neither warm nor cold.

"Can you tell me how to get to the cafeteria?" Beth asked.

"There are six cafeterias on board the *Orion*. One is for command personnel only, two are located towards the stern, two are—"

"Just the one nearest our cabin, please."

If the avatar was upset at being interrupted, it didn't show it.

"The nearest cafeteria is one hundred metres away. Turn round and follow the corridor until it branches. Take the left corridor. I will show these directions on the screen."

The panel next to Ship blinked and a little figure appeared in orange. A line traced out from the figure, back along the corridor.

"Thank you," said Beth.

"You are welcome," said Ship, and disappeared.

Turning round, Beth followed the line. As she passed each panel it lit up with her trail, and at the junction it blinked and she obediently turned left. She realised there was someone up ahead, coming towards her, chattering and feet pounding. For a moment she—

"Argh!"

Someone ricocheted round the corner and crashed into her, knocking her to the ground. Pads and other gadgets bounced around them.

"Oops! Sorry! Ha ha!" It was a small girl in a pink T-shirt, who was now scurrying around and picking up her things. She had black braided hair decorated with butterfly clips. Beth realised dazedly that she was the girl from the transport.

"*Up* you come, hello!" She pulled Beth up and then stared at her, then at one of her pads, then at Beth again.

"Hello … Beth!" she said proudly. She peered again. "Beth McKay, hello! I'm Limit. Isn't this *awesome?*"

"Sorry, what?"

"This *ship*. Isn't she great? Have you seen the gravity? It's fantastic, it's like field lines, have you seen how it changes in waves? *Awesome*. You were on the transport!"

Beth blinked.

"And then you were *sooooooo* sick, it was *awesome*. Mikkel – this is her, the girl who was sick! It's the zero-g, it totally messes with you, plus it's completely unhealthy long-term and does stuff with your bones which is why they put in the gravity here even though it's so expensive and uses power like crazy. *Have* you noticed the field lines?"

"Wait!" croaked Beth. She held up one hand. "Wait a minute. Er. Hello. I'm Beth."

"I *know*, you're Beth McKay, and your mum is … comms ops, and your dad is … *cool*, applied agriculture –" the girl read the information off her pad – "and you're in Cabin Sixteen/Thirty-two and, and—"

"Lauryn, she knows this."

For the first time, Beth noticed the boy next to them. He was shorter than Beth, thin and pale with white-blonde hair, and he wore rumpled jeans and a grey jumper. His

15

eyes were grey too, and pale, peering through his fringe. He spoke with a soft Norwegian accent, or perhaps Swedish, and his face had a slightly dreamy look, as if he was only half there. He smiled gently at Beth.

The girl stopped and grinned. "Hello," she said cheerfully.

"Hello … Lauryn?"

Lauryn nodded. "Yeah, but that's just my normal name. My *handle* is –" she raised a hand and made some sort of gesture – "*Limit*. You should call me that."

"Limit?"

"Totally! What's your handle?"

"I'm just Beth."

"That's OK, you'll think of something. This is Mikkel; he doesn't have a proper name yet either." Mikkel nodded.

Lauryn/Limit pointed her pad at Beth. "We've been tracking you!"

"What?"

"On the pad! I've figured out how! We saw you coming down the corridor."

"I told her we could ask Ship," said Mikkel, shrugging, "But she wanted to work it out herself."

"Why were you tracking me?"

"Well … you were the only one I could find. The tracker's got a limited range. But also because you were so *cool* when you threw up – *bleurghhhh!*" She mimed being sick, then turned to Mikkel. "You should have seen it, zero-g sick, it just went *everywhere*, and then all these cool flying robots came down, and *sucked* it up, and everyone was, like, *eeeeeewww*, and—"

"OK!" snapped Beth. "Yes, I was sick. It was the zero grav—"

"That's what I *said*. That's why the gravity here is so awesome. In fact, this ship is awesome all *over*. Have you scanned the engines yet?"

"Er, no?"

"You should! They have some sweet automation, it's all wired to Ship, it's completely routable everywhere and all the cabling is embedded into the infrastructure and, and…"

"It's awesome?" ventured Beth.

Lauryn nodded wildly. "*Totally*." She trotted off down the hallway. "C'mon," she said, waving her pad. "I want to try this some more."

Mikkel followed her and Beth found herself pulled along in their wake. "Try what? Where are we going?"

Mikkel said, "We are trying Lauryn's app. It works out who people are by—"

"By scanning their faces and matching them to the pre-flight profiles they put up, you know, where they

17

introduced everyone. Look—" Lauryn thrust the pad at Beth, who saw a brief glimpse of her passport photo. "It taps into Ship's processors for the face recognition. Anyway, I want to try it out with a crowd, so – here goes!"

She paused, and Beth realised that they were at the entrance to the cafeteria. Lauryn dived in, and Mikkel too, leaving Beth standing outside on her own. She shook her head in bemusement, and then grinned.

Here goes, she thought, and followed them in.

3

Vihaan

The cafeteria was a large, brightly lit space, part refectory, part coffee house, with tables scattered around and a few sofas at the back. The serving area was automated and staffed by small kitchen robots.

It was noisy, with groups of kids from about nine and up chattering, shouting and running around. There were no adults – instead, Ship was keeping order. She was everywhere, her disembodied blue heads holding dozens of conversations.

Lauryn was already heading at speed towards a group near the door. They seemed older than Beth, fifteen or so, and she realised that everyone had more or less clumped together into age groups. Lauryn wielded the pad at them and talked rapidly.

"—Marcus Ackar, you're from Germany, cool, and you're Fiona Howard, you're a gymnast – awesome! – and you like dogs…" The teenagers looked at her with a mix of bemusement, humour and mild contempt, but Lauryn didn't seem to notice.

Mikkel and Beth watched her.

"She's enthusiastic, isn't she?" said Beth.

Mikkel smiled. "She found me when I was ten metres out of my cabin," he said in his soft, precise voice, "and I think she has not stopped talking yet."

They ordered milkshakes from the little serving droids and took them over to the empty end of a table. Mikkel nodded towards a large bright mural of a landscape under a red sun, occupying one whole wall of the cafeteria. "Look," he said. "Our new world."

Beth realised it was a moving simulation of a landscape, with a title: "EOS FIVE". Their new home… It looked similar to Earth, though the colours were different. Eos was a dwarf star and its light was redder, giving the scene an orange cast. The grass was slightly blue, genetically altered to cope better with the alien light and soil. It stretched across the world under orange-blue skies and soft clouds.

"It's beautiful," she said.

"Yes… But it does not look like that, hey?"

"I know," said Beth. "They're still cooking it. I saw the stream about the terraforming machines." Right now, she knew, the colony point at Eos Five was covered in hundreds of machines, robots and terraformers; planting the seeds, carving rivers, encouraging soil microbes, preparing the land. It would be years – decades, centuries, perhaps – before the whole planet was transformed.

"It's all really rough and wild out there just now," she said.

"Yes," he said, nodding seriously. "But we are rugged and adventurous." After a moment Beth realised he was joking and sniggered.

"That's me, for sure," she agreed.

"I am studying Advanced and Xeno Languages," he said. "This colony, it is all English speakers, but if we meet an alien I will be ready. I know the Videshi for *I surrender – please do not kill me*." Again, his face was absolutely serious, and then he gave a very tiny smile.

Beth laughed. "Always a handy skill," she said. "Better than me. I'm doing Command Training." She always felt slightly embarrassed to say it out loud. "It's what they give you if you don't have any actual skills, I think. I don't know if I'm really the leader type."

"I should salute, yes?"

"Oh, for sure," she said. "I wish— Hey, is that Lauryn?"

Mikkel turned. At the other end of the cafeteria a row was breaking out. A large boy was laughing and holding a pad up in the air, and Lauryn was jumping up for it.

21

"C'mon, tiny!" he yelled, "You can make it! C'mon!" Lauryn nearly reached it, but the boy pushed her and she fell over.

"I think it is—" started Mikkel, but he was already alone.

Lauryn had picked herself up. She was blinking, as if trying not to cry.

"Please give it back," she said in a small voice.

The boy held it out, but he was still grinning.

"Listen up, tiny," he said. "You keep your nerdy little toys away from us. Go back to your own end with the preschoolers, OK? Or next time—"

"Or next time *what*?" snapped Beth. She shot in between Lauryn and the boy and squared up to him. "You give it back to her *now*." Her blood pumped in her ears and she felt the hot, slightly dizzy sensation of knowing she was about to do something reckless.

The boy looked surprised. "What?"

"NOW!" Beth shouted. People turned and stared, and the boy looked uncertain, but he didn't back down. Beth, meanwhile, was realising that he was a good head taller than her and looked like he could fight. But her anger kept her going.

The boy's eyes flicked to someone behind Beth, as if for help. Beth whirled round. Sitting across from them, leaning back on a chair, sat another boy – about her age, maybe older, with light brown skin and black, short-cropped hair. He wore a military-style jumpsuit that should have looked dorky but on him seemed *right*. He gazed at them and smiled, as if he found the scene amusing.

He stood up and walked across. "Why are you screaming?" he asked Beth. He kept his voice low and calm, but looked at her as if she was an unruly servant.

But Beth wasn't about to be intimidated. "This lummock yours?" she demanded. "You like watching him bully people? You *proud* of that?"

The boy grinned. His teeth were straight and very white. "Arnold," he said, without looking away from Beth, "give the little girl back her toy."

The other boy – Arnold – threw the pad on to the ground near Lauryn, and Beth heard it scrape as it landed. Lauryn pounced on it and then shouted, "I'm *not* a little girl!"

The boy smiled again. "You're a girl, and you are certainly little. Arnold has explained that you shouldn't be bothering your elders and betters."

His voice stayed calm, quiet. It was hypnotic. Beth felt herself deflating.

"And who are you to be so bloody mighty?" she

managed. "You think you're so *special?*"

He laughed, and so did some of the others around her. But before he could answer, the face of Ship appeared between them.

"Excuse me," it said. "This activity is disturbing the other children. Also, property damage has occurred. Is everything all right?"

"Absolutely," said the boy smoothly. "We were just advising some of the less *mature* children on proper behaviour around others."

"That's a lie!" snapped Beth.

Ship paused for a second and then said, "Your account is inconsistent with the actions recorded in this area, Vihaan. Please clarify."

"My apologies," said Vihaan, still smiling. "I'm sure everything is fine now."

Beth hissed, but Lauryn was pulling her away. She heard Ship say, "Your father has asked me to discuss all such interactions with him, Vihaan. Is there anything you wish me to add?" and to her satisfaction she saw a scowl cloud the boy's face.

Then they were away, Lauryn on one side and Mikkel on the other. Lauryn stared up at Beth in wonder.

"You. Were. *Awesome.*" she said.

"Not leadership material, hey?" asked Mikkel.

"Um." Now it was over, Beth felt only embarrassment. And she noticed the scrape on Lauryn's pad. *If I hadn't done that, she'd probably have got it back in one piece*, she thought. *Why did I go rushing in like that?*

"Do you know who that *was*? Do you know? *Do* you?" Lauryn was almost dancing along beside her.

"What? Er, no. Should I?"

Even Mikkel laughed. "That was *Vihaan Joshi*," he said. "Son of *Amarjeet* Joshi, yes?"

Beth stopped. "What, really?"

Amarjeet Joshi. *Captain* Amarjeet Joshi, commander of the *Orion* and everyone on it.

"Oh no." She clapped a hand over her face. "Mum's going to *kill* me."

4

Sleeping

A week later, the *Orion* had her official launch party.

By now she was travelling at over a hundred thousand kilometres an hour and they were far from Earth, well beyond the Moon, and a sizeable fraction of the distance to Mars. The ship had settled in now, with last-minute repairs and reorganisations complete, and they were nearing their first Jump point. The essential part of their journey was about to start, and so Captain Joshi had arranged the launch party to celebrate.

He stood at the front in his white formal dress uniform, next to a screen that showed a maintenance hatch on the outer hull. As the crowd watched, one of the Gizmos – the large maintenance robots aboard ship – left the ship, carrying a small bottle of champagne. It smashed the bottle against the side of the hull and the champagne vaporised into space, and the sky burst into glorious colour as hundreds of tiny firework microsatellites created a laser lightshow.

A man came out of the crowd and nodded to the captain. He too wore a white dress uniform, although Beth thought that he looked rather better in his than Captain Joshi. He was younger, and a little shorter; he had high cheekbones and deep brown, almost black, eyes, a very crisp black quiff of hair and a neat stubble beard. He was smiling at the light show.

"Who's the man next to the captain?" Beth asked.

Beth's mum looked up. "That would be Captain Kier," she said. "He's captain of the *Sparrowhawk*, our scout ship. He'll be joining us for the whole trip." She glanced across at Beth. "Handsome, isn't he?" she asked, sounding amused.

"Mu-um," muttered Beth. She felt her face go a little red and ducked her head, and it took her a few moments to realise there was someone standing next to her chair.

"Good evening, Lieutenant McKay," said Captain Joshi.

Beth looked up.

Captain Joshi was very tall, and his gleaming bald head made him seem taller. He had a long, slightly curved nose, dark eyes and thick eyebrows. He was smiling politely, but his manner suggested he would rather be under enemy fire than at a party. Next to him stood Captain Kier, with one hand tucked in a pocket and a glass of champagne in the other.

"Good evening, captains," said Beth's mum. "May I introduce my husband, Douglas? And this is my daughter, Beth."

The captains and Beth's dad nodded to each other. Captain Joshi started asking questions about the farm, and Kier turned to Beth.

"Hey," he said. "I'm Henry."

"Hi," she said.

He *was* handsome, she thought, and seemed far too young to be a captain, but he carried himself with a smiling confidence, somehow relaxed and ready for action at the same time. Unlike most adults, whose gaze tended to drift over the children in search of someone more interesting to talk to, he looked directly at her – as if he was genuinely interested in what she thought.

It was such a surprise she realised that she couldn't, in fact, think of anything. She coughed. "So, ah… You're a captain then?" she managed. A tiny voice inside her wailed in embarrassment. *Stupid, stupid question.* But he didn't seem to mind.

"No, I'm just a glorified pilot," he said, and shrugged. "The *Sparrowhawk* is a one-person scout ship – she's tiny, really. But they gave me this suit for free, so I thought I'd

28

try it out." He held his arms out and posed. "What do you think?"

She grinned. "Pretty sharp."

"Why, thank you." He grinned back. His accent was Californian, and he spoke with a humorous and self-deprecating twang.

"It sounds dangerous," said Beth. "Mum was a scout once, for the army. Some of her stories are a bit scary."

But Kier shook his head. "It's usually very boring. Most missions, the hardest thing I have to do is stay awake! Don't believe her – you can't trust anything grown-ups tell you, you know."

She smiled. "Even you?"

Kier laughed. "Oh, especially me!"

Captain Joshi turned. "Ah, Beth," he said. "Good evening. I've been hearing about *you* already. I understand you've already met my son?"

Beth's mouth went dry. Kier lifted an eyebrow. "Um…"

The captain leaned slightly towards her and held a hand up. "Ship showed me the footage of the incident," he said. "It takes courage to put yourself between your friends and danger. *But* – your mother would tell you that courage is useless without discipline, hmm?" He stood up straight. "I understand you'll be taking the Command classes," he said. "I'm sure my son will be delighted to see you there." He smiled at them in a distracted way, as if checking it off a to-do list, nodded to them all and turned to another table. As they left, Captain Kier gave Beth a wink.

Beth stared at her plate for a moment, red-faced. When she looked up, Mum was looking at her with a strange, appraising expression. Was she smiling?

"Well," said Beth's dad. "First week and already the captain knows your name. You're clearly on the fast track to success – cheers!" He raised his glass and grinned, and Beth laughed despite herself.

With the *Orion* officially launched, they were ready for their first big step across space. The week of acceleration had lifted her up to enormous speed; at her current velocity the *Orion* could go all the way round the Earth in only twenty minutes. But Eos, the tiny star they were heading towards, was twenty-six light years away – hundreds of millions, *billions* of kilometres. It would take almost three hundred thousand years to reach it, travelling normally.

That was why they Jumped.

"It's like this," her mum had explained, many months before, when they were still back on Earth. They'd been eating dinner, and she pinched two points in the tablecloth in front of them.

"How far apart are these points?"

Beth had shrugged. "Half a metre?"

"Sure. Now, imagine we could do … *this*." She lifted the cloth up and pulled the points together so that they touched.

"Now how far?"

"But…" Beth had frowned. "But we can't just do that with space, can we? I mean, what about everyone else … living there?"

"That's the freaky thing," said Mum. "It's *already* like that. We think space is like a big room where you go forward, backward, up, down, left, right; but it's more like … like a ball of string. It seems solid, but it's actually one long strand wrapped over and over, bumping up against itself. When we Jump, we skip across the bumps."

Beth looked at the tablecloth. "Really?"

Her mum laughed. "Well … honestly, no, it's a lot more complicated than that. How about this – the universe is *really weird*, and sometimes we can do *really weird* stuff and pretend it makes sense. Someone understands it, but it sure ain't me, kiddo."

"Oh. So why do we have to Sleep?"

"Well … turns out it's a bit *too* weird. The Jump does something to our consciousness. Scrambles it. Anything more complicated than a lugworm comes out comatose

31

and never wakes up. It happens to computers as well – circuits fry, CPUs crash. There's just no way to go through the Jump with your mind intact.

"So…" She shrugged. "We cheat. We make a copy of our consciousness – everything we know, everything that makes us who we are. The ship copies its memories too. Then we go to Sleep, the ship sets course for a Jump, hibernates … and wakes up a second later. It boots up, downloads its backup, then it downloads *our* backups, then we Wake – and we've travelled about two hundred billion klicks."

"*Seriously?*"

Mum nodded. "Seriously. I mean, it's a bit more complex than that. Getting the ship to wake up again was a tricky problem."

"But … does the ship know all your thoughts, then?"

"No – but good thinking! No. People thought it could, but mind-state is just too complex. The ship can't read your state, or change it. It can only store it and transfer it back. It's weird, but it works, and we've never had a failed Jump."

They'd gone on to talk about Eos Five, their new home, and what would have to be left behind, and the habitat they would live in, and Beth never gave the Jump another thought.

Now it was time. The children would Sleep first, then non-essential crew, then the rest. They would Jump, and then they would be Woken in reverse order – essential crew, non-essential, and finally the children.

So Beth and the others now stood in a cargo container filled with sleep pods, ready to climb in. Each child had an adult with them; Beth was with her mum. Beth thought the other children looked a little nervous, except for Lauryn, who had to be physically restrained from tapping at her pod's control panel.

Ship's hologram floated at the front of the room, and on its signal they climbed up and into their pods. They were comfortable; each one had a foam mattress and a pillow.

Beth's mum looked in over the top. "OK?"

"Sure."

Ship said, "The Jump will take less than zero point zero five seconds to complete; however, your Wake-up will be delayed while the crew ensure everything is safe. When you Wake you may experience some disorientation; this is normal and will pass.

"When you are ready, please let your carer know."

Beth looked up at her mum and gave the thumbs-up. A few seconds later, the sides of the pod slid up, then across, then completely over her…

…and Beth McKay was gone.

It was pitch black. All the lights were out. There had never been light. There was no memory of light. There was nothing.

Then … something. A thought? An idea that there had been something before; an awareness of something now. A feeling. *Thump … thump … thump…*

It was something familiar, it was something, it was … a *heartbeat*.

The thing in the darkness listened to the sound of this *heartbeat* for a long time. Then it thought: I am alive. The black was now a red glow, although there was still nothing to see. And there was a thin soft sound that went in … out … in…

Breathing. I am alive. There is somebody I *was*.

"Beth?"

That was new. A sound, but from outside, not part of her.

A word floated up from within: *Mum*.

And suddenly Beth McKay remembered who she was, and where and why and when and what she was doing. She was lying in this sleep pod and they'd put her into Sleep, but now she was waking up and Mum was waiting for her, the red glow was light filtering through her closed eyelids. She was awake.

She opened her eyes. It stayed dark.

She opened her eyes again, but nothing happened. She had sleep dust gumming them shut, she thought. She tried to lift her hand to rub it away, but couldn't move.

She couldn't move.

She tried again, and again. Nothing happened. She started to panic. She felt/heard her heartbeat speeding up, *thump-thump, thump-thump, thump-thump*, and her breathing increase, but nothing else.

"I'm trapped!" she shouted, but made no sound. "I can't move! Help! Mum! Help me!"

Thump-thump-thump-thump-thump—

"Beth? Beth, if you can hear me, relax." Mum's voice poured down on to her like cool water, soft and gentle. "You might be finding it hard to move. That's OK, it's OK. Relax. Listen to my voice.

"You're in the pod and we've completed the Jump. Your memories have returned, but you're finding it hard to reconnect with your nervous system. Your mind will figure it out. Take your time."

Thump-thump-thump, thump-thump, thump-thump, thump, thump, thump … thump … thump…

Gradually she calmed. She realised she could feel something on her arm, stroking her. The nerves on her skin were sending signals and her mind was picking them up. She concentrated on that, thought about the short, pale hairs on her arm, relaxed…

…and opened her eyes.

Her mum looked down at her, smiling. After a long time, Beth managed to smile back.

5

School

With the *Orion* officially launched, and the first Jump completed, life settled into its new normality. For the children, that meant school.

Aboard *Orion*, school was a collection of cargo units converted into small classrooms, with desks and fold-up screens. Beth's class had only six pupils – Beth, Mikkel and Lauryn sitting on one side, and on the other, Vihaan, Arnold and another girl Beth hadn't seen before.

At the front of the classroom stood a very large, smiling woman. She had dark skin, pink hair and a dress covered in a floral pattern so bright you could probably still see it from Earth.

"Good morning, children!" she trilled. She had a soft accent, like a bird, and she bobbed as she talked. "I am Ms Cordoso, and I will be your teacher this year." She beamed at them and Beth found it impossible not to smile back. The rest of the class were the same, except

Vihaan; he sat straight in his chair with a polite, waiting expression. A word popped into Beth's head: *aloof.* That's what he was being. Arnold, seeing him like that, stopped smiling and tried to copy his expression.

"I will be looking after you for group lessons and shared time, and you will use your monitors for your own subjects," Ms Cordoso said cheerfully. "If you have any questions, just ask.

"Now – let us introduce ourselves. My name is Gabriella Isadora Cordoso, and I come from a small town south of Fortaleza, which is in Brazil. I was born there, I lived most of my life there, and now –" she laughed – "I am in space! I am a teacher and a botanist, and … I can juggle." She looked round the class. "Who's next?"

There was an awkward pause. Eventually the girl Beth didn't recognise stood up.

"Hello," she said. "I am Lucille. I am from Toulouse, that is in France. I have two little brothers; they are very annoying. I am happy to be here. I, ah … I like to make cakes … *merci.*"

She sat down.

"Excellent!" Ms Cordoso clapped. "Well done, Lucille. Who's next?"

"I'm Arnold Sanchez Junior," said Arnold. "I'm from Milwaukee. That's in America. My mom's a marine. I'm doing Security Systems. I can do fifty press-ups. That's, like, a *lot* of press-ups."

"I am Mikkel," said Mikkel. "I like logic puzzles. I have a rat." He shrugged. "And a brother."

"I am Vihaan Joshi. I am the son of Captain Joshi."

"I'm Lauryn but you should call me Limit cos that's my proper name, and I'm a programmer and so's my dad and my mum's a systems engineer which is like a programmer for hardware, and our rooms are just down the corridor from here, and I can find them all the time because I wrote this app here, see, this is it here, and these dots are us and when we get to Eos Five I want to work on the environmental-control software, which is *awesome*—"

"Um. I'm Beth. My dad runs the farm; my mum's a lieutenant. I, um…"

I what? she wondered. *I'm scared about leaving Earth? I'm excited about moving to a new world? I miss my old friends? What is there about me?*

Caught in the headlights of the watching class, she said the first true thing that popped into her head:

"I've wanted to command a starship since I was five years old."

Vihaan snorted and Arnold smirked, but Ms Cordoso just smiled and said, "Thank you, Beth," and Beth sat down in relief.

Ms Cordoso split them into small groups and went through their timetables and setup. The desks folded out into learning stations, with screens that ran individual lessons. Mikkel and Lauryn were far better than Beth at the Maths and Physics modules, and Lauryn skipped straight over the Programming Introduction to some complex page of code and started typing. But Beth did well at Ship Systems – she seemed to have absorbed more than she thought. And she was looking forward to the afternoon, when Ms Cordoso had told them they would be starting their Command classes.

They broke for lunch and sat in the canteen. The lights had changed to a warm yellow, like the sun on a bright day, and at one end a group of kids played football on a temporary pitch. Beth and Mikkel ate and chatted about the classes, while Lauryn stared at her screen and tapped at it in bursts. Occasionally she blurted out random noises – "Hah!", "Eh?", "No-no-no-no" or "Argh!"

Mikkel said, "After the Jump, I stabbed myself in the lip."

"What?"

He shrugged. "I was eating dinner. When I tried to lift the food my hand moved the wrong way." He pointed to a tiny dark scar on his lip. "Ship cauterised it to stop the bleeding."

"Oh, wow."

"Yes." He nodded.

Beth said, "The whole thing was weird to me. I felt paralysed."

"That is common," he said. "I felt it too."

Beth shook her head. By the time she could sit up, Mikkel had already been talking to one of his dads, moving his legs. Vihaan had been climbing out by himself – stiffly, but successfully. Lauryn had *already* climbed out and was asking Ship a dozen questions.

"It took me forever," Beth said. "They had to lift me out of the pod. I couldn't do anything. I was trapped; I— I couldn't do *anything*." She felt her heart pounding just thinking about it, prickles running down her arms. "It was…" *Horrible. Terrifying. Awful.* "It was pretty rough, I guess." She looked at Mikkel. "Didn't it freak you out?"

He shrugged. "It was strange. But the adults said it would happen. I knew it would be fine in the end."

"Huh. Lauryn, what about you?"

"Hmm?"

"Waking up, after the Jump. How come you were bouncing about so quickly?"

Lauryn looked up, although her hands still typed, apparently by themselves.

"Oh. Well, we're all just computer systems, right?

We rebooted and I just had to figure out how to restart everything. It was pretty cool, wasn't it?" Looking down at the screen again, she stabbed at something, stared for a second and then shouted "Hah!"

Beth smiled. "Lauryn, *what* are you doing?"

"Ship comms protocol," she said, still staring at the display.

"Oh, *sure*," said Beth. "Ship *comms protocol*." She winked at Mikkel.

"I've cracked the encryption," said Lauryn. She looked at their blank faces. "You know? Ship comms protocol. Like – all the stuff Ship sees, going back to the central processor?"

"OK…"

"Right, so, the data's encrypted, obviously, but the encryption is *poor*, dude, it's like *weeks* out of date, and I knew there was this zero-day hack for ship operating systems and I tried it and I figured out the packet structure and—"

"Stop!" Beth laughed. "I swear, Lauryn, your head must be like a swarm of bees. What does all that mean?"

Lauryn grinned. "Here – listen!" She clicked a button and a voice came from her screen:

"—pass me the wrench? Ta. Reckon this is the last relay, once it's in place—"

Lauryn clicked again.

"—so tired this morning. We were up all night with the twins; they both had nightmares and wouldn't settle down—"

And again.

"—to me! To me, Roddy! Pass the ball! Pass the – argh! Why didn't you pass, knucklehead?"

Beth stared across at the football game, where two boys were arguing.

"Wait," she said slowly. "Are these *real*? Are these, like … *bugs*?"

"No! No. Well, yes. I mean, you know there's cameras all over the ship, right? Everywhere?" Lauryn looked at them expectantly. "Well, there are. Like, *everywhere*. Pretty much everything you say and do. And this is the audio feed. Pretty cool, eh?"

She clicked the button again.

"—no, *I'm* sorry. It's just I was in a bad mood. I promise it's OK—"

Beth shook her head. "I don't think you should be doing this," she said. "This is… Are they really listening to everything we say?"

"Yup."

"Lauryn Hopper, explain your activity."

They looked up into the face of Ship's avatar.

"Oh!" said Lauryn. "Er … nothing! Nothing, just, you know, goofing around…" She touched the screen and the voices stopped.

"Lauryn, we have discussed this. You are not authorised to interface with Ship systems."

"I wasn't interfacing! I was just, you know, testing the security—"

"Please refrain from further unauthorised access, or you will be restricted from all computer use. Do you understand?"

Lauryn's face paled, and she nodded.

Ship said, "Thank you," and faded away.

Mikkel, Lauryn and Beth looked at each other.

"You are in *trouble*, Lauryn," said Mikkel in an appalled voice, and they laughed.

Lauryn shrugged. Once she'd solved the problem it was boring anyway.

They had a new teacher in the afternoon, one very different from Ms Cordoso.

She was tall and thin; too thin, as if she'd lost weight recently in a hurry. Her clothes – a white shirt and black trousers – hung loose about her. She was in her sixties maybe, with grey hair cropped very short, and her face looked weather-beaten and harsh. There was a patch of artificial skin on one cheek, and she walked with a slight limp.

The children sat up instinctively when she walked in. Vihaan, Beth noticed, was straight as iron in his chair, face alert and serious.

"I am Major Greyling," the woman said. Her voice was scratched and rough. "You may call me Major, or Ms Greyling, or Ma'am, if you prefer. I am here to teach you Command."

Beth grinned. The woman ignored her.

"This course is about the role of command within a starship, the techniques of effective command, and the proper behaviour of those *in* and *under* command. You will learn how to organise, train and manage a team in order to effectively achieve your goals, and the command protocols you will be expected to follow."

She examined each of them in turn. "Let us begin. Who can tell me the fundamental principle of the command chain?"

Nobody spoke, though Vihaan gave a small smile. The major scanned the class. "Ms McKay?"

Beth started. "Um … to protect the ship?"

The major gazed at her for a long two seconds, then without turning away she asked, "Mr Joshi?"

Vihaan spoke with confidence. "Ma'am, the

45

fundamental principle of the command chain is the concept of unity of command."

"Indeed. And what is that concept?"

"Unity of command states that a subordinate within a command chain has one and only one superior officer."

"Correct, Mr Joshi." Major Greyling gave a pale smile. "Ms McKay, your answer was heart-warming. To protect the ship… Heart-warming and irrelevant. What would happen were the ship to be destroyed and we were all in life pods – do you think the command chain should simply stop? Or on away missions? Hmm?"

"Um … no."

"No."

She turned to the screen behind her. As she did so, Vihaan smirked and Beth's face blazed red.

"The command chain," said the major, writing, "is one of the most important principles of military structure. It is very simple. It states that everyone in the command chain has *one* person they report to. You report to your lieutenant. She reports to her captain. He reports to his major, she reports to her general, all the way up the chain.

"You have one job, and that is to do what you are told by that person. You are not there to make decisions. You are not there to *think*. You are there to do what you have been told, and only what you've been told, by your superior.

"It is not *democratic*. It is not *fair*. It is not even particularly *efficient*. So why does it matter? Anyone?"

The room was silent. Arnold was frowning as if wondering whether he'd walked into the wrong class.

The major sighed. "Mr Joshi, tell them."

Vihaan somehow sat up even taller. "Ma'am, the command chain is critical in emergencies where the situation is confused and fluid. Each subordinate knows their own area of responsibility and who to report to for further orders."

Major Greyling nodded. "Exactly. The command chain means that whatever else is happening, *you know what you have to do*. You do not have to think about it; you simply follow your orders. So, Ms McKay, should a critical situation arise, you will not be responsible for resolving the emergency. You only have to do what your commanding officer –" she waved her hand casually towards Vihaan – "orders you to."

She turned back to the screen again and wrote FUNDAMENTALS OF COMMAND across the top.

"Open your monitors. I have prepared study material. For the next few days we will concentrate on basic command principles. Later, we will move on to more advanced concepts. Proceed."

For the next hour they worked through the exercises. The material was tailored to each of them already – from the conversations Vihaan was having with the major, he was clearly on a more advanced module. Beth sneaked a look at later chapters. *Clausewitz's Principles of War*, she read. *The Prince by Machiavelli. World Order Systems in the Twenty-second Century. Plato's Republic.* She sighed.

At the end of the afternoon the major let them go, informing them cheerfully that she had assigned them homework and expected it back tomorrow. Vihaan strode out with his back still straight and his arms swinging. Arnold followed him, grinning back at Beth as he left.

"*Protect the ship!*" he muttered dramatically, and Beth felt the blood hot in her cheeks again.

She was last to leave. As she did, Major Greyling stopped her. "Ms McKay?"

Beth turned.

"Your answer was wrong," the major said. "But not so wrong as you might think.

"The command chain *is* more important than the ship, but it is not more important than the *crew*. The crew are the reason it is there in the first place. Sometimes those who understand the mechanics of command do not always understand *why it matters*."

She nodded to Beth and limped away.

6

Videshi

They Jumped four more times that month. Each time, Beth climbed into the pod and felt the long blink of unconsciousness, and the endless winding path back to herself. And each time she went through the same terrifying sensation of having no control, no way to reconnect.

She tried passively waiting, like Mikkel, trusting in the grown-ups and their reassurance that the feeling would go away, but it always seemed too long. She tried thinking of it like a computer problem, like Lauryn, but she couldn't work out the right code. But each time she did Wake eventually, and hauled herself, cursing, out of the pod, stumbling to the ground. At least she could manage that now.

With each Jump, the *Orion* and its crew skipped unimaginable distances. Billions of kilometres, spans that would have taken hundreds of years in normal space.

49

Each one was only a tiny step towards their destination.

They were out of regular communications range now. Signals home would take far too long, so the *Orion* used messaging shuttles – tiny unmanned spacecraft that could Jump, and which quickly travelled back to Earth with messages from the crew. Occasionally they returned with updates, but these were rare; to all intents and purposes they were alone.

On the fourth Jump, they were not alone.

They were in class when it happened. Ms Cordoso was showing them pictures of Eos Five, its landmasses, oceans and seas, major rivers.

"Almost none of these geographical features have been named," she said. "When you arrive as some of the first colonists, one of your duties will be to name them. Arnold, what name would you give this mountain?"

"Um … I don't know. Mount Everest?"

She gave him a warm smile. "Sure, we might name some of them after points at home. Lots of colonists did – New Amsterdam, which became New York, for example. Or we might name them after the colonists themselves – like *Rondônia* in my country. Or after someone special. Who would you pick?"

The large, clumsy boy looked lost for words, and he fidgeted. "Uh … Mount … Gloria, ma'am? That's, uh –

that's my mom's name."

Some of the children sniggered and Arnold blushed, but Ms Cordoso smiled again. "That's a lovely idea. I'm sure your mother would be very pleased with—"

"ATTENTION. ATTENTION. STOP ALL NON-ESSENTIAL ACTIVITY. PROCEED TO SLEEP PODS IMMEDIATELY. REPEAT: PROCEED TO SLEEP PODS IMMEDIATELY."

Ship's head appeared on the classroom screens. "Please exit this class and follow these lights to the sleep pods. Please leave all bags behind." Its face looked as calm as ever. The children stared.

"Th-thank you, Ship," said Ms Cordoso. "Children, could you—"

"What is happening?" asked Lucille, the small French girl. "What is— What is happening? *Que se passe-t-il?* Are we in danger? What is—"

Ms Cordoso held up her hands. "It's all right, everybody; this is just a Jump. Come on, as we practised, everybody up."

Vihaan and Arnold were already standing, ready to move, and so was Mikkel. Beth stood and nudged Lauryn on the shoulder. Lauryn was tapping furiously at her pad and Beth had to haul her to her feet.

She leaned over to Lucille. "It's OK, Lucy," she said,

as cheerfully as she could manage. "It's probably just a drill."

Lucille looked at her with a face full of worry, but nodded back. "*Oui.*"

They went out of the classroom, joining a stream of older and younger children. The younger ones seemed excited; the older ones tried to look bored, as if it was all routine. Beth wasn't fooled. This wasn't a drill. She could feel it.

"What do you think it is?" she asked Mikkel.

He thought. "It could be Scrapers."

Beth shuddered.

Across all of known space, it seemed inevitable that the most likely threat was not the vacuum, not asteroids, not even alien life forms – it was other humans. Nomadic groups of thieves, pirates and murderers, living off the supplies of their victims. Some claimed to be legitimate organisations with genuine grievances; some claimed they were persecuted and only wanted to live their own lives. Others made no such claim, and simply took everything they could. Food, fuel, equipment – even slaves. They could strip a colony ship down to dust floating in space. The groups had different names, but collectively they were known as Scrapers.

Whispers raced along the line. *Scrapers. Could be Scrapers.*

We've been boarded by Scrapers. They've taken the cargo bay. They're cutting into the bridge—

Ship's head appeared. In fact, its head appeared in several points along the line of children, all speaking in unison.

"Please stay calm," it said. "This is not a Scraper attack. Proceed to the sleep pods. I repeat: this is not a Scraper attack."

"You heard Ship," called Vihaan with a voice full of authority. "All we have to do is get to the pods – without any more scaremongering." He gave Mikkel a stern glare, but Mikkel shrugged.

They stumbled down to their pod room. There were no parents this time; the adults were all at their posts.

Lucille said, "If we have to Jump, what will happen to the crew?"

"They have Sleep discs on their necks," said Mikkel. "So they can do emergency Sleeps."

Beth turned round. "Come *on*, Lauryn," she blurted in exasperation. "Get to your pod!"

Lauryn hadn't stopped tapping all the way down the corridor; Beth had practically had to steer her the whole way. Now Lauryn pressed a button and gazed at the screen. "*There*," she whispered. She looked up and waved the pad. "That's what's out there."

The screen was an image of space, with a tiny dot of light in one corner. Lauryn activated the projector on her pad and zoomed in on the dot of light, and it became a ship.

"*Non*," whispered Lucille.

Scrapers were terrifying, ruthless and cruel, barbaric. They were mostly awful people, living off others' misery. But still, they were human. There was a connection of some sort.

This … was *alien*.

Videshi.

It was difficult to tell how big it was. It was like no human ship ever built. Long, thin tendrils wafted out behind its hull, like a jellyfish floating through space. The tendrils were many times the length of the *Orion*. It was lit up all over in some way, as if fluorescent, with a pale, pinkish-blue glow.

It had no name, nor any marking that Beth could make out. After a long silence, Mikkel said, "It is a Protector class. That means it is … like a border guard."

"Is it going to attack?"

Mikkel raised his arms in a shrug. "Maybe. If they thought we were being hostile, or entering their space…"

"What's that?" asked Beth. There was a smaller dot between the *Orion* and the alien vessel. It was darting back and forth, but always keeping between the two.

"It's a ship," said Arnold. "Hey, it's the *Sparrowhawk*!"

"Captain Kier!" gasped Lauryn. She made a sudden, odd squeaking sound and nearly dropped her pad, and Beth looked at her in surprise.

"Is it him?" Lauryn asked. She sounded as if she'd inhaled helium.

Vihaan rolled his eyes but nodded. "Yes," he said. "He is keeping himself between us and the enemy."

"They're not the enemy," Beth said. "They're just different."

Vihaan shrugged.

"It's moving," said Arnold. His eyes glittered in excitement. "It's heading towards us."

He was right. The peculiar, jellyfish-like ship was closer now, and its tendrils seemed less random. The *Sparrowhawk* was forced to retreat, and the children stared, breathless, as the alien craft came closer … closer…

The screen blanked suddenly and Ship's head appeared. "Please get into your sleep pods now," it said.

"Are we being attacked?" asked Vihaan, his voice steady.

"No. We are being approached. By the terms of our agreements with the Videshi, we are leaving this point in space immediately."

"But if we do not, they will attack, yes?" asked Lucille.

Ship said, "We are leaving immediately. Please get into your pods or I will contact your parents. Please do so now."

Reluctantly they climbed into the sleep pods. Beth smelled the now familiar scent of disinfected plastic around her and looked up for her mum, but of course she wasn't there. She could hear Lucille in the next pod trying not to cry. She could hear her own heart, beating in a disjointed, frantic rhythm.

We will be fine, she thought. *We will be fine.*

We will be fine.

She closed her eyes.

7

Small Lies

Later, Beth wrote: *Mum and Dad were there when I Woke. They said the Jump went fine; there was nothing to worry about.*

She looked around the tiny niche where she was sitting, an awkward gap behind her desk just big enough to squeeze into. With her back against the wall it was actually quite comfortable.

Lauryn's in trouble for hacking the system again. Ship was going to take her pad away!

Ship had been ready to do it, too. But to Beth's own surprise she'd found herself stepping forward.

"I ordered her to do that," she'd said.

Lauryn had stared. Ship's face had been as expressionless as ever.

"I have reviewed my surveillance videos," it had said. "You did not give this order. You have no command authority over Lauryn."

"It was ... a secret command," Beth had said lamely. "I

57

said it came from you."

Ship had gazed at her. "Very well. Lauryn, you are on your last warning. Beth, you lied to your colleague and used her to interfere with ship systems. This will be reported."

"Fine." Beth had turned away, then turned back. "But you could have just told us what was going on!"

"Lauryn's actions caused panic and delayed our Jump. My programming directs me to limit access to information that could reduce safety. Beth, please write a report describing the code you used to pass orders to Lauryn and send it to me."

Beth wrote, *I had to make up a pretend thing I did and say it was a code for "go hack the system and report back". It was so stupid. Ship won't let us have any secrets. It watches us all the time; it listens to conversations… It's actually pretty creepy…*

That was the other thing she liked about the niche. She'd checked a dozen times and she was sure there were no cameras anywhere within her line of sight; this was one of the few spots on *Orion* where Ship couldn't spy on her.

The next day, when they entered the schoolroom, Ms Cordoso wasn't there. Instead, Captain Kier was waiting for them.

He wasn't wearing his white formal suit this time, but a battered grey flight jacket and heavy black boots. He leaned against Ms Cordoso's desk with his arms folded, and smiled at each of them as they entered; when Lauryn saw him she made a tiny 'eek' noise and her face went bright red, and she tripped over her terminal.

No one spoke. The children looked at each other with raised eyebrows but stayed silent. When everyone had sat down, Kier coughed.

"Good morning, guys," he said. "Ms Cordoso will be along in a little while, but I wanted to talk to you first. For those of you who don't know me, I'm Captain Kier. I fly the *Sparrowhawk*, and my job is to watch for any dangerous or strange situations and check them out."

He grinned. "So, yesterday was a fun day for me."

The class smiled back.

Captain Kier nodded. "I'm here because you've probably got questions about what happened. I'm working my way round the classes. They thought I might be a friendly face. Apparently half the crew are more scared of Captain Joshi than they are of the Videshi."

The children laughed and Kier winked at Vihaan. "Just kidding, Vee. Don't tell your dad I said that." Vihaan nodded and smiled, and Beth stared, amazed. He obviously knew Kier already, she realised. The expression on Vihaan's face was part embarrassment, part hero worship.

"So – yesterday we had an unexpected encounter with a Videshi Protector-class vessel, and everyone got spooked, and I'm here to explain what happened. Here's the story.

"The Videshi are a little mysterious, and we don't always know what they want. But they're not aggressive and there's never been a major conflict with them. Sometimes we come across their ships when we Jump, like we did yesterday. When that happens … we go away."

He shrugged. "And that's what happened. That's all there is to it."

He smiled as he talked, and he was relaxed, and Beth felt the others relaxing in turn. It wasn't so much the words as the way he said them – the confident captain reassuring his crew. His arms were still loosely folded, his manner was casual. Everything was OK.

Without even thinking about it, she spoke up. "That's not true."

Kier frowned. "Pardon me?"

Beth almost slapped her hands over her mouth. The others turned and stared at her. Vihaan looked angry. Arnold rolled his eyes.

"Shut *up*," he hissed, but Kier raised a hand and shushed him. He looked at Beth.

"Something you want to say?"

He didn't seem angry, only surprised, and, she thought, a little amused. Beth stared back, sweat pricking across her forehead and heat radiating from her cheeks. *Shut. Up.* But there was no alternative, so she pressed ahead.

"That's not all there was to it," she said. "Everyone was *scared* yesterday. Not just us. Grown-ups. Ms Cordoso. Even Ship. You were in the *Sparrowhawk*. I mean … there was more to it. Something you're not telling us."

Vihaan seemed furious now. "This is Captain *Kier*—"

But Kier was shaking his head and laughing. He rubbed a hand over his face and waved to Vihaan to stop him.

"It's Beth, right?" he asked. "Beth McKay?"

"Um … yes."

He nodded. "We met before, I remember. You know, I've given this speech six times so far. I've talked to three maintenance crews and all the older kids." He grinned. "You're the first one who's realised it's rubbish."

Beth stared at him. Arnold spoke up. "Is she … *right*, then?"

Kier shrugged. "Well … what I've told you is the official line. But—"

There was a shimmer in the corner of the classroom, and Ship's head appeared.

"Captain Kier," it said, "please remember to keep all

61

communications within official guidelines."

The children looked at it, and then at Kier. His mouth twisted as if eating something sour. "Yes, thank you, Ship," he said. "I think I can handle it. Goodbye."

Ship said, "The guidelines are there for the safety of the crew—"

"*Goodbye*, Ship," said Kier.

His voice was dismissive, and after a moment the image faded out. Kier gave the class a lopsided smile. "Look – there aren't any big secrets here," he said. "But some things we play down."

He turned to the screen behind him. "Here's what we know about the Videshi," he said. He wrote:

– *Technologically advanced*

– *Protective*

– *Non-aggressive?*

"And here's what we don't."

– *Where they come from*

– *What they look like*

– *What they want*

– *Everything else*

He stepped back.

"We know some of their language," he said. "A few of you are studying Videshi, yeah?" Mikkel nodded. "They can understand our words, and we can understand theirs, a little.

"But they just don't want to talk. They don't want to be near us; they don't even want us to know what they look like. We've never even *seen* a Videshi, we've never seen inside their ships, we've never seen a Videshi colony, we don't know where their home world is." He shrugged. "The Videshi are … *strange*."

"Are they more powerful than us?" asked Lucille.

"No," said Arnold scornfully.

"Yes," said Mikkel.

Vihaan stayed silent.

"…Kind of." Kier seemed to be choosing his words. "Their ships are very tough. Our normal weapons pretty much bounce off them. In a fight they could Jump away before we could do any real damage. They've been in space a lot longer than we have."

He shook his head. "We just don't know. So when we pop out of Jump and see a *Protector* sitting there, yeah, we get spooked. And I go out and do my little dance in front of them, although I've *no* idea what I'm supposed to be doing. And we leave, and we don't use that Jump point any more."

He looked straight at Beth. "So, there you go. There's *probably* nothing to worry about. How's that?"

She grinned back and said, "Better."

"What about the Scrapers?" asked Arnold.

The captain frowned. "How do you mean?"

"Well … what aren't they telling us about them?"

Kier laughed and held his hands up. "Guys, I'm not suddenly your snitch! And it's not like these are secrets. It's just some things are complicated."

He shrugged. "Scrapers are complicated. Some of them are genuine pirates – real kill-you-dead scum. Some are different. Earth doesn't have as tight a hold out here as we like to think. There are colonies that have broken off contact with us, and we tend to call *them* Scrapers, too.

"They're not all bad. I even know some of them. I've dealt with them…"

He shook his head. "That's it," he said. "Ms Cordoso will be here soon for your normal classes. I've got three other groups to reassure. Do me a favour?" He smiled. "Don't repeat this to anyone, OK?"

They smiled back, just as Ms Cordoso returned to the class, and Captain Kier nodded to her and left. She looked at the screen for a moment, wiped it and then turned and beamed at the children.

"Good morning, class," she said in a bright voice. "We will continue now with our Eos Five studies – please open your monitors and log in."

She carried on from before and didn't mention the

Videshi, ignoring any questions about them during the day. At break-time, Beth noticed Vihaan was still frowning and chewing the inside of his cheek. When he saw her, he hesitated, and then gave her a short nod before turning and walking away.

And that was all the adults would say about it, no matter how much the children pried. A week later they had a regular Jump, and nothing happened. A week after that they Jumped again. And after that, nobody thought about the Videshi again.

8

End of Term

Space, Beth had discovered, was *boring*. When she'd been discussing the journey, months before with Mum and Dad, she'd assumed it would be full of interesting sights and experiences. Nebulae! Binary star systems! Asteroids and black holes!

Once aboard the *Orion*, though, she realised that these were all things that grown-ups thought were good to see *from a long way off*. In space, apparently, 'exciting' equalled 'very bad', and *Orion*'s navigators seemed to spend most of their time making sure they were far away from anything worth seeing.

So they drifted, between Jumps, through the dullest backwaters of the sky. There weren't many windows on the ship – just the observation decks and the odd maintenance inspection hatch – but video from cameras on the hull showed the same sight every day, a black blanket dotted with points of light that changed position but never seemed to come any closer.

They were two months in, seven still to go, and their world was the inside of a steel egg. Their old social groupings were long gone. Instead, Ship and Captain Joshi organised events – dances, performances, game arenas – and gradually their life before *Orion* slipped away.

At the end of that month the children went into exams. Beth scraped a pass in Programming and managed better in Ship Systems. Mikkel, in his quiet way, scored well in Physics and Linguistics, and Lauryn achieved a technically impossible 107% in her Computing assessment by exploiting a security flaw in the test machine. She was awarded a medal of distinction and told never to do it again.

Command Training exams were different. They had written elements, and parts where Ship asked questions, and coursework. But the final test was an old-fashioned oral exam, with a real human being – the major.

Beth's heart had sunk when she learned about that. She'd spent the whole term spatting with Major Greyling, trying to figure out what she wanted, without success. Every question seemed to be a trap; every answer she gave was met with an incredulous shake of the head or a sarcastic comment that wrecked her carefully planned arguments and left her red-faced and foolish. And most aggravating of all had been Vihaan, sitting crisp and correct at the other side of the classroom with the right answer always on tap.

The exam took place in the classroom. Beth waited outside for her turn, feeling her back sweat against the plastic chair and checking the time every few seconds. At last the door opened and Arnold sauntered out, frowning, hands in his pockets and a black smudge of grease on one cheek. Arnold wasn't interested in Command Training. He'd spent the term stripping and reassembling one of the ship's booster rockets as part of his engineering course. Now he nodded to Beth.

"She says to go in," he drawled, and wandered away. Beth drew a long breath and entered.

The major sat behind her desk, writing on a pad. Beth sat in the empty chair across from her and waited.

"Ms McKay," the major said as she wrote, "this is the fourth and final part of your exams for Command Training Term One. This is an interview exam. Are you ready to begin?"

"Y-yes. Yes."

"Good." The major looked up. "On your first day aboard ship, there was an altercation between Lauryn Hopper, yourself, and Arnold Sanchez. Please describe it."

Beth blinked. "What?"

The major raised an eyebrow. "Please describe what happened," she said with heavy patience. "On the first day. In the canteen."

"Um. Well, there was a… I mean… Hang on – is this part of the exam?"

"Ms McKay, everything from the moment you walked into this room is part of the exam. Everything from the moment you came aboard this *ship*. This is Command Training! You don't get to decide when you will be tested. Answer the question!"

She seemed quite serious.

"Sorry," said Beth. "OK. On the first day…" She tried to remember. "Arnold and Lauryn were having a spat. No. I mean, Arnold created a spat. He took Lauryn's pad and wouldn't return it. I, uh, interceded."

Major Greyling checked her notes.

"You moved towards him aggressively, you shouted at him and insulted him, and you demanded he return the pad."

"I – yeah."

"And did that work?"

"Kind of."

"No, it did not. Why did it not work?"

"It did work; she got the pad back!"

"Lauryn got the pad back because Vihaan Joshi ordered Arnold to return it. Tell me, what do you think would have happened if Vihaan hadn't been there?"

Beth remembered how big Arnold had suddenly seemed when she was in front of him.

"He probably would have flattened me," she admitted.

Major Greyling's lip twitched. Was that a smile?

"Why did you do it, then?"

"Well, you know … Lauryn is small, and he was… It just didn't seem like—"

"Compared to Arnold, everyone is small, including you. You'd known Lauryn for all of twenty minutes and you had no understanding of the tactical situation, and yet you ran across the room and threatened him without a moment's thought. And the results were nearly disastrous."

"What else could I *do*?" Beth snapped. "Sorry. I mean, I didn't think. She was in trouble."

"Hmm." The major wrote something on her pad. She said, without looking up, "Tell me about Vihaan."

Beth chewed the inside of her cheek, baffled. Was this another kind of trap? To see if she was loyal or something? What should she say? What kind of exam *was* this?

"He's good at command," she managed at last. "He knows all his stuff about, you know, command structures and theory and techniques. And he's good at the *practical* stuff. Like – he can get people to obey him. They listen to him."

"Why?"

Beth shrugged. "I don't know. They just do."

The major snorted. "Dear me, what a terrible answer. Try again."

"Well…" Beth took a deep breath and concentrated. "He has confidence," she said. "He talks as if people are going to do what he says … so they do. He looks like he always knows what to do." Then she suddenly said, "And he sits right."

The major frowned. "What do you mean?"

Beth wasn't sure. It had just popped into her head.

"I mean … in the canteen, he sprawls out, like … relaxed. At school he's different. With Ms Cordoso, he's…" She remembered the word she'd thought of at the time. "Aloof. But in Command Training, he's like a soldier at attention. He keeps changing."

"So what? Why does that matter?" The major leaned forward and stared at Beth as if trying to read the answer off her face. Beth thought, *I don't know! Why did I say that? Think.*

She thought. The major tapped her stylus on the side of her pad; Beth ignored her. She thought.

"When he's with other kids, he's relaxed," she said slowly. "He's showing that he's completely confident. He tells Arnold or the others to do stuff and they do, because he talks like he knows they'll do it. And he encourages them, and they like it. He's like Captain Kier. He makes people want to impress him."

"Oh, of course, the marvellous Captain Kier," drawled the major.

Beth didn't know what to say to that, so she ignored it. "And then, when he's in class, Ms Cordoso is the relaxed one. So he becomes like … like the son of the king with a tutor. He's saying that Ms Cordoso is just a … *servant*. He's refusing her authority."

"But in Command Training he knows *you* have the authority. You're his commanding officer. So instead he's the good soldier. He can't take over, so he becomes the second-in-command. Every time he meets a new situation, he knows how to take the most control he can."

The major leaned back, no expression on her face. "Is Vihaan a good leader?"

Beth shrugged. "Probably. He knows his stuff. He's good at taking control. He stays calm."

"And that makes him a good leader?"

"Yes. I mean … it makes him good at leading." She considered this, and then shook her head. "No. I don't…"

She hesitated. "I don't think he cares about people," she said at last. "He watched Arnold bully Lauryn and he didn't step in until it became public. He's good at command, but he's not a good leader, because he doesn't *care*."

It felt horribly disloyal. But it was true.

"And what about you?" asked the major in a soft voice. "Are you a good leader?"

And Beth laughed as she realised the answer.

"No," she said, with almost a sense of relief. "No, I'm not. I care, but I have no control. I'd *like* to be a good leader, but I'm not."

"Hmm," said the major. "Well." She made more notes on her pad. "Thank you, Ms McKay," she said. "That will be all."

She carried on writing, and after a few seconds Beth realised the interview was over, stood up clumsily, and left.

She told her mum later, on their way to the sleep pods for the weekly Jump. Beth's mum strode down the corridor in the soldier's gait that seemed effortless and ate up distance; Beth had to trot every second step to keep up.

"I think I blew the Command exam," she said.

Her mum slowed. "Really?"

"Yeah. The interview bit."

They were nearly at the pods.

Her mum stopped outside. "Major Greyling told you this?"

Beth shrugged. "Not really. In fact, I kind of told *her*."

Her mum started to say something, but a faint tremor rippled through the ship, just enough to notice. She looked to the wall screens and frowned. "Hang on," she said. "Ship? What's going on?"

Ship appeared in front of them. "A small anomaly has been detected three hundred kilometres from the ship. It will be investigated prior to Jump."

As the avatar spoke, they heard fast footsteps round the corner and Captain Kier trotted past, fastening his flight suit as he went. He looked distracted; worried, Beth thought. But his face cleared when he saw them.

"Here I go again," he said, and laughed. "Hey, Beth."

Beth's mum said, "Any idea what's happening?" but he shook his head.

"No. Probably nothing. Or an alien invasion. The usual."

She smiled. "Go get 'em, Henry."

"Will do." He grinned at Beth. "Look after the ship for me, eh?"

Beth grinned back. "Sure."

He jogged away. Beth's mum watched him for a second

and seemed about to say something, but shook her head instead and ushered Beth into the Sleep room. Ship was in there, preparing everyone.

"Juvenile Sleep cycle will begin in five minutes," the hologram said. "Please make sure you are in your sleep pods. Young adult Sleep cycle will begin in thirty minutes. Please head to your pod rooms."

Beth clambered into her pod and looked up. Her mum smiled down at her.

"I've spoken to the major about you, you know," she said. "She likes you. I bet you didn't do as badly as you thought."

Beth almost laughed.

Her mum shrugged. "And it's only the first term."

"Juvenile Sleep cycle will begin in four minutes," said Ship.

"Besides," said her mum, "I've heard that … that… What the—"

WHUMP.

There was a massive sound, so loud that it was more like a wall of pressure that crashed against Beth's ears and stunned her. Her mum stumbled. And the ship *lurched*.

A klaxon blared and red emergency lights rotated inside the room, firing danger signals all around them.

"ATTENTION. ATTENTION. PREPARE FOR

IMMEDIATE JUMP. REPEAT: IMMEDIATE JUMP. ASSUME JUMP POSITION. ATTENTION. ATTENTION—"

"Status!" shouted Beth's mum. "Ship, status! Ship!"

"EMERGENCY JUMP IN FIVE, FOUR—"

"Mum!" Beth reached up but the glass cover of the sleep pod had already slammed shut, trapping her inside. "*Mum!*"

Her mum stared down at her. "It's OK!" she shouted. "You'll be OK!"

"TWO, ONE—"

Beth's mum disappeared. The pod disappeared. The room and Ship and the emergency lights disappeared.

Beth disappeared.

9

Awake

I'm alive, Beth thought. *I'm alive. The noise I hear is …
breathing. I'm breathing.*

I've done this before. I've been like this. I'm…

"Beth."

A sound from outside, but one that she was somehow
expecting. This had happened before as well. The voice
called her back and suddenly she was Beth again, and she
was climbing up the long dark path into her body—

The ship is in danger!

"Beth."

The ship, the ship was in danger, she remembered.
And Mum was there and then…

"Beth, you will be experiencing some disorientation.
This will pass. Do not panic. Control will return
momentarily."

Mum's voice sounded odd, cold somehow. Beth
couldn't put her finger on what was wrong…

She opened her eyes.

The ship's hologram stared down at her.

Beth tried to yell but couldn't move her mouth. She tried to sit up, but her body ignored her.

"Beth McKay, you are awake," the hologram said. "You will start to regain control over your body soon."

Where's Mum? Where's Dad? The ship is in danger!

"Beth, you must listen carefully to what I am about to tell you," said Ship.

Beth looked back, helpless. She tried to move her lips.

"There has been an accident. There was an Event. As a result of this Event, it was necessary to carry out an emergency Jump."

"Mmmuuum," managed Beth.

Ship ignored her. "The emergency Jump was compromised. Sleep storage was compromised. All crew members not in sleep pods were compromised."

"Mmumm. Wherrrrezzz, Mmummm?"

"Beth, please pay attention. Your parents and the rest of the crew are physically unharmed, however their Sleep has been compromised. I am unable to Wake them."

Beth realised she could move one hand in a slow twitch. She wriggled it around a little, trying to get life back into it.

"I am unable to Wake anyone not in sleep pods at the

time of the Event. In this situation there are protocols I must follow.

"In the event of the loss of the entire bridge crew, command passes down in order of seniority for active members of the ship's crew. In the event of no active crew members, command falls to any viable crew member with sufficient Command Training."

Beth's hand was moving properly now. She gripped the side of the sleep pod and feebly pulled herself up, a centimetre at a time, into a sitting position, and swung her head towards the other pods. They were all still sealed.

Ship continued. "Of the personnel and passengers who can be Woken, six have Command Training. Four have insufficient Command exam scores.

"The remaining candidates are Vihaan Joshi and Beth McKay."

"Ship," muttered Beth with a thick tongue. "Where is everyone?"

"Beth, please listen carefully. The remaining candidates are of equal rank and are therefore ordered by Command exam scores. Vihaan Joshi's most recent exam score is fifty-four per cent. Beth McKay's most recent exam score is fifty-four-point-five per cent.

"Beth McKay, you are the most senior viable candidate for command. You are therefore designated acting captain of the starship *Orion* and all its crew. Please acknowledge this communication."

Beth swung her head back and gazed at Ship, with her mouth hanging slightly open, for a full minute.

Eventually she said, "What?"

10

Second-in-Command

Beth flopped out of the sleep pod and landed awkwardly on the floor. Her legs still weren't working properly; she could make them move, but she had to think about each instruction. *Move up, left leg. Move to the right, right foot. Take my weight. Take my weight. Ready… Up!*

Eventually she could stand, holding the side of the pod. Ship watched her.

It was dark; she could hardly see the people in the other pods. The main lights were off, and the only illumination was from thin pale strip lights round the side of the walls, and the tiny monitors blinking away on the sleep pods.

"Ship, why is it so dark?"

"Emergency energy protocols are in place. Generators are in safety mode. Batteries are running at seventy-two per cent. Estimated time to failure: seven hours three minutes."

"Where are my parents?"

"Carol McKay and Douglas Anderson are in Sleeping Berth Five."

Beth tried to turn, slipped, caught herself, worked out how to walk, and carefully lurched towards the doorway, grabbing at pods as she passed to hold herself up.

Ship said, "Please designate your second-in-command."

"What?"

"Please designate your second-in-command."

"I don't… What do you mean?"

"Ship protocol requires the captain to designate their second-in-command. The designated crew member will be Woken now."

"Ship, I'm not the captain."

"Of all the crew members with Command Training who can be revived, you are the most senior. Command protocol states that in this event you are the acting captain."

Beth stared at the hologram. It looked back. *This is not a joke*, she thought.

Ship said, "Please designate your second-in-command."

Beth made it to the doorway. Sleeping Berth Five was across the corridor and to the left. She sniffed; there was a faint smell of something … ozone? Smoke?

"Ship, is something burning?"

"Yes. There is a fire in Generator Room Three."

"*What?*"

Ship seemed completely relaxed. "There is a fire in Generator Room Three. Gizmos have been assigned. The fire is under control, however Generator Room Three cannot be accessed and all generators are locked into safety mode. Please designate your second-in-command."

Walk, thought Beth to her legs. *Walk*. She tottered out of the doorway, made it two metres across the corridor and grabbed the rail on the other side, feeling triumphant. Then she slowly made her way to Sleeping Berth Five.

"What happened?" she asked, concentrating on her walking.

"Please be more specific."

Beth snorted. "All this!" she said, waving. "What happened with the Jump? Why did it go wrong?"

"There was an Event. Emergency Jump was initiated. Damage resulted from the Event and the Jump. The crew were placed into emergency Sleep."

"But what *caused* it?"

"Ship systems were compromised during the Jump. Log entries have been lost."

Beth stopped. "You mean you can't remember?"

"Log entries have been lost."

She was at Berth Five now; her legs were starting to feel more like they belonged to her and she was able to stumble into the room without falling over. Her parents' pods were near the front. Beth reached the first one, her dad's, and peered inside.

He was there, his chest rising and falling very slowly as he breathed. He seemed unharmed. Beth looked for a long time, and then went to her mum's pod.

"Why can't you Wake them?" she asked. Her voice seemed steady, she thought.

Ship said, "There was no time for proper Sleep operation. Emergency Sleep was carried out instead. This appears to have failed. The memory records for all crew members were corrupted.

"Are they... Are they *gone*?"

"The memory records were corrupted, but they can be repaired. This ship does not contain the necessary equipment to repair them. Repairs can be carried out on Earth or any major colony."

Relief pounded in on Beth so hard that she thought she was going to faint. *They can be repaired.*

"OK," she said. Her voice sounded oddly muffled, as if far away. "What happens now?"

"Please designate your second-in-command."

She laughed. "Ship, I'm *not the captain*! I can't be! I'm only thirteen! I'm a *kid*!"

"You are the most senior available crew member with

Command Training. My programming states that in the event of there being a crew member with acceptable Command Training, that crew member must assume command. You must assume command."

Beth stared at the hologram, and it stared back. It seemed completely serious. *You must assume command.*

This is a glitch, she thought. *It's just a glitch. I'll be 'captain', but Ship will keep things actually running, and when we get home, we … we fix Mum and Dad. This is fine.*

"OK," she said slowly. "Let's pretend I'm the captain." She shook her head but continued. "What happens now?"

"Please designate your second-in-command."

"Lauryn," she said. "Lauryn Hopper."

"Lauryn Hopper does not have sufficient Command scores and cannot be selected as second-in-command."

Beth blinked. "I thought I was captain? Don't I get to choose?"

"Lauryn Hopper does not have sufficient Command scores and cannot be selected as second-in-command."

"OK… Mikkel Eklund."

"Mikkel Eklund does not have sufficient Command scores and cannot be selected as second-in-command."

"Well, who *can* I pick, then?"

"Available crew members with acceptable Command scores include: Vihaan Joshi."

Beth waited. Eventually she said, "That's it?"

"Please designate your second-in-command."

"Wow, what a list." Beth closed her eyes for a second, and then grinned as she imagined the look on Vihaan's face when he discovered who his captain was…

"OK," she said. "Fine. Ship, I designate Vihaan Joshi as my second-in-command. Let's Wake him up and give him the good news."

With a final pat on the lid of her mum's pod, Beth made her way back to the kids' berth. Her body was mostly working now, although she had to be careful; it was like walking with pins and needles.

Ship was already waking Vihaan up. By the time Beth made it back, his pod was open and his breathing had returned to normal.

"Vihaan," said Ship.

Vihaan's eyes opened. He looked up at the hologram without moving.

"Vihaan Joshi, you are awake. You will start to regain control over your body soon."

His eyes flicked to Beth and stared at her. She returned his gaze, surprisingly nervous. After a second, he looked back at Ship. He moved his jaw back and forward a little as if stretching. "Dad," he whispered.

"Vihaan, you must listen carefully to what I am about

to tell you," said the avatar. "There has been an accident."

Vihaan lay quiet as Ship repeated the words it had said to her, and didn't react until he heard "All crew members not in sleep pods were compromised." Then he blinked. "Dad," he said again.

Ship said, "Your father is safe but cannot be Woken. Command has reverted to the highest-ranking available crew member. Beth McKay is acting captain."

Vihaan stared at the hologram, blinked several times and then croaked, "*Her?*" Even half paralysed, the astonished contempt in his voice was enough to make blood rush to Beth's cheeks.

"That's *sir*, actually," she snapped. "Or *captain*, if you prefer."

Vihaan stretched his mouth again and his hands twitched. Beth could see him willing them into action, fingers moving one after the other on his right hand, then his left, waking up and taking control. *How does he do that?* she wondered.

"What happened?" he asked. His voice sounded almost normal already.

"Ship doesn't know. It lost its memories. We Jumped, and when I Woke we were like this."

He pulled himself up into a sitting position and started wiggling his toes methodically. His face looked calm, but he seemed to be thinking hard.

"Where is my father?" he said at last. He asked it in a deliberately off-hand way, as if only curious. Beth could tell that he was worried and didn't want her to know.

"He's next door. I'll show you when you can move."

"I can move now," he said, and hoisted himself out of the pod with a sudden push. He landed awkwardly but didn't fall, and his feet stayed under him. He held tight to the pod for a moment and then shuffled away. Beth tried to help him, but he stopped until she backed off.

He stumbled towards the adults' berth. When he got to the corridor, she was sure he would reach out an arm to her, but he didn't; he closed his eyes for a second, muttered something under his breath and *lunged* across the room in two tottering steps, grabbing the handrail with a grunt. Then he continued as if she wasn't there.

They reached Berth Five and she showed him Captain Joshi's pod. Vihaan looked in.

"Is he all right?" he asked softly. "Can he be … fixed?"

"Ship thinks so. It says we just need to get to a colony, or to Earth." Vihaan nodded and ducked his head for a second. When he looked up his face was calm.

"Very well," he said. "And you are … captain, now." She sensed again his bemusement but before she could answer he called out, "Ship? Where is the nearest colony?"

"The nearest colony is on Mina Three, approximately seven light years from here."

"Can we Jump there?"

"Jump drive is offline. Jump navigation is offline."

"Can we repair it?"

"There are no crew members who can be revived and who have sufficient expertise to repair Jump."

"Very well," said Vihaan, appearing unfazed. "Send a message shuttle with our location to—"

"There are no message shuttles remaining."

Vihaan frowned. "Where did they go?"

Ship seemed to think about this. Not long; a half-second perhaps. But noticeable. Then it said, "Many systems were damaged in the Event. Log entries have been lost."

"Could we send a radio signal?" asked Beth. "I mean, if it's quite close—"

Vihaan gave her a scornful look. Ship said, "A radio signal travelling at the speed of light would take seven years, six months and three days to reach Mina Three, and would be very weak on arrival. It is unlikely to be picked up."

"If it gets picked up at *all*," added Vihaan, "it will be by nearby Scrapers."

Beth felt embarrassed but tried not to show it. "OK, OK, bad idea. But what about—"

"Ship," interrupted Vihaan, ignoring her, "status report."

"The ship is damaged but structurally intact. Generators are in safety mode. Propulsion is offline. Jump drive is offline. Jump navigation is offline. Oxygen generation is damaged but functioning. Gravity is online. Internal sensors are damaged. External sensors are damaged. Batteries are running at sixty-eight per cent. Estimated time to failure: six hours thirty-nine minutes. There is a fire in Generator Room Three."

"*What?*"

"Yes," said Beth, "but it's OK, Ship says it's under control—"

A crash rumbled up the corridors from the rear of the ship and they stumbled.

"ATTENTION. ATTENTION. FIRE IN GENERATOR ROOM TWO. ATTENTION. ATTENTION. FIRE IN GENERATOR ROOM THREE."

Klaxons broke out across the ship and there was a sound, far away, of emergency doors slamming shut.

"Correction," said Ship. "The fire is no longer under control."

11

Fire

Vihaan spun to face Beth. "What have you *done*?" he spat. "Ship! Status of fire!"

Ship appeared as calm as ever. "The fire has spread to Generator Room Two. All generators are now offline. Emergency measures in place. The fire is no longer under control. Gizmos have been damaged. Remaining Gizmos are insufficient to control the fire. Short circuits in Generator Room Two. Explosion in Generator Room Two. Batteries damaged. Time to battery failure: eighteen minutes."

Vihaan half ran down the corridor, still groggy but almost recovered. Beth staggered after him. "Where are you going?" she panted.

"To the generators, of course! Ship! Options!"

Ship's hologram followed them as they stumbled along. "Options include: evacuate ship; detach generator module."

"Show me the fire!"

"Camera systems in generator rooms are offline."

Vihaan muttered a word under his breath and sped up. Beth still felt as if her legs were on puppet strings.

"How long has it been burning?" he demanded.

"I … don't know," said Beth. "Since I woke up. Twenty minutes?"

"And you didn't think to put it *out*?"

"Ship said it was under control!" she snapped. "And I was distracted! It kept asking me to designate a second-in-command!"

Vihaan grunted, accelerated and left Beth behind. She swore and forced her legs to move properly. *Left-right-left-right, come on, come on, left-right-left—*

"Caution," said Ship. "Gravity systems have been reduced to preserve battery life."

Beth's feet weren't hitting the floor properly. Each step launched her further than she expected, and it was hard to maintain balance. Her stomach churned.

"Oh no," she muttered, clinging to the handrail.

The corridor ended in a door marked with yellow and black stripes and a sign that read "GENERATOR ROOMS – Engineer Personnel Only". Beth hurried through, into an unfamiliar area with a further four doors; the door to Generator Room Two was open and she stumbled through it. The walls were hot to the touch and the smell here was stronger, a sharpness in the air that made her lungs hurt.

She lurched round the corner and nearly collided with Vihaan. He was peering through a thick super-glass inspection window. She didn't even need to look through it herself; she saw the flames reflected on his face. She looked anyway.

There wasn't just a fire burning in the room – the room *was* the fire. The massive steel generator was burning. The cross braces were burning. The floor was burning and the paint was burning off the walls. It was almost too bright to look at. And it *roared*; she could feel it through the insulation, through the glass, raging. With gravity almost gone the fire wasn't burning upwards, but spread around, floating, balls of blueish red plasma impossible to control.

A white cloud of gas was spraying from sprinklers in the ceiling, but it seemed far too thin to stop the fire. Below, six Gizmo robots directed jets of more spray. They looked tiny. One wall of the room was completely wrecked, and through it she saw the remains of Generator Room Three.

Vihaan said, "Can we detach just these two generator modules?" Somehow he still sounded calm.

"No," said Ship. "Modules are too badly damaged. Time to battery failure: sixteen minutes."

"Why isn't the spray putting it out?" panted Beth.

"Supplies of halon gas are very low. Sprays cannot maintain pressure."

"Can we use water?"

"Spraying water will cause both electrical and chemical explosions."

"OK, OK … something else then. What else puts out fire?"

Vihaan shook his head. "It is not enough," he said. "It is not enough."

He was right. Even as she watched, a beam buckled and crushed one of the Gizmos, and the fire ballooned out. The noise seemed louder.

"We have to detach all the generator modules!" she shouted.

"And then what?" demanded Vihaan. "We'll still be out of batteries! We'll have no power! We'll freeze to death!"

We could burn the generators to keep warm, thought Beth hysterically. *Come on. Think. Think. Detach the generators or die. Detach the generators and die. Evacuate, fire themselves into the vacuum of space in tiny escape craft … and die. What puts out a fire like this? Nothing. Nothing on Earth.* Nothing…

"Ship!" she shouted. "Open both airlock access doors

to Generator Room Two!"

Vihaan gaped at her. "You want to go *in*?" he roared. The noise was so loud now she could barely hear him.

"Vacuum!" she shouted. "Vacuum!"

She saw his face change as he understood. The external access doors were an airlock, but if they opened both the outer and inner doors … the room would be exposed to the vacuum of space.

Next to her, Ship said, "Opening both airlock doors will cause massive atmospheric decompression. In their current state, Generator Rooms Two and Three could lose structural containment. Please confirm your—"

"Yes! Just do it! Confirmed!"

"Confirmed."

Through the glass she saw the external hatch open. There was a … *shudder*, and as the inner and outer doors opened, it was as if a wind swept through the room. Everything, suddenly, was leaning towards the hatch: the fire, the equipment, the Gizmos, all pulled towards the vacuum of space.

The Gizmos! But they'd already stopped trying to fight the fire and were now clamping on to nearby fixtures. There was a noise, a low whistle, that steadily rose in pitch and grew louder until she wanted to hold her hands over her ears. It filled the room and cut into her head; it was the sound of everything being sucked out through the hatch. As the flames leaned towards the exit they stretched and pulled and for a moment they seemed even worse than before.

Small pieces of wreckage trembled and danced towards the hatch before lifting and flying out, crashing against the walls as they did so. Now the flames were stretched so thin they became insubstantial, invisible; then they started to die out.

"It's working!" she shouted.

Generator Room Two slowly emptied. Spanners, hammers and other smaller items spun through the air. Desks and chairs crashed into still larger pieces and kicked them up towards the hatch. They jammed together at the exit and Beth thought they were going to block it, but they burst through.

The generator in the centre of the room stayed fastened to the floor, though it shook. Room Two was almost empty now, and the flames were nearly out. Through the blasted wall Beth could see the fire still burning in Room Three, but weakened.

She turned to Vihaan, triumphant. "It's working!" she shouted again. But he was scowling at the exit hatch.

"The hatch has been damaged," he said. "I do not know if it can be closed."

"So what? We can leave the whole area exposed if we have to. It's not like we need to get to these rooms. We've got the other two generators—"

A faint crash from within caught her attention; one of the Gizmos in Room Three had lost its grip and hurtled into the remains of the generator there, smacking straight into it. There was a rumble beneath her feet and a *wrenching* sound, and the generator broke free of its bearings ... and drifted across the room.

It moved quite slowly at first, but accelerating. And it was so massive that it seemed inevitable at any speed, a colossus of red-hot metal pushing or destroying anything in its path: fixtures, clutter, one of the other Gizmos... It *crumped* through the remains of the shattered wall.

"Oh no," she had time to say, before it slammed into Generator Two.

There was very little atmosphere left in the rooms now, and the collision was surprisingly quiet. But she felt it through her feet on the deck, through the glass she was leaning against. It was a feeling like a vast paper model being scrunched up. It felt ... *big*.

Equipment scattered off both generators, and Generator Three itself *bounced* and hurtled off at an angle. She watched it. It looked like it was heading for them.

"Run," said Vihaan.

It was definitely heading for them.

"*RUN!*"

Vihaan grabbed her by her top and yanked her back. She stumbled, almost landed on him, recovered and staggered after him.

"Close the airlock!" shouted Vihaan. "Ship, close the airlock!"

"The airlock cannot be closed," said Ship. "Structural damage has occurred. Internal and external hatches are both dama—"

Generator Three smashed into the wall behind them.

Looking back, Beth saw in terrified astonishment that the wall held. The bulkheads were designed to cope with engine explosions; they bent, but didn't break.

The window shattered, disintegrating into thousands of pieces that hurtled towards them. Vihaan and Beth fell through the next doorway and Ship closed it with a slam behind them; the glass shrapnel rattled against the door like a sudden squall of rain on a window, and was gone. Spinning slightly in the reduced gravity, Beth stared back through the tiny window in the door.

The glass, having used up its momentum, was now being sucked back towards the airlock. Behind it, Generator Three had bounced off the wall and was also moving away from them and towards the hatch. Beth watched with her hand over her mouth as it careened towards the exit, and hit…

…and stopped.

The frame round the hatch bent with the impact but held, and the generator jammed into the gap, almost covering it. Other small items pattered against it and bounced off, but the generator itself stayed fixed in place, wedged into the exit.

She became aware of klaxons blaring. Ship was saying, "ATTENTION. ATTENTION. STRUCTURAL DAMAGE IN GENERATOR ROOM TWO. STRUCTURAL DAMAGE IN GENERATOR ROOM THREE. ALL GENERATORS OFFLINE. BATTERY LIFE REMAINING: SIX MINUTES. PREPARE FOR LIFE SUPPORT SHUTDOWN. PROCEED TO EVACUATION PODS. ATTENTION. ATTENTION—"

"Ship," croaked Vihaan, "is the fire out? Can we activate the other generators now?"

"Fires in Generator Rooms Two and Three have been extinguished. Generators One and Four can now be activated."

"Activate Generator One and Four!"

"And switch off the damn klaxons!" shouted Beth.

The klaxons fell silent. "Generators One and Four are

starting ignition process," said Ship. "Stand by. Battery life remaining: five minutes."

They waited, panting.

"Ignition stage one confirmed," said Ship. "Generator diagnostics in progress."

Beth's breath sounded harsh in the sudden silence, and her ears rang with a faint whine that wouldn't stop. Her hands were clenched, but she couldn't seem to make them relax.

Ship spoke: "Generators One and Four are online. Ignition complete. Battery status: recharging. Normal lighting resumed. Normal gravity resumed." The lights were suddenly very bright, and to Beth's utter relief she felt the tug of gravity pulling them down until they collapsed to the deck, leaning against the door.

For a while they said nothing, just stared ahead with expressions of stunned bewilderment. Beth listened to her heart hammer in her throat; it didn't seem to want to slow down.

Eventually Vihaan gave a long, shaking sigh. "You chose me as your second-in-command."

Beth shrugged. "Yeah."

"Why?"

"I… You were the best candidate." *The only candidate*, she didn't say.

"And yet I was not suitable to be captain."

"That's *right*," she said. "*I'm* the captain."

"Why?"

"My exam score was higher."

"That is unlikely." He said it in a matter-of-fact voice. "My coursework was excellent, and my theory exam score was the highest in class."

"Maybe you flunked the interview?" asked Beth innocently.

Vihaan studied her for a long time, then turned away, muttering something under his breath. She ignored him, and concentrated on the feel of her breath, in and out.

"Well," said Vihaan at last. "What do we do now … Captain?"

Beth shook her head. "Get the Jump drive working, I guess," she said. "Ship? What's the status of the Jump drive again?"

"Jump drive is offline," said Ship. "Jump field emitters must be repaired. Jump navigation is offline. Jump navigation computers must be repaired."

"How do we repair the emitters?"

"Jump drive emitters are placed round the surface of the ship. Emitters must be realigned."

The surface of the ship… Beth rubbed her scalp and

felt her hair, gritty and greasy.

"Could the droids do it?"

"Housekeeping droids cannot survive external conditions. Only Gizmos are designed for space use."

"In that case—"

"Four Gizmos are currently functioning. Three are damaged. All Gizmos are currently in Generator Room Two. Generator Room Two cannot be accessed."

"OK… How do we get the Gizmos out?"

"Generator Room Two must be sealed before internal bulkheads can be opened. Its airlock must be repaired."

"And let me guess," Beth said, closing her eyes, "we'd need a Gizmo to go out to the surface to repair the airlock."

"Correct."

Vihaan snorted. "So, we can't get to the Gizmos until we repair the airlock, and we can't repair the *airlock* until we get the Gizmos."

"We'll have to fix the emitters ourselves," said Beth.

"How?"

Beth looked around the corridor. *No idea*, she thought. *And even if we get them working, how do I fix the computer? The only person I know who could manage that is…*

Hmmm.

"I think we should Wake the others," she said.

12

Captain

They started with Mikkel and Arnold. Beth stood above Mikkel's pod and listened as Ship went through its Wake-up script.

Mikkel Eklund, you are awake… You will start to regain control over your body soon…

Mikkel Woke slowly, as if from a long Saturday lie-in. His breathing changed, his lips moved as if muttering, and then he frowned and opened his eyes, gazing up at Ship with an expression of mild curiosity.

"Hey, Mikkel," said Beth. He looked across at her.

"Mikkel, there's been an accident," she said. "Your dads are OK, and your brother, but Ship can't Wake them up. It can't Wake any of the grown-ups."

Now he reacted; his eyes darted between Beth's face and Ship's hologram and his mouth stretched.

Ship said, "Captain McKay is correct. All senior crew members were put into emergency Sleep and have been compromised."

"It's OK, Mikkel," said Beth, holding a hand up. "They can all be fixed; we just have to get to a colony. They're all fine, I promise." He stared at her, but his breathing slowed, and he seemed to relax.

"*Captain* McKay?" he whispered at last.

Beth blushed. "Um. Yeah. Acting. It's a long story."

Mikkel considered this. "I'm not going to call you 'sir'," he said and Beth grinned.

Across the room, Vihaan was having a similar conversation with Arnold. Arnold was already sitting up, albeit shakily, and as they talked Beth saw him turn and stare at her. She pretended not to notice.

They Woke the others in their year, Lauryn and Lucille. The rest of the children on board were too young; Ship refused to Wake them. It also objected to Lauryn, to Beth's surprise.

"Lauryn Hopper is too young to be Woken," it said.

Beth frowned. "I thought she was the same age as us?"

"Lauryn Hopper is eleven years old. She is too young to be part of the emergency crew."

Eleven? No wonder she's so small, thought Beth. "Well, it doesn't matter; she's in all of our classes so she counts as us. Wake her up."

"Lauryn Hopper is too young."

"But she's the one we need to fix the Jump navigation!"

Ship's face was impassive and final. "Lauryn Hopper will not be able to fix the Jump navigation. Lauryn Hopper is too young."

"But that's—" Beth exhaled in frustration. "Well … *fine*. Fine."

"Fine?" asked Vihaan, from across the room. His voice was scornful. "This is how you respond?"

Beth said, "You heard Ship: she's too young."

"I see," he said, "and you will do what Ship tells you. And now I understand why it made *you* the 'captain'."

Beth's cheeks flushed and a rush of anger raced up the back of her neck so hard it left her feeling light-headed. How *dare* he—

"Ship!" she barked. "As captain I *order* you to Wake Lauryn Hopper and enlist her to the emergency crew."

"Is this a direct order?" asked Ship.

"Yes! Do it!"

"Very well. Lauryn Hopper is being Woken. Your order has been logged."

Vihaan turned and muttered something to Arnold, who snorted. Beth seethed. Had she proved that she was in command? Or just allowed herself to be manipulated by Vihaan?

It was crazy, anyway. Lauryn was the best systems

hacker they had. Beth couldn't understand why Ship was so reluctant to Wake her at all.

Once the others were awake, still sitting in the opened sleep pods, Beth, Vihaan and Ship explained the situation.

Standing in front of them, Beth was aware of how she and Vihaan must look – their clothes, faces and hair covered in grey dust shaken loose during the generator disaster, marked with streaks of sweat. Vihaan stood with his arms folded, facing slightly away from her.

"So, um… Hi," Beth said. They looked at her, waiting. She coughed.

"Um, right. This is the… OK, so there's been a … an *Event*. We're not sure what happened, and neither is Ship, but it had to Jump really quickly, really … unexpectedly. It had to put everyone into emergency Sleep."

"Why?" asked Arnold.

"We don't know," said Beth. "But there's been damage. Maybe an attack. I remember an explosion, or something hitting us? Something bad, anyway. The Sleep discs seemed to have failed too."

"Does Ship not know what happened?" asked Lucille.

Beth shook her head. "Ship's logs were damaged in the Jump. Its logs are like its memory. It basically can't remember.

"Anyway, we Jumped, and we're here, and we're not

106

being attacked. There's no immediate danger –" *now we've put out the damn fire*, she thought, giving Ship's hologram a hostile sideways look – "and we have power, and oxygen.

"All we have to do is get to a colony, and they can fix everyone. Ship Woke me up because of my Command score, and I Woke Vihaan. So we're in... That is, we have command – I mean. I mean, I'm the acting captain."

"Why just us?" asked Mikkel.

Beth nodded. "Ship says everyone younger than us is too young to have a crew role. Everyone *older* was still awake when the Jump happened, and they can't be revived. It's just us."

The children looked at each other.

"So," said Beth. "Problem: we can't Jump." She nodded at Ship, who created a hologram of the *Orion* in front of them.

"The areas in red are where the ship's damaged," said Beth.

There was a pause.

"But ... it's *all* red," said Arnold eventually.

"Yeah."

"*Mon dieu*," whispered Lucille.

"Where's my pad?" asked Lauryn. She'd clambered out of her sleep pod and was searching beneath it. "I left my pad here when I went to Sleep. Where is it?"

"I don't know. Ship? Where's Lauryn's pad?"

"It is not here," said Ship.

"But I need it to see what's going on!"

"We'll find it in a bit," said Beth. "You can ask Ship in the meantime."

"But I don't *trust*—" Lauryn stopped. "I mean, I like to see for myself," she muttered, looking cross. Her fingers twitched.

Beth shrugged. "Well, trust *me* for now. We'll find it, OK?"

Lauryn nodded, doubtfully, and stuck her hands into the pockets of her jumpsuit. Beth looked back at the hologram.

"OK. Critical stuff is working. Life support stuff. But we've got no Jump drive, and no message shuttles – we can't get anywhere and we can't call anyone."

"Perhaps we should just wait for help?" asked Mikkel. "We must be at a Jump point, and there are other colony ships. We could wait for one of them?"

"Well, that's another thing," said Beth. "We're not where you'd expect us to be. I mean, we're *nowhere* you'd expect us to be. Ship, show the map."

The image of the *Orion* faded away and was replaced by a large three-dimensional map of space with tiny dots representing stars.

"This is Earth's sun, here." Beth pointed. "And this is Eos, where we were heading to, here." The hologram lit up with a jerky path that Jumped across the map.

"And where we are now ... is *here*."

Another point appeared, fully round the other side of the map, hundreds of light years from where they should be.

"How the hell did we get there?" asked Arnold.

"No idea. My guess is that the emergency Jump failed, and we ended up by chance on a strand all the way over here."

She pointed again. "There's a tiny colony nearby – Mina Three – about seven light years away. But there's only one common route to it, and we're not on it. So we can't wait, because no one's coming. We have to fix the Jump, and the Jump navigation."

Beth's throat felt sore. Talking like this was surprisingly hard work. Vihaan still hadn't said a thing and was looking around as if bored.

"So we fix the Jump drive, Jump to this colony and we're safe?" asked Arnold. "That's it?"

"Exactly!" said Beth. "Only there's another, ah, problem."

She recounted the events in the generator rooms. Lucille stared with dismay, though Arnold and Lauryn seemed pretty excited by the descriptions of the fire.

"We have to fix the Jump emitters," Beth said. "But we need Gizmos for that, and the only ones left are trapped inside the generator room. We can't get them out."

"Well, then we can't fix the drive!" exclaimed Arnold. "Why are we even discussing it?"

"Well…" Beth chewed her lip. "I don't—"

"We're stuck here!" wailed Lucille. "We cannot move—"

"Yes, but—"

"What are we going to do?" asked Arnold. "We can't survive *forever* here—"

"Hang on, it's not—"

"And what if the other generators give out? We'll lose all our power and freeze to death!"

"Stop! Calm down—"

"You're supposed to be the captain and you're telling us you've got no idea what to do—"

"Well, if you *listen*," snapped Beth, "I'm *trying* to explain—"

"But what are we going to *do*—"

"Quiet!" snapped Vihaan. "Everybody be quiet *now*."

He stepped forward, his face stern. "Listen to me, all of you. This is an unexpected situation, but it is not a *disaster* situation. You will *remain calm*."

He gestured around him. "We have life support. There is no emergency. We will investigate, evaluate and establish a plan.

"Lauryn, you will interface with Ship and get a status report on the Jump systems. Arnold: you're our engineer. Check out the state of Generators One and Four, make sure they're OK."

He seemed to grow taller as he spoke; his voice stayed calm but cut clean across their panic. It was a kind of magic. Beth was as mesmerised as the others.

"Lucille, navigation. Mikkel, communications – can we send a signal, is there anyone out there? Check the gravity and oxygen systems too."

He faced them all. "This is what we were training to do. This is *why* we were training. We are the crew and we will *not* panic. Yes?"

Sheepishly the others nodded, Beth included.

"Good. Are there any questions?" asked Vihaan.

In the silence Arnold drawled, "Yeah. Why is Beth the captain?"

Everyone looked at Beth.

Oh no.

"Um, well…" said Beth. "Ship, ah, selected me as having the best command abilities." Said out loud, it sounded ridiculous even to her. Vihaan said nothing.

"So we should do what Ship says here?" asked Arnold. "I mean, it's just us. Shouldn't *we* decide?"

"Well, no, because this is how it works, you know, the command structure—"

"Perhaps we should vote?" asked Lucille.

"No! Look, Ship put me in charge—"

"And what have you done?" asked Arnold. "Lost the Gizmos so we can't repair the Jump drive."

"What? I put out the fire! I *saved* us all!"

Arnold shrugged. "Well, so you say. But so far, your first command has left us kind of stranded here. Maybe we should consider someone else."

Vihaan was staying quiet, Beth noticed, letting things unfold; worryingly, so was Ship. The situation was slipping away from her; she could feel them turning, turning to Vihaan…

Perhaps they're right, she thought, biting her lip. *Perhaps I should let Vihaan take over. It was only half a percentage between us after all. It was a mistake. He* is *better at command.*

But then she remembered her interview with Major Greyling. *He's good at command … but he's not a good leader.* Beth had said that, and she knew she was right, somehow. Vihaan was missing something important. It wasn't just about giving orders; there was more to it. If only she could figure out what that was…

She stood straight. She had to be confident, take control. Remember what she'd learned.

"OK, listen up," she announced, raising her hands. *Project confidence.* "This is a starship, not a colony, and Ship has selected me as captain. You all understand how this works –" she glanced across at Vihaan – "and so does he. But I'm not going to waste my time, so here's the deal: we'll take a vote, one time, me or Vihaan. And once you've voted, there's no going back, understand?"

She spread her arms. "Hey, I'm not slick, I admit it. I'm still figuring this out." *Head high. Firm voice.* "But Ship didn't pick me by luck. It picked me because my Command scores are higher. Major *Greyling's* scores. You know her. *She* chose me. I *will* figure this out. I *will* get us home. Trust me. OK?"

She looked round the group. "Arnold?"

He shrugged. "Vihaan."

Beth nodded. "OK. Lauryn?"

"You," said Lauryn without hesitation, and Beth smiled at her.

"One each. Lucy?"

"I … ah … I do not know." Lucille squirmed, looking from one to the other, avoiding eye contact. She'd suggested the vote, but didn't seem to like the idea now. "I theenk –" her accent had become very strong – "I will

… abstain? I do not know. I am sorry."

"That's OK," said Beth. "Don't worry." *I thought Lucille would vote for me.* "It's OK."

She took a deep breath. "Mikkel?"

Mikkel was sitting with his arms loosely wrapped round his knees, looking down. He didn't react when Beth spoke; she wondered at first if he'd even heard her. After a moment, though, he nodded and looked up.

He said, "I think Vihaan is better at leading, yes?" He nodded again. "Yes. He would be better maybe. I would vote for him."

Beth's heart sank, and Vihaan stood taller.

"But …" Mikkel continued calmly, "this is not a vote place. This is a starship. We follow the captain. We do not have a game of who will be captain today. We have a … like the rope, yes?"

"Chain of command," said Vihaan flatly, not looking at him. "You mean we have a chain of command."

"Yes, a chain, yes," said Mikkel. "On a starship, we follow the chain of command. So I say, the captain is the captain, and we do not vote the captain out. Yes?"

There was a silence.

"Thank you," said Beth in a thin gasp. She realised she hadn't breathed out the whole time.

And that was it. Arnold shook his head. Vihaan raised

his eyes to the ceiling, but then nodded.

"OK," he said calmly. "It is settled. From now on Beth is captain, and we do what she says, understand?"

They nodded.

Vihaan glared at Arnold. "Understand?"

"Sure," said Arnold, shrugging. "If you say so."

"I do."

Vihaan turned to Beth. "Well, Captain," he said, as if nothing had happened. "What are your orders?"

13

Investigations

What are your orders?

Beth faced them. This was it. She was the captain, this was her crew, and her job was to get them home.

"Right," she said, as confidently as she could manage. "Like Vihaan said, this is an unexpected situation but not an emergency. We have a ship that can keep us alive for as long as we need. We don't know how to repair the Jump drive, *yet* – but we'll figure it out. We're not helpless, and we're not alone. We've got Ship to help us, keep us safe. We *will* get home. It's just a question of figuring out how. Now," she said, looking round. "Does anyone have any other questions?"

"Yeah," said Arnold. "Is there anything to eat? 'Cos I'm starving."

They ate in the main canteen. The little kitchen droids still worked, and they served up a table full of fresh sandwiches, plus some salad that nobody touched.

The canteen seemed strange with only the six of them. One wall was still playing the simulation of the Eos Five landscape, its blue-green grass waving in an imaginary breeze. Whenever she saw the movement at the corner of her eye Beth thought someone was walking in on them. All the lights were on, which was inefficient, but at least there were no shadows in the corners of the room.

They didn't talk much. Lauryn munched quickly and absently, her hand twitching on her knee. Arnold had gathered a ludicrous number of sandwiches and was working through them with mechanical determination. Lucille wasn't eating at all. She sat with her knees tucked up and her arms wrapped round them, staring at the simulation without seeing.

Beth sighed, and sat down next to her. "Hey."

"Hey," said Lucille, in a small voice.

"Have a sandwich," said Beth. "They've got peanut butter and jelly. It's the USA's contribution to world cuisine. It's a travesty, and bizarrely delicious. Want to try?" She held it up, but Lucille didn't take it.

Beth nodded. "It's going to be OK, Lucy. We'll get the Jump working, or build a new message shuttle, or something like that. And then we'll get to a colony, and they'll Wake everyone up, easy. And then we'll be heroes, right?"

"I do not want to be a hero," said Lucille softly. She pressed her face against her knees. "I want *Maman et Papa.*"

"Yeah. Me too." Beth remembered standing over her mum's sleep pod, resting her hand on the glass as if she could reach in and wake her up. She put an arm round Lucille. "We'll just have to look after each other for a bit," she said. "But that's OK."

After a few seconds, Lucille nodded and lifted her head, wiping her face on one arm. She looked at the sandwich in Beth's hand.

"That looks disgusting," she said. She took it and ate a bite and nodded. "This is the worst thing I have ever tasted."

"You're welcome," said Beth.

After lunch, Beth sent Arnold and Vihaan off to look at the ship stores, and Mikkel and Lucille to check life support and communications, and to try to figure out the navigation systems. She wanted Lauryn to help, but Lauryn was still trying to find her pad.

"Maybe I left it in my quarters," she said doubtfully. "I'll have a look."

"I'll come with you," said Beth. "We shouldn't

go off alone."

Lauryn shrugged and waved at a camera. "We're never alone. Ship is always watching us." But she waited for Beth.

The corridors were quiet. Although the generators were running again, Beth and Lauryn's feet still seemed to echo against silence as they walked. The side panels that usually showed all the activity on board were almost dark, just six tiny white dots moving around the ship. It was creepy.

It seemed to bother Lauryn as well; she wasn't as chirpy as usual. Her hands kept twitching, reaching for a pad that wasn't there. She sped up as they approached her cabin and jabbed the door button eagerly.

The door stayed closed.

"Ship, the door won't open," said Lauryn. She kept pressing the button over and over, jab-jab-jab. "Ship, open the door."

Ship's hologram appeared next to them. "This room cannot be accessed," it said.

"Why not?"

"Some rooms have been destroyed or damaged and are not safe. Structural damage has occurred throughout the ship. This room cannot be accessed."

"But I need to get in there!" said Lauryn.

"This room cannot be accessed."

"Beth! Order Ship to open the door!" beseeched Lauryn. "Let me in!"

Beth frowned. "Sorry," she said. "If Ship thinks it's not safe, then we can't go in."

"But my *pad*! All my stuff, it's all on my pad! I *need* it!" Lauryn was almost wailing now.

"Look, we can get you another pad. We have supplies. We can—"

"It won't be the *same*!" she cried. "It'll be some rubbish with a sub-processor that you can just about play *Pong* on; it won't be security hardened or have any scanning modules or—"

"Stop!" snapped Beth. "Get a hold of yourself!"

Lauryn stopped. "You told me we'd get my pad back," she muttered. "You *promised*."

"Look, I'm sorry," said Beth. "We can't get it and that's that. We'll get you one from Supplies." She held up a hand. "A *good* one. Best we can find. Come on."

They headed back towards the canteen. Lauryn was quiet, but her face was dark and ugly, angrier than Beth had ever seen. She hissed something about Ship as she walked, but Beth pretended she hadn't heard.

Mikkel and Lucille returned at about the same time. The first part of their report was fine. Mikkel believed the life support systems were all intact – power, oxygen, gravity, water purifiers. They needed servicing occasionally, but in theory they could keep everyone on board alive pretty much forever. Navigation hardware was working too; they just needed the software to talk to it. Lucille had tried to figure out how their Jump had taken them so far, but was struggling to make sense of the readings. And, of course, they still had to work out how to fix the emitters on the ship's hull without Gizmos. But it was a start. Lucille seemed happier now that she had something to do.

Communications were less promising. There was no way to build message shuttles, and no relay station close enough to send a message to – unless they wanted to wait five years for a reply. Beth nodded; it was what she had expected. And she was starting to realise that part of her job was to nod calmly and look as if everything that happened was under her control. Never dismayed, surprised or alarmed. Always confident.

"There is something else," said Mikkel. "The *Sparrowhawk* is gone. And Captain Kier is gone also."

Beth gasped. She suddenly remembered Kier jogging past her and her mum, as they'd been walking towards the sleep pods. He'd been sent out to check a nearby anomaly, she remembered. *Probably nothing*, he'd said, grinning. *Or an alien invasion.*

"He made it out," she said. "He escaped!"

Mikkel shrugged. "Perhaps. Or something happened to him as well, yes?"

But Beth shook her head. "No," she said. "He's out there. And the *Sparrowhawk* can Jump, like us. Maybe he Jumped home to tell everyone. Or maybe … maybe he's *looking* for us."

"It's unlikely," said Lauryn. But Beth could see that part of her wanted to believe it. She chewed her lip. "We're a long way away; how would he find us?"

"Still. Maybe, eh?"

It was another twenty minutes before Vihaan and Arnold signalled them, appearing on a large display above the table. Vihaan was standing with his arms folded, too cool to look into the camera, but Arnold seemed very pleased with himself.

"Hey, guys!" he shouted. "Wait, I – Arnold and Vihaan reporting to the captain, sir! Ma'am. I – sorry, sir. I mean, ma'am."

"Arnold, shut up," said Beth, grinning. "What have you got?"

"Captain, we've got *this*." Arnold reached up, lifting the camera from wherever it had been perched and swinging it round towards a large container door. He wrenched the door open with a flourish.

Six white spacesuits hung on a rack along one side of the container. On the other side were backpacks, and the far wall was lined with boots and helmets.

Beth stared. Arnold swung the camera back to his beaming face. "What do you think, captain?"

Spacesuits...

Beth grinned. "We'll be right down."

"We checked the equipment lockers," said Vihaan. "We found where the suits should have been, but they were all gone." He and Arnold walked down aisles of shelves stuffed with thousands of plastic containers, with the others following.

"Then I remembered the supply run," said Arnold. He grinned at them.

"My mom," he said. "When she was a recruit, she *hated* the supply run. If you were late, or your boots weren't polished, or you spoke back to the sergeant, they'd send you down to Supplies and make you carry back a whole suit − backpack, helmet, the works. Then they'd send you back down again with it. And they'd make you do it again, I don't know, maybe five times.

"Those suits weigh about sixty kilos. And the backpack's awkward to carry and the helmet's a total *b*—" He stopped. "I mean, my mom, uh, really hated the helmet."

He turned left down an aisle that looked identical to the others.

"So, Mom used to say, if I was slow picking up my room or whatever, that she'd *send me on the supply run*, you know, just foolin'. But then I thought, maybe it's worth a look. So I looked. And … look!"

He waved his hand like a magician towards the back wall and a stack of cargo containers. One of them was open and had lights on, and Beth could see the suits inside.

"Right," she said, nodding. "Let's take a look."

"It was good work, Arnold," said Vihaan. Arnold beamed.

"Oh, I mean, yeah, good work," said Beth, frowning. *Giving praise, that's something you're supposed to do*, she thought. *So many things you're supposed to do.*

They went inside.

The container was bright white. Each suit hung in front of a locker that contained layers of underclothes, like old-fashioned long johns. The suits themselves were large, though not as bulky as she'd expected, but the backpacks – with their oxygen tanks, power supplies and manoeuvring thrusters – were huge and unwieldy. She lifted one off its hook and gasped.

She tried on one of the helmets. It was large, with

a wide visor, and she could see surprisingly well from inside. There were two thin tubes near her mouth; water and liquid food, she guessed. She was very aware of her breathing, and the way it pushed back into her face when she exhaled. It felt quite claustrophobic and after a second or two she took it off.

The others were trying out the equipment too – boots, gloves, helmets, even climbing into the suits. Arnold was juggling some of the gloves, laughing, and Lauryn seemed to be trying to dismantle a helmet with her pocket screwdriver kit.

"Stop!" Beth called out. "STOP!"

They stopped. Beth said, "We'd better be careful. We're going to need these." She looked around. "Six suits. I guess we could all go out."

"Not Lauryn," snorted Arnold.

"Hey!" shouted Lauryn. "Why not? I'd be as good as you!"

"Sure, I know you would," said Beth. She frowned at Arnold, but Vihaan shook his head.

"He's right," he said. "Lauryn is too small."

Beth realised what he meant. The suits were designed for adults, of course; Lauryn would be bouncing around inside it. Arnold and Vihaan would be OK. Beth, too, and perhaps Mikkel. Lucille would struggle – although

Beth felt that getting Lucille out on to the surface of the ship was never really an option.

"OK," she said. "Sorry, Lauryn, but it's true. Anyway, we'll need support from inside while we go out, and you're our best techie."

Lauryn grumbled but didn't object.

"So what do you think, captain?" asked Arnold.

Beth stared at the suits. Was it feasible? To fix the emitters by hand? To go out on to the surface of the ship by themselves?

"OK," she said. "We'll bring four up to the main airlocks for now, figure out how to get them working. Arnold, you find the instructions and safety protocols. And then…" Beth grinned. "Maybe we'll go for a little walk."

14

Suits

They spent the afternoon heaving the spacesuits from the supply room to the main airlocks, three decks up and halfway round the ship. Mikkel found a trolley, but the suits were *heavy*, and the backpacks worse, and the helmets – large, shiny and difficult to hold – were everything that Arnold's mom had claimed. It took three trips and a fair amount of bad temper before they were done.

Arnold wanted to try them on right away, but Beth refused. Everyone was tired, and the suit fastenings and safety systems looked complicated. She called it a day and they gathered in the canteen again for dinner. They were weary but hopeful; finding the spacesuits gave everyone a feeling that there was a plan. Arnold and Vihaan spread the instructions out and argued over them between mouthfuls of pizza. Lucille and Mikkel discussed their navigation investigations, and how close they were to working out what needed doing, and Lauryn had retrieved a shiny, expensive pad from Supplies and was reinstalling her old setup on to it.

The image of Eos Five behind them dimmed, and the room lights too, as the ship dropped into evening mode. Beth was tired; her muscles ached, and it was hard to keep her eyes open. It had been a long day. But as the shadows grew she realised that once she left the canteen, the only place to go was her old room. Alone.

The thought flicked across them all, one by one. It cast a gloom over the group; they fell silent, thinking about the walk back along the corridors, the smell of unused air. The coldness of a room with no other people, no brothers or sisters, no parents.

Suddenly Mikkel said, "We should try to save energy."

Beth shrugged. With two generators and only six active crew, it wasn't really a priority.

But Mikkel persisted. "Lighting and heating all our individual rooms, it is not efficient, yes?"

There was a thoughtful pause.

Vihaan said, "Also, it leaves us scattered around the ship. That's not very good in an emergency."

"Well … we could set up a dorm room," said Arnold. "Or two rooms. Then we won't be alone— I mean, it would be more efficient than being alone."

And everyone breathed out a long sigh, and nodded,

and smiled. And that was that.

They converted a storage area into two dorms, one for the girls and one for the boys, near the canteen. The dorms were basic, just long boxes with low ceilings, but they looked good once they were set up. Cosy, Beth thought. The children went back to their old rooms for bedding and any personal items. Beth and Lauryn went together to Beth's room.

Entering her quarters was creepy. The room felt unused, the air stale. There was a thin layer of dust over everything, perhaps shaken loose from the Event. It felt like a long time since she'd last been there, and her own tiny bed seemed both comforting and strange. She looked wistfully at a small stuffed rabbit on her shelf but decided to leave it. It didn't seem very Captain.

She reached under her pillow for her diary, but it wasn't there. She looked all over the bed, and then in the few drawers and cupboards she had, and in the small gap behind the bed, but couldn't find it.

"Ship, where did I leave my diary?" she asked, but Ship couldn't tell her. She sighed and made a mental note to find out if there was another book in stores. You could get pads easily enough, but physical books were rare, heavy and expensive. It would turn up, no doubt.

She didn't look back as they left. The room was silent

behind her; the dust made her eyes water and she walked away quickly.

By the time they reached the dorms the corridors were almost dark, with only a little pocket of dim light that stayed ahead of them as they walked, just enough to see where they were going.

"Well," called Beth, as she climbed into her new bed, "goodnight, then." There was a drowsy chorus of goodnights from the others, but Beth hardly heard them; she was asleep almost before the words were out of her mouth.

She woke in darkness to the sound of rain pelting against the window. No, not rain. A hard, tapping sound. Tapping? She opened her eyes and saw Lauryn sitting up in bed and typing at her new pad. The shine of the screen turned the deep brown skin of her face into a white-ish blue.

"Lauryn," Beth whispered. "What are you *doing*?"

Lauryn looked up and blinked. "I'm rebuilding my system," she whispered back. "I won't be long."

"It's two a.m.," hissed Beth. "Go to sleep."

"I'm nearly done."

"Go to sleep, or I'll have you thrown off the ship."

Lauryn stopped typing and grinned. "Yes, captain."

She turned it off and settled down. Beth lay in the darkness, staring at the ceiling and listening to Lauryn's breath as it deepened into sleep.

She thought about Captain Kier. Was he really out there? Was he really looking for them? Vihaan was right; it was unlikely. Almost impossible. But she knew that even Vihaan had wanted to believe it.

Look after the ship, Kier had told her.

I'm trying, she thought.

They woke early the next day. No one said much; Beth could feel a tight wire of tension running between them. The spacesuits were calling.

She pushed away her breakfast, half finished, and saw that the others were all done too. They were looking at her.

"Well," she said. "I guess we could—"

Her voice was drowned out by the scrape of chairs and excited chatter of voices as they got to work. Lauryn and Lucille went to the bridge to have another look at the navigation systems; everyone else headed for the suits.

Arnold had clearly been reading instruction manuals all night. He strode to the airlock area with a fixed look on his face, as if he was holding an image of an assembled suit in his mind and didn't want to lose it. As soon as he arrived he lifted one of the piles and spread it carefully out on the floor.

"It's easy," he said confidently. "The underclothes are heated, see, and then the suit goes on top. The suit's carbon fibre, so it's pretty much indestructible. Then the boots, gloves, Life Support Unit –" he pointed to the backpack – "and then the helmet. The LSU plugs into the suit here, and locks here. Piece of cake."

"How do you adjust the size?" asked Vihaan. Arnold pointed out a number – a large number, Beth thought – of straps, fastenings and adjusters. Then Mikkel asked about the controls – how did you fire the manoeuvring thrusters? Arnold went through the procedures. Vihaan asked about safety checks. The talk became quite technical, as they discussed subsystems, modules, communications…

As she watched, Beth became uncomfortably aware of how far they were from the core of the ship. The artificial gravity was weak here, and her stomach floated uneasily.

The side panel next to her lit up and Lauryn's face appeared. "Hey, Beth."

Beth swallowed the bubble of spit that was forming in her throat and tried to look relaxed. "Hey, Lauryn, what's up?"

"We're looking at navigation and the repairs you need for the Jump. Want to see?"

"I'll be right along."

She left them to it and headed to the bridge.

She'd been on the bridge once before; there had been a tour for the children, and they'd been led – *very carefully now and very quiet please or you'll disturb the crew* – through the back of the room, seeing the captain and the other crew members in their seats, facing large banks of screens with scrolling information.

This time most of the screens were off, and the only crew members were two children at a set of navigation computers, arguing.

"Hello," said Beth.

They turned.

"Captain on the bridge!" shouted Lauryn, and she and Lucille stood to attention.

Beth grinned. "Thanks. I mean –" she coughed and looked formal – "as you were."

She looked at the captain's chair. Like the others, it was padded, with a headrest and controls in the arms. She climbed into it and admired the bridge, feeling the leather against her back and the smooth glass of the panel under her fingers.

"Pretty cool, eh?" asked Lauryn.

Beth grinned. "So what's the problem?" she asked.

"These readings," said Lauryn. "They make no sense." She pointed to her screen and Beth reluctantly clambered out of the chair and came across. The screen displayed an enormous grid of numbers. Lauryn reached over and swiped at it and Beth saw, to her dismay, that the chart was actually in three dimensions – not just a table, but a *cube* of numbers.

"Um…" she said cautiously.

"These are the Jump readings," said Lauryn. "They show the ribbons of space-time near us and how they intersect. We're in the middle, see? This cluster of zeros here, that's us at our Jump point."

"Er, OK."

"And *this* –" Lauryn zoomed the screen out, swiped far to one side and back in again to an apparently identical cube – "is the last known location, before the Event."

"Right," said Beth, nodding. She glanced up. Lauryn was looking at her expectantly. "So…?"

"Well, look! How did we get from there to here? None of the tau settings are the same, the trajectories are in completely the wrong directions and all of the staging points lead to totally different ribbons. It doesn't make *sense*."

Beth gazed at Lauryn, and then at Lucille, and then back to the screens.

"OK," she said. "Let's pretend that I'm an idiot and this means nothing to me and try again."

Lauryn looked surprised but Lucille said, "We do not know how we could start at this point *here*, and get to this point *here*, in one Jump. There's no connection between these points."

"So, what are you saying – we Jumped more than once?"

"Ship says we did not."

"Could we have Jumped without Ship knowing?"

Lucille shrugged. "Maybe. But we do not know."

"We *could* know," said Lauryn, "if we could get to my pad. I was recording all the ship stats, and if we'd Jumped more than once, I'd know. But all I have is this –" she slapped her shiny new pad – "piece of *junk*."

Beth nodded. "Yeah. It's weird, I know. It doesn't make sense." She looked around the bridge. "But, look, all we really need to know is this: *can we Jump again?*"

Lauryn shrugged. "Sure."

Lucille shook her head vehemently. "*Absolument pas!*"

Beth sighed. "Guys…"

Lauryn said, "We know we need to fix the emitters outside. They create the Jump field, but they're misaligned – which is another really weird thing, by the way – but we can fix them."

135

Lucille nodded. "*Oui*. But we must fix *all* the misaligned emitters before we Jump."

"How many are there?"

"Two hundred and thirty-eight," said Lucille.

Beth stared at them. "We need to fix two hundred and thirty-eight emitters *by hand*?"

Lucille nodded.

Beth rubbed her forehead. "OK, then what?"

"We also need to sort out the navigation software," said Lauryn. "It's behaving really weirdly. We can see the maps, we can pick points, but when we look out the *window* –" she gestured at another screen – "the stars are in the wrong place."

"That sounds … bad?"

"Yeah, maybe. But only by a tiny bit. We can still Jump."

"But if we do, we might get the same thing as before!" said Lucille. "We might get sent all the way across the galaxy!"

"That's not going to *happen*," said Lauryn. "I tell you, these readings are hokum; this can't be what happened—"

"And I tell *you*, they look correct to me and they are showing—"

"Enough!" shouted Beth.

The two girls stopped.

"Look," she said. "Let's start by figuring out how to fix the emitters – at least then we can decide. And it seems like it's going to take a while, so I'll … leave you to it. I'm sure you'll figure it out."

"But—"

"Good luck!"

And Beth fled, back to the perils of low gravity, but away from the squabbling of maths geeks.

Back at the airlock, Arnold was clambering into a suit. He was wearing the long johns and looked like a large grey teddy bear.

"This is really uncomfortable," he said in a grouchy voice.

They helped him fasten up, then lifted the backpack on to him, and finally the helmet. Vihaan adjusted it and plugged connectors from the pack to the suit until a series of lights pinged green.

"How does it feel?" he asked. Arnold said nothing. Vihaan tried again through the radio link.

"It's hot," said Arnold's voice over the ship's speakers. "It's *really* uncomfortable."

"Who is next?" asked Mikkel.

One by one they went off to change into their space long johns, then climbed into the suits, heaved the packs on, and felt the helmets go over their heads. Lucille came down to help, and then went to the airlock controls.

Beth looked around. The pack was awkward, even in low gravity. And the suit was far too big; folds of material gathered at her knees and elbows, and her shoulders slipped around inside as if wearing one of her dad's jackets. The helmet muffled the sounds around her.

They stood in a circle, shifting as they turned to look at each other. Beth's heartbeat thudded inside her helmet. Everything seemed suddenly very *real*. Up until now, getting the spacesuits to work had felt like a puzzle to solve, a game, even. Now... Were they actually going to do this? Were they actually going to step out of the ship? Into space? Into *space*?

She shook her head, hard, and toggled the radio. "Ready?" she asked, as if confident. The others gave thumbs-up. Lucille checked their suit seals, twice, and then opened the inner door of the airlock.

They shambled inside and the door closed hard behind them.

15

Outside

They waited until the light above the airlock door flicked green. Beth realised she could make out a faint hiss as Lucille decompressed the airlock, removing the air to match the vacuum of space outside.

Arnold's voice came over the radio. "OK... Is everyone still breathing?" Beth snorted, but she held up a thumb and so did the others.

"Well, congratulations, folks – we all ain't dead."

They looked at each other, helmets dipping slightly.

"The boots have magnets, so we won't drift off," said Arnold's voice. "The tethers will retract when we get to the surface." He patted clumsily at the reel clipped to his hip, connecting his suit to the wall. "If we *do* seem like we're drifting, they'll shoot back to the hull again automatically."

"Remember," said Beth. "This is just a trial run. We're just going to step outside for a little bit. If everything seems fine, we'll look at one of the Jump emitters and figure out how to fix it. We're going to keep things simple, OK?"

"Agreed," said Vihaan, followed by the others.

Lucille's face appeared at the window of the inner door. "Everyone ready?" she asked over the radio.

"Check off one by one," called Arnold. "Arnold, ready."

"Beth, ready."

"Mikkel, ready."

"Vihaan, ready."

Arnold said, "We are ready for outer door. Commence outer door."

Slowly, the door above their heads opened.

Beth had slightly expected to be pulled out, but of course with the air already removed, the pressure was the same inside and out. She tried to look up; the suit wouldn't move very far, but she could see stars. *Billions* of stars. She was gazing straight at the thick white stripe of the Milky Way, closer here than from Earth, the mass of suns and solar systems at the heart of their galaxy, a savage tear in the sky.

Don't be sick don't be sick don't be sick.

"Is everybody all right out there?" asked Lucille's voice.

Beth croaked a reply.

Arnold shouted, "Weeeeeeeeee-hooooo!"

"Vihaan to Lauryn, we are on the surface. Roll-call check. Vihaan: OK."

"Arnold: A-OK."

"Mikkel: OK."

"…Beth?"

Beth was still staring at the stars. It took her a moment to realise someone was talking.

"Sorry," she managed. "Beth: OK."

"OK. Lauryn?"

"Hello, campers, are we having a lovely day today?" Lauryn's voice sounded breezy and happy. Beth suspected she was tapping on her new pad while she spoke.

"Hey, Lauryn," she said. "We're, ah, OK. It's…" *Awesome. Incredible. Nauseating. Awful.* "…pretty cool out here."

"I'm sending you the path to the first emitter. You should be able to see it ahead of you, about two o'clock."

With an effort, Beth lowered her head from the vast sky and turned slightly to the right, and saw what looked like a small satellite dish. The screen displayed a path towards it.

"Confirmed," she said.

"Great! Head for that and we'll talk you through what you have to do next."

Their tethers disconnected and zipped back into the reels at their hips, and slowly they made their way across the skin of the ship.

The magnetised boots were odd to walk in. They required a strange technique of stepping – you had to peel your foot off the 'ground', heel to toe; swing it, carefully; and place it down, sensing the gentle *suck* as you made contact again.

Beth's breathing sounded loud inside her helmet. It was the only thing she could hear; the clump-clump of her boots was something she felt through her feet. But the breathing sound was good. The clumping feeling was good. Everything, anything that distracted her from what she was doing was good.

Because what she was doing was *terrifying*.

The massive black above her was like a different form of gravity. It shrank her, made her tiny, insignificant. The magnets on her boot were irrelevant. The thin tether cables were irrelevant, and the boosters on her suit. There was nothing stopping her from flaking off this tiny lump of tin and into endless space, with the stars of the Milky Way always ahead, always out of reach, until she became nothing but a drifting speck of dust...

"—you hear me? Beth! Guys, I can't hear Beth. Can you—"

Beth shook herself. "What? Sorry, I was… What?" She realised the others were ahead and had turned back to look at her. She must have stopped walking.

"You OK, captain?" Arnold's voice sounded concerned.

Beth blinked. Her heart was battering inside her chest. There was sweat on her face that she couldn't wipe off.

"I-I'm fine," she managed. "I just stopped to look at the stars. Carry on."

They turned back towards the dish and kept walking.

After a while she looked up. The dish was larger than she'd first thought, and further away. She walked, and tried to push the black space out of her head. Was everyone feeling this? How could they not be? Step. Step.

After a long time, she bumped into someone and stopped, looking up.

They were at the dish, and it was *huge*. It was as big as a house. The base it sat on was a metre high, the dish itself ten metres wide.

They were going to fix *this*?

She became aware of Lauryn's voice through the radio. "—control panel round one side. It's square. It should be lit up."

They walked round. Arnold said, "I've found a square, but it's not lit."

"Yes, that must be it," said Mikkel. "That is why we

cannot fix it ourselves. The controls are broken. We will have to do it manually."

"How do we do that?" asked Vihaan.

Mikkel pointed. "There are wheels on the dish mount; do you see?"

They looked up at the dish.

"We need to climb it?" asked Vihaan. His voice sounded calm.

"We can jump!" shouted Arnold. Beth winced. One of the suits – Arnold's, she guessed – suddenly leapt up and on to the platform. *He must have switched off the boot magnets*, she thought.

Oh god.

Vihaan jumped after him, and then Mikkel. Beth thought about switching her magnets off and was nearly sick inside her suit. She couldn't move, she just *couldn't*; her feet refused, her legs ignored her. She stayed on the hull.

"How far do we move it?"

Two of the suits turned towards her, and then back to each other.

"Thirteen degrees to the right," said Mikkel. "There is a marker, see?"

"I see it." That was Vihaan, taking charge. "Arnold, you turn it." Beth watched, helpless, as the larger figure gripped the wheel and heaved at it.

"It moved!"

"That's it! Eleven … twelve … thirteen. That's it."

"Very good." Lauryn's voice. "The other wheel has to be set to seventy-eight."

Arnold groaned but gripped the other wheel. "Here we go – *heave*."

Gradually, laboriously, he turned the wheel while the others watched and Beth stood at the base. She tried to move. She swore at her legs: *move! MOVE!* She was paralysed.

"Seventy-six … seventy-seven … seventy-eight! Stop! Stop, that's it!"

The suit stopped and slumped.

"Confirmed," said Lauryn. "That's it aligned."

Beth swallowed. "We'll head back now," she said. Her voice wavered.

Arnold said, "But we could do another – there's one not far away—"

"*Now!*" she snapped.

After a moment Vihaan said, "You heard her. This was a practice run only."

The group turned and trudged back to the airlock. Beth concentrated on the route on her display and ignored everything else. The others bounded ahead, obviously delighted.

They made it back to the airlock, and as the platform sank back down, Beth felt the tiny increase in gravity and watched the outer door close over them. And then there was the hiss of recompression and the inner door was opening and Lucille was there, and they could unfasten their helmets and breathe the ship air.

"Woo-hoo!" shouted Arnold. "That was *amazing*!"

"Well done, everyone," said Vihaan. He was even smiling.

"Is that it then?" asked Arnold. "Are we good? Have we done it?"

"No," muttered Beth. She felt cross and oddly betrayed. How had she failed when everyone else had done so well? "There are more emitters to fix."

"How many?"

"Two hundred and thirty-seven."

The group fell quiet, and Beth felt meanly satisfied.

"Get me out of this suit," she snapped to Lucille. "We all need to rest."

They unsuited in subdued silence and went back to the dorms.

But by lunchtime the mood of cheerfulness had resumed, and the crew were laughing and exchanging stories. Beth sat to one side, ignoring them all, and chewed on a sandwich without tasting it. Now that she was back inside, everything seemed normal again. She couldn't understand what had happened. It was ridiculous! How had no one else felt it, that paralysing, all-encompassing terror? Could they not *see*? Were they lying? How could she be afraid of *space*?

Vihaan and Mikkel approached. Vihaan seemed to have something on his mind.

"Do you think we can repair all the emitters?" he asked bluntly.

"What?" Beth realised she hadn't even considered it. She'd been so wrapped in her own failure she'd forgotten about what they were trying to do.

"Well," she said, thinking. "That's one done, and it went OK. So, ah…"

One done. Two hundred and thirty-seven to go. If we manage two per day, that's still nearly four months. And that's assuming nothing goes wrong, and no one gets hurt—

There was *no way* they could repair all the emitters.

"I, ah…" she fumbled. What to say? A leader should be confident, right? Say something positive. But it was clearly impossible.

"I think, maybe," she said cautiously, "if we were careful, and, uh, if we … I mean…"

Vihaan watched her taper off into silence. Then he said,

in a flat voice, "I do not. I think that we could fix one, two, maybe ten. But two hundred – that is not feasible. We should understand what is possible and what is not."

"Yes," she admitted. Why hadn't she just said that?

"Mikkel has an idea." Vihaan turned to Mikkel, who nodded.

"I thought, there are Gizmos in the generator rooms, yes? One is working, maybe others we could repair. Perhaps we could get them out?"

Beth shrugged. "Yeah, but the whole of Generator Three is wedged in the exit hatch. And we can't open the internal doors because the rooms are exposed to space – it smashed the airlock."

Mikkel nodded. "Yes, but maybe we could cover the outer hatch? If we got a big sheet of metal and welded it over the outside, we could make a seal. Then the ship could pump air back into the generator room, and then we could—"

"We could open the internal doors and let the Gizmo out!" said Beth. Excitement lifted her out of her mood. "Fantastic! Can we do it?"

Mikkel shrugged. "I think so. There are vacuum welder fittings for the spacesuits. We could get a sheet of metal from Supplies."

"And once we had the Gizmo," said Vihaan, "we could

program it to fix the emitters for us."

"Mikkel, that's *genius*." said Beth. "Arnold! How'd you fancy a bit of welding?"

Arnold looked up. Mikkel explained the plan, and he grinned. "Sounds good!" The others started chattering, and Beth watched them, smiling. Fix the hatch, rescue the Gizmo, repair the emitters, go home. Easy!

Fix the hatch. The thought crawled up her back and Beth shivered suddenly. *Leave the ship. Walk across the surface again, under the black sky. Under that terrible, awful void...*

She shook her head and tried to push the thought away.

16

Repairs

They ran the idea past Ship, who did agree, eventually, that it might work. It even pointed them to sheets of titanium alloy they could use from Supplies. Arnold found the welding kits, which attached on to the backpacks and worked even in the vacuum of space, and spent the day figuring out how to operate them safely. He seemed very confident, although the thought of Arnold waving around a white-hot welding arc in space made Beth want to sit down in a dark room.

The others brought up six metal sheets from Supplies. The plan was to weld two to each side of the hatch and then the last two over the middle. The sheets were huge and heavy, and it took all of them to lumber each one on to the trolley, but finally they dragged them to the airlock floor. Arnold fitted the welding sets to their suits. They were ready.

Everyone had agreed that this was preparation only,

and that the mission itself would be the next day. They'd get some sleep, be ready and refreshed. But by four o'clock ship time it was all done, and they all stood in front of the suits and metal sheets. Nobody made a move to leave.

After a minute Beth said, "Oh, let's just do it."

"*Yes!*" shouted Arnold, and they all surged towards the suits.

"We could do this with three people, if you prefer," said Vihaan.

Beth stopped. "What?"

He gestured towards the airlock. "The walk. We could do it with three. If you wanted to stay here and … command."

The others stopped. Nobody looked at Beth.

"I don't know what you mean," she said at last. "Four would be better. You need four."

Arnold murmured, "We only had three last time."

"Last time was a glitch," snapped Beth. "There was something wrong with my suit."

Mikkel and Lauryn frowned. Mikkel said, "I do not think—"

"It was a *glitch*," insisted Beth. "I'm perfectly fine."

She ignored the tremble in her hands, the butterflies in her stomach, and tried to push them down and away. *I'm the captain.* Just for a moment she wondered if Vihaan was right. Perhaps she *should* stay behind and let them do this. Stay behind … while Vihaan led the mission and saved the ship…

No chance.

"Thanks, Vihaan," she said smoothly. "I'm sure if you're feeling tired you could do ground control here. But if you think you're up for it, we should probably push on, don't you think?"

He didn't react; just looked steadily at her and then, after a second, nodded. "Very well." He turned away.

They changed back into the underclothes, still clammy from that morning's walk, and clambered into their suits. Then they put the large helmets on again and felt the air solidify around them, external noise wiped out and replaced with the sound of their own breathing and the crackle of radio, and they walked into the airlock, standing on the metal sheets, and fastened their tethers.

Beth listened as the air hissed out around them. She was fine. The large doors above their heads opened, and the floor started to rise to the surface of the ship. She was fine. The floor stopped moving. They were on the hull of the ship. She looked up at the naked sky.

She was not fine.

She thought she'd be ready this time, but the black

open space exhaled around her, covered her, crushed her as if she was nothing. She wondered if she was going to faint. She could hear her heartbeat, feel a thudding pulse behind her ears. It was all too *big*.

Mechanically, barely listening, Beth stomped after the others, moved into position, lifted up the sheets – now weighing almost nothing – and trudged towards the hatch. She focused on her gloves, her fingers holding the sheet, not looking up. There was an odd, grey sparkling fog at the edges of her vision; the longer she walked, the more it closed in on her. She walked.

They crept across the hull, towards the generator-room hatchway.

"How's it going, Beth?" asked Lauryn's voice over the radio. Beth ignored it.

"I'm only asking 'cos I'm monitoring your heart rates over here and, I don't know, maybe it's glitchy because yours is showing, like, a hundred and eighty beats." Lauryn gave a nervous laugh. "Are you OK?"

Foot up. Foot down. The grey around her vision was so thick she could see only a tiny circle ahead of her, like looking down a telescope at something far away, her hands on the ends of arms too long for her, her fingers impossible to control.

Foot up…

Slowly, calmly, Beth let her other foot peel off the surface of the ship and float up behind her. She released the metal sheet and drifted upwards, away from the others and the ship and her hands and feet, drifted up and looked at it all as if it was something she was watching on a screen, far away. Drifted…

"—can anyone see—"

"—eth! Beth, what are you—"

"BETH! BETH, WAKE *UP*!"

She came to with a start and suddenly realised what was happening, what she was doing. She screamed and thrashed her arms around with absolutely no effect.

"*Help!*"

"—ckets, use the—"

Rockets. She stabbed at the buttons that controlled the tiny steering rockets on her backpack, but she couldn't remember which buttons to press; she mashed her hand on them all and pushed herself further away. Space was reaching for her just as she'd feared; she was a fleck of dust and she had been brushed off the surface…

And then she was being tugged *hard* back towards the hull so fast that her arms stretched out in front of her, and now she was colliding with something or someone and there was a suit there and she looked up and it was Arnold; she could see his face from behind

154

the visor, staring at her and saying something.

She stared back. Her fingers clamped tight round his arm and she didn't seem to be able to let go.

"—weren't very far up," he was saying. His voice was gruff, almost embarrassed. "Your tether fired. You were connected to the surface. I jumped up and grabbed you and used the boosters to pull you back down. Came down a little fast, sorry."

She was crying, she realised. "You saved my life," she gasped.

"You were never in danger," crackled Vihaan scornfully. "You were about three metres off the deck."

Beth's breathing slowly started to return to normal. Her heartbeat strummed in her ears. The air inside her suit smelled of scared sweat.

After a moment, Vihaan said, "She won't make it to the hatch. We'll have to push on."

"Don't leave me!"

"No." Vihaan sighed. "We can't leave you either." He paused. "Arnold, you've got the experience with the welder. Mikkel – I'm sorry. Take Beth back to the airlock."

Mikkel turned his suit towards Beth. For a moment he didn't move. Then, in a resigned voice, he said, "OK," and clumped towards her, back towards the airlock. She stumbled alongside him, feeling his arm under her fingers, and wishing that her voice would work normally.

There was silence for a while on the radio. For once Lauryn was quiet. Then, when they were halfway back, they heard Vihaan say, "Lauryn, we're at the hatch."

Beth and Mikkel walked back, listening to the sounds of two people doing a job that needed at least three. They were still at it when Mikkel nudged Beth to let her know they'd reached the airlock. She stood silently as the floor descended, as the outer door closed, as air hissed back in, as the inner door opened.

Mikkel unclamped Beth's hand from his suit and led her out of the airlock. Lucille unfastened her helmet and helped her from her suit. Beth walked out of the airlock room without looking at anyone, and showered and changed her clothes. Then she went back to her dorm and lay on her bed.

Some time later, there was a knock on the door and Mikkel looked in.

"Hey," he said.

Beth sighed. "Hey."

Mikkel said, "It looks like it worked. Ship says the welding is a bit rough, but it's sealed."

Beth nodded. "They did a good job," she said quietly.

"Yes."

He coughed. "They can't pump the air in yet. Ship won't let them without the, uh, captain's authorisation." He half smiled. "Vihaan is cross about that."

Beth nodded. "OK," she said. "I'll come out."

"OK."

He waited a little longer and then turned to leave.

"Mikkel?"

"Yes?"

"I'm sorry you didn't get to work on it. On the welding. It was your idea, after all. I messed it up."

Mikkel didn't disagree. He stuck his hands in his pockets and stared at the doorframe as if it was fascinating. After a few seconds, he sighed.

"It's a form of agoraphobia," he said. "A fear of open spaces. It affects some people when they spacewalk. It is not a thing to be ashamed of." He shrugged. "There are things I cannot do. Things you can do, or Lauryn, or Arnold. That is OK – I am good at other things instead. I do the things I can and leave the rest to others. I do not worry about what I can't do. You're good at some things too. It's not your fault you have agoraphobia."

He took a deep breath. "But when you *knew* you couldn't do it, and did it anyway, you risked the mission. You risked *us*. And that was…" He looked away.

"A bit rubbish," said Beth quietly.

157

"Yes." He looked around, embarrassed, and kicked his heels. "I will tell them you are coming, yes?"

"Yeah."

"OK." And he left.

She waited another five minutes, staring at the ceiling. Then she sighed, wiped at her eyes and went out to face the others.

17

Training

Beth walked into the canteen, where the others were waiting. Vihaan unfolded from his seat and stood up straight. In a cold, formal voice he gave a report of the rest of the mission and asked her to order Ship to pump the air back in. Beth did so.

There was a long pause, before Ship said, "Atmospheric pressure is rising in Generator Room Two. Repairs are holding."

Arnold cheered, and the others breathed out, and laughed, and gave each other high fives. They grinned at Beth too, and she sighed with relief.

Vihaan didn't cheer. He stared past her, with no expression, and said nothing.

By the next morning the damaged generator rooms were nearly at the same pressure as the rest of the ship, and Ship agreed to open the inner doors and let the Gizmos out.

The cameras in the rooms were destroyed; the children could only listen to the distant *clump-clump-clump* as the one surviving Gizmo walked out, dragging the remains of three more on a trolley.

The crew met the Gizmo as it came through the last door. It was tall, taller than an adult, and it stooped under the low ceiling of the corridor. It had been blue and red once, but it was now charred black, its surfaces pockmarked with thousands of chips and scrapes. Its left foot seemed fused, and one side of its face was caved in.

"It's a Type Three," said Arnold, looking it over critically. "Old but good. Could be worse. Say hello, Gizmo."

"Hello," said the robot. It had a deep, slightly rasping voice.

"Status, Gizmo," said Arnold.

"Status: emergency repair mode activated. Damage to left ankle. Cosmetic damage to surface and face. Internal systems intact. Power intact. Warning: this droid needs servicing and repair. If you continue to use this droid, your warranty may be invalidated. Why not contact Jones and Yamaguchi, Droid Repair Services, for all your Gizmo needs? We're only a call away!"

It fell silent again.

"Hmm," said Mikkel. "Maybe Jones and Yamaguchi

do house calls, yes?"

"What about the others?" asked Beth.

Arnold examined the broken Gizmos on the trolley and shook his head. "Don't know, they look burned up. We might fix one, two maybe – want me to try?"

"Later," said Beth. "Take them to the repair shop, and we'll see what this one can do."

Arnold nodded and gave the orders, and the Gizmo dragged the trolley away down the corridor.

They did a trial run that morning, sending the one working Gizmo out to the surface of the ship and watching from cameras. The Gizmo was designed for repairs and had magnets built into its soles, and despite its damaged foot it managed the peculiar peel-off-peel-on walking style effortlessly. It trudged towards the nearest emitter and climbed on to the platform.

Back on the bridge, Lauryn stared at a screen full of diagnostic messages and muttered into a microphone, and the Gizmo turned first one wheel, and then the other. Ten minutes later, it stepped back off the platform, sank gently to the deck, and stood to attention.

"Checking…" said Mikkel "Yes. It is fine."

"Hah!" shouted Arnold, and Lucille gave a little smile. Beth said, "Can it do the rest?"

"Sure," said Lauryn. "Me and Mikkel have been

161

looking at it. It's pretty simple – we just need to give it directions to the emitters and their new settings. In fact, I was rooting around and found a program in the ship's database, does just that." She snorted. "It was rubbish. *Totally* wrong. But I fixed it."

"How long will it take?"

Lauryn screwed up her face. "I reckon… It's got to walk to each one, and it has to recharge. And we want to be careful. Let's say, eight a day?" Mikkel nodded. "Yeah," said Lauryn. "So that's, uh, thirty days."

Thirty days. We could be home in a month.

"Well done," said Beth warmly, and Lauryn, Mikkel and Lucille beamed.

"So, we just sit and wait for the Gizmo now?" asked Arnold. "Nothing else?"

"Don't see why not," said Beth. "What else is there for us to do?"

"*School?*" she exclaimed.

The Gizmo had completed three emitters so far, and Mikkel and Lucille seemed confident. Now Beth stood in her dorm, facing Ship's hologram.

"That's *ridiculous!*" she snapped. "We're in an emergency situation. You can't seriously think we should be spending our days learning … *history* or something!"

Ship stayed as calm as ever. "This is no longer an emergency situation. Imminent danger has been avoided. All children under the age of sixteen must follow a school curriculum. History is not a required subject."

"But we're *crew!*"

This didn't have any effect either.

"As crew members, you have all demonstrated skill levels far below that required for your positions. Corrective action takes the form of mandatory training."

Beth scowled. "You mean," she said, "if we're kids, we have to go to school, and if we're crew, we have to go to training."

"Correct."

"Which is just school."

"Training consists of a number of theory and practice sessions within a learning environment."

"Just like school."

"Correct."

Beth put her hands on her hips. "What if I said no?"

Was there a pause? For a moment? She wasn't sure.

Ship said, "As captain, you are authorised to override this directive—"

"Then I will!"

"—however, this would be inadvisable."

Beth snorted. "I don't think anyone died for missing a

month of school, Ship."

"The risks associated with operating this vessel with minimal training and experience are high. Immediate repair work is required in: Jump emitters—"

"We're already *fixing* them—"

"Gravity and oxygen generators, Generator Room One, propulsion, Jump navigation—"

"Yes, but—"

"Life support systems, food generators, hydroponic farm—"

"But we don't need all of that stuff to—"

"Weapon systems, tactical defence systems—"

"We're not going to be fighting—"

"And sleep pods."

Beth hesitated.

"Sleep pods?"

"Sleep pods require maintenance. They have been in constant operation for longer than the recommended interval."

She scratched her chin. "Defence systems?"

"This area, and the areas we will Jump through, have known Scraper presence. We are currently unable to move. Tactical defence should be a high priority."

Beth said slowly, "I sort of thought we were done. You know, with the Gizmo and being able to Jump."

Ship said nothing.

We'll be home in a month, thought Beth. *We could just not worry about it. Seriously, what could happen?*

She thought about what could happen.

"OK…" she said. "So we need to repair and maintain all these systems."

"Correct."

"And it's got to be us."

"Gizmos are unavailable."

Sleep pods. Weapon systems. Life support.

Beth closed her eyes and sighed. "OK. Let me tell the others."

She and Vihaan worked out a schedule. In the mornings, daily rounds: checking status reports, making sure the gravity and oxygen weren't about to fail or the generators blow up. Then training, then lunch, then more training. Then repairs and servicing work as required, and then dinner and free time. A day off from training every five days. Thankfully most of the ship was self-cleaning; all they had to do was put their own rubbish in the bins and their own laundry in the machines and the little housekeeping droids took care of them.

Mikkel was assigned life support, communications and scanning, listening for messages and spotting anything unusual. Arnold was on engineering and tactical – weapons and defences. Lauryn looked after the computer systems, and Beth and Vihaan did a bit of everything.

Lucille got navigation and Jump mechanics, and worked on finding the shortest path to a colony.

"You cannot just pick a point you want to Jump to and go there," she said, two days later. She stood in front of a hologram map of the surrounding space. "Space-time is twisted, curled in on itself. Maybe you Jump here to here –" she pinched her thumb and forefinger together into a tiny gap – "but in our space, you have crossed from *here* to *here*," and she tapped two parts of the map on opposite sides.

"And where we are … it is very difficult to get to. We are so close to a colony, but we cannot Jump to there from here. So, we must go like this…"

A path of a dozen or more steps lit up on the map, zigzagging across the galaxy, ending at a tiny colony near the centre.

Arnold whistled. "What is that, ten Jumps?"

"Thirteen," said Lucille. "It is the only way I can see."

Vihaan said nothing. Beth felt dismayed but tried not to show it. Thirteen Jumps! Thirteen Sleeps. Thirteen times struggling to regain control of her own body.

"Is there no shorter route?" she asked. "To *anywhere*?"

Lucille shrugged. "Space is big, you know? And there are only fifty colonies. And, look." She tapped on the hologram at the point where they were, and it zoomed in to show arrows pointing outwards.

"These are the paths we can take from here. These ones, they go nowhere. They are dead ends, yes? These ones – here, here, here – they go to asteroid fields, very bad. These ones, we do not know – anywhere, nowhere, they are uncharted. And *these* ones –" she tapped several of them – "they go to Videshi space." Her finger shook slightly as she pointed. "We do not go on these ones, *ever*."

She shook her head. "So we must Jump far away, over here, where there is no one. And then again, and again."

"OK," said Beth. "Well. Good work, Lucille." Lucille looked pleased and gave a little bow. Beth turned to the others. "You heard her, folks," she said brightly. "Once Stumpy up there gets done –" she pointed above her head towards the surface of the ship and the Gizmo, clumping around – "we have a route home."

Thirteen Jumps. Not for the first time she wondered how they had got to this point.

Mikkel's report was fairly upbeat. The *Orion* was a little battered, but it was designed to keep a crew of hundreds alive and active, and now it only had to support six;

167

passengers in Sleep mode needed a fraction of the food, water and oxygen resources. They could keep going for years if they had to.

More worrying were the scans of the hull.

"Here are scorch marks, yes?" Mikkel said, pointing to Beth's screen. "That is laser fire. Here … and here. Someone has been shooting at us. And there is more on this side. Lasers cannot turn corners – someone must have been firing from this side too. That means there was more than one attacker. And there is another thing." He zoomed in to show a service hatch that seemed to be dented and scratched.

"I think someone was trying to force their way in," he said.

The others stared at him, stunned.

"Are you…" Beth cleared her throat. "Are you saying that someone has been trying to *board* us?"

"I think so, yes," said Mikkel calmly. "But I do not know how, or when. All of the sensors and internal cameras in that area have been damaged."

"Ship," called Beth, "have we been attacked recently?"

Ship's hologram appeared. "The *Orion* has been attacked three times in its history," it said.

"Yeah, but I mean recently."

"The *Orion* has not been attacked since you were

Woken from Sleep."

"O-K ... but what about before?"

"The *Orion* has not been attacked between the colony mission launch and the unknown Event."

There was something ridiculous and maddeningly pedantic about its replies. "Yes, but what about *since* the Event!"

There was a pause, and then Ship said, "Logs have been damaged."

Beth frowned. "Hmm." A horrible thought struck her. "Mikkel, that hatch – they didn't *manage* to get in, did they?"

Everyone stood up very straight. Lucille put her hand to her mouth and made a squeaking noise. But Mikkel said, "No. It is bolted on the inside, and the security seals are still in place – it hasn't been forced."

They breathed out again. "Well, that's something anyway," said Beth. "OK – who's next?"

Beth received Command Training. It felt unending.

"Command consists of different areas of personality and training," recited Ship, using material prepared by Major Greyling. "These include: mental toughness; charisma; confidence; situational awareness; empathy; loyalty; discipline; fairness; self-control; and ruthlessness.

"Some of these are transient. Charisma will give you a free ride until you fail once, twice perhaps, but if you have nothing else it will soon become apparent to your subordinates. Most traits can be developed through training.

"Your report from Major Greyling suggests you score well in some areas but poorly in discipline and ruthlessness. Please comment."

"I score low in ruthlessness?" asked Beth. "Isn't that a good thing?"

"Ruthlessness is required in emergencies. Command requires hard decisions."

"I blew up the generator room!" she snapped, rising out of her seat. "That was a pretty hard decision, wouldn't you say?"

"Ms McKay has the makings of a fine officer," said Ship. This time it really was in the major's voice, rasping and familiar, and Beth stopped in surprise. "She has strong empathy skills and commendable diligence. Her theory work is satisfactory. But she lacks steel and self-control. She's a collection of chaos. In the next term we will concentrate on those areas. End of report."

Beth sank back into her chair and tried to slow her breathing to normal. In its own voice, Ship said, "Your training will emphasise techniques of self-control in order to become an effective captain."

"Sounds like fun," she muttered.

"We will begin now. Lesson One: Take Ownership of Your Attitude."

Beth groaned and sank her head down on to the desk.

Ship drilled Beth, and the others, until they looked forward to their servicing jobs as a chance to escape. Theory and practice, over and over, trying to cram in the knowledge they needed to run the *Orion* and its complex systems.

On their morning routes Ship's avatar followed each of them, pointing out more learning opportunities, and in the evenings it suggested videos and interactive tutorials they could run in their spare time. It seemed to Beth that Ship was following her even into sleep, to pester her dreams.

"Imagine you are the captain of a ship, sailing out to sea," it told her. It was quoting from Major Greyling again. "The wind blows and the sea swells around you, and all you have is your ship and your crew. The wind batters you. You cannot change the wind. The sea crashes against you. You cannot change the sea. These things are *out of your control*. If you rage against the wind, or rail against the sea, will it stop? No. Of course not.

"But you are the master of your ship. You control the

heart that beats within you, and the voice that shouts out from you, and the hands that turn the wheel. You can steer your ship towards or against the wind, into or alongside the waves. You can raise or lower your sails. You cannot control the sea, but you can control *how you react*. And by your reactions will you live or die.

"You are the master of your own ship. In everything you do and everywhere you go, you will be met with forces you cannot control. They will thwart you, or spite you, or simply ignore you when you want to be heard. But in every case this one fact holds true: *You* are the master of your own ship."

Again and again, Ship made her repeat this like a mantra, until she heard it in her sleep, until she mumbled it when half awake.

"I do not control the seas. I cannot control the wind. But I am the master of my own ship. I do not control the seas…"

18

The Wanderer

"I don't have a presentation," said Arnold, rubbing the back of his head. "I didn't know we were supposed to … OK. Um… I've been looking at the guns, yeah, and the, uh, defence systems."

Beth and Vihaan were sitting in the captain's room, just off the bridge, and Arnold was standing in front of them. He looked terrified. "I'm, uh. I'm not very good at this. I mean … talking."

"It's OK," said Beth. "Don't worry about a presentation. Just tell us what you know." Inspiration struck her. "Do we actually *have* any guns?" she asked innocently.

He gave her a look of bemused contempt. "Of *course* we have guns! We've got sixteen banks of long-range surface-to-space capability with auto-target and remote coordination." Enthusiasm overcame his nervousness. "We've got short-range defence cluster, laser banks and scatter shot that will take out anything entering a one-K radius of the ship. We are *armed*."

"OK, then—" started Beth.

"What we *don't* have is ammo," said Arnold.

Beth rubbed the bridge of her nose. "No ammo."

"Nope. We've only got about a hundred racks of long; that's enough for ten seconds of firing. We're better with short; we've got enough to hold defence for maybe ten minutes. Against incoming, or asteroids, that kind of thing.

"Lasers are fine; they recharge. But they don't do serious damage; at least, ours don't. So yeah. Great guns, zero ammo. That's what I got."

He put his hands in his pockets.

"How could we have left home like this?" asked Beth.

Arnold shrugged.

After he'd left, Vihaan said, "I'm concerned about Arnold's report."

His voice was flat. He was still angry with her about the spacewalk, she knew, and the way she'd endangered the mission. And he clearly thought he should be captain. But he'd managed to stay civil. He behaved like a proper second-in-command, reporting to her, carrying out her orders, supporting her in public. As Beth had told the major, Vihaan always knew how best to play whatever part he had.

But she'd come to realise it was more than that. Vihaan really *believed* in the chain of command. Beth was his captain, and it was his duty to follow her, no matter what he thought. Beth couldn't decide if that made him a pig-headed fool, or a better person than she was.

She nodded. "It's worrying," she said. "I'm amazed we set off with so little ammo. Unless we've used some already…"

Vihaan said, "Arnold is unreliable. He shouldn't be looking after tactical."

Beth looked at him. She wondered if Arnold knew how ready Vihaan was to jettison him.

"He wouldn't be my first choice," she admitted. "But everyone else is busy. It can't be you – if we do run into trouble, you need to be running operations."

Vihaan said nothing.

"Besides…" To Beth's surprise, she was starting to like Arnold. He'd put away his earlier bullying tendencies and seemed willing to help. "I think he cares about it more than you think. We could do worse."

"Very well," he said, his face blank. "If those are your orders."

"That's *right*," she snapped, and then stopped. *Take Ownership of Your Attitude*. She took a breath and tried again.

"They are," she said. "I have faith in him – I think he'd do OK in an emergency." She snorted. "Hopefully we won't have to find out."

A week later, they found out.

Mikkel noticed it first, during one of the long-range communication sweeps he ran every morning.

"Captain?" he called. He always called her 'Captain' now, and seemed to take her title seriously. "There is something unusual."

Beth wandered over. "What's up?" She peered at a screen covered in small white dots moving at different speeds and in different directions. It was almost all smashed asteroid fragments, with one or two tiny pieces of metal.

Mikkel pointed to one. "That one," he said. "Ship picked it up at oh-four-hundred this morning. It just drifted in."

"What is it?"

Mikkel gazed at the screen. "I don't know. It could just be another asteroid, yes? Or wreckage from an old ship…" His voice trailed off and he frowned at the screen.

"But you don't think it is," said Beth.

He shook his head. "It does not … *wamble* enough," he said at last. "It is not like these ones."

Beth raised an eyebrow, but he pointed to the other dots and she watched them, and after a while she understood what he meant. The others, while still heading in their straight lines, were turning slightly, or flipping over, changing their shapes by just a tiny amount over a long time. The newcomer wasn't. It was slow, but deliberate.

"Could it be…" She stopped. Then she said, "Could it be a search scout?"

Mikkel shrugged. "Maybe," he said. He didn't sound too sure. "It's not sending out a radio beacon."

"OK. Worth a look anyway. How long until it gets close enough to see?"

"About an hour?"

"I'll wait here with you."

An hour later, Beth and Mikkel stood on the bridge, surrounded by the others. Everyone had heard about the mysterious dot and had somehow all managed to find something that needed to be done on the bridge.

"How far is it now?" asked Beth.

"About eight hundred kilometres," said Mikkel. "This is the best picture we can get. But there's also…" He turned on a couple of extra displays. "This is spectrographic data. It's what Ship can work out about the thing's chemical composition – what it's made of." He looked at it. "I don't know what it means. Ship, what is the entity made of?"

Ship's hologram appeared. "The surface of the entity contains a mixture of iron, alloyed metals and superconductors," it said.

"What does that mean?" asked Lucille.

"It means it's the same as us," said Arnold. He nodded to the hologram. "That's right, ain't it?"

"Yes. This is most likely a human space vessel – either a message shuttle, a scout or the remains of a larger craft."

A human space vessel.

Everyone pulled themselves up.

"Is it heading for us?" asked Beth, her throat dry.

"On its current trajectory, the entity will pass ahead of us by five hundred kilometres."

"Have we tried to contact it yet?"

"Negative," said Ship.

Beth faced the others. "Well … should we send it a message?"

"We don't know what it is," said Vihaan.

Lauryn said, "Could be a search mission!"

Lucille looked excited too. Arnold was staring at the screen and frowning. Mikkel shrugged.

Beth chewed her lip for a moment.

"OK," she said. "Mikkel, send a ping." A ping was a very short burst of radio noise, like the single dit of ancient Morse code messages. "Lauryn, keep an eye on the sensor readings. Ready? Go."

Mikkel pressed a button on his console and nodded. The children watched.

Nothing happened at first. The little craft didn't change its route. But after a few seconds Mikkel said, "That's a ping back." He sounded like he was discussing the weather.

Beth took a deep breath. "OK," she said. "Let's wait and—"

"And more," he said, studying the screen. "That's a welcome signal, I think, yes? And that is communication protocol. Ship's translating it—"

A metallic voice suddenly echoed around the bridge. "Greetings, alien ship!" it said cheerfully. "Come a please banana on the relay to twice happy intervals!"

There was a pause, and then Arnold sniggered.

"Er … was there a problem in the comms link, Mikkel?" asked Beth.

Mikkel was tapping away at his screen but shook his head. "No, that's really what it said. It's sending data to Ship as well. I think it's uploading log files. There's gigabytes, terabytes of data."

He considered it. "I think it is an automated navigation scout, yes? Someone has sent it to look for Jump routes and report back what it finds."

"Can we reply to it?"

He shrugged. "For sure. Wait… OK, talk into the mike." He handed Beth a small microphone.

Feeling very self-conscious, Beth said, "Hello?" She coughed and tried again. "Alien vessel, this is, er, Captain McKay of the colony ship *Orion*. Can you hear me?"

The speakers crackled back into life. "Hello! Chortle joy! Listening and with the merry breath one station two station adjust sigma variation please." The voice was full of happiness and seemed to bounce around the bridge.

"I think you might have a problem with your speech systems," said Beth. "Do you understand us?"

"Indeedly doodly! Speeching on the snicker-snack, so sad boohoo. Cor blimey governor! What to do? Hello? I'm so pleased to see you!"

Still grinning, Beth said, "Ship – is there anything we can do to help with its talking?"

"Processing log upload," said Ship. "Please wait."

They waited. Beth said, "Where are you from, craft?"

The metallic voice chuckled. "Mostly on the far side, flip side, hoppity-hop, oh such a long, long, longitude, latitude, who can tell? Long ago, far way, so much to see, yes? Sorry, burbling, so lonely long time. Friends, yes? Yes, friends!"

"I think its AI is maybe a bit fritzed," said Lauryn.

"Yeah," said Beth. "Or maybe it's been on its own for a loooong time." She activated the mike again. "Alien vessel, what is your name and designation?"

"A name!" The voice laughed. "I had a name, that's right! Yes indeed, remember the name? I don't. Do you?"

"Well, what should we call you?"

"Call me anything! Call me any time! Call me Ishmael! No. Bob. Bob the Happy Wanderer."

Arnold snorted. "So, it really is nuts."

"I thought it was looking for us," murmured Lucille. Her head dropped.

"Yes, but it doesn't matter," said Beth. "All that matters is, does it have a working Jump drive?"

"Oh, yeah!" said Lauryn. "We could get it to send a message!"

"Mikkel, does it have Jump drive?" asked Beth.

Mikkel peered at his screen again. "It is hard to tell," he said. "It's waking up, I think. Something's changing. It's starting up other systems. Ship, what's the other vessel doing?"

"Processing log upload," said Ship again. "Please wait. Please wait."

"Hang on," said Lauryn, frowning. "I'll cancel that." She tapped at her console.

"Cancelling," said Ship. "Cancelling. Processing log upload. Please wait. Please. Processing."

"Stupid thing," muttered Lauryn.

Beth said, "Alien vessel, please cancel your data stream to our ship."

"Affirmative! *Absolument!* Steady, drip-drip, too much chaos. Never-ending, never-ending." Its cheerfulness was relentless. "Better now? All better? So many things to tell you!"

Lauryn shook her head. "No, Ship's still struggling. It's weird, hang on." She tapped again. "Ship, are you back?"

"Processing log upload," said Ship.

"Alien vessel, you're still streaming data," said Beth.

"Processing," muttered Ship. "Please— Processing log upload. Wait. Processing log up— Attack. Please— Emergency log upload, upload, upload, upload— SYSTEM REBOOT IN TWO SECONDS."

"Alien vessel, your data stream is causing problems for our systems. Please stop *at once*," said Beth.

"Oh noes!" said the voice, sounding heartbroken. "No with the badness! So sorry, so sorry – oops, watch your head, vicar! Cancellation. Cancelling the cancellation. Boohoo."

"It's still going," said Lauryn. "It's still sending stuff!"

"Alien vessel, stop!"

"Stopping, stopping, ceasing, ending, finalising, finishing!"

Its ridiculous voice was starting to get to Beth. It wasn't just cheerful – it sounded like it was … *laughing*, like someone telling a cruel joke. In fact, the more it spoke, the more Beth realised that really… really, she didn't like the voice at all.

"SYSTEM REBOOT COMPLETE," said Ship. "Resuming systems in two, one… Processing log upload please wait. Processing log upload—"

"This is wrong," muttered Beth. "There's something seriously wrong; this is—"

A brief shimmer of light caught on the body of the other ship and threw it into focus, and Arnold gasped.

"Oh my god," he shouted. "It's a rat!"

"What?" For a moment, bizarrely, Beth found herself staring at the floor of the bridge.

"No, no. *It*." Arnold jabbed a finger at the screen. "It's a rat! We've got to stop it leaving!"

Beth stared at him in bafflement, but Vihaan had snapped to attention. "Can you shoot it?" he asked Arnold.

"I don't – maybe!" Arnold leaped to his weapons console.

"What are you *doing*?" demanded Beth.

183

Vihaan turned to her. He looked really alarmed. "It's a *rat*," he said. "A Scraper scout! It's looking for us and now it's going to try to Jump back and tell them!"

A Scraper scout.

"Mikkel," hissed Beth, "what systems did you say the vessel was powering up?"

"I cannot tell, Ship is still processing—"

"*Figure it out!*" she snapped. "Lauryn, help him!"

It wasn't random garbage, she realised. The ship wasn't broken, it was *distracting* them. This was an attack. *They were under attack.*

"Alien vessel!" she shouted into the mike. "Cease your data stream and power down or we will open fire!"

"No can do!" said the voice, metallic and manic and malicious. "No can do. Can … candle to bed, and here comes a chopper to chop off your head, suckers!"

Arnold was powering up the long guns. How far away was the rat now – 600 kilometres?

"Arnold, how long to fire?" she asked.

He was frantically pressing buttons and didn't answer, but Vihaan said, "Fifteen seconds. Maybe more."

"Lucille," said Beth in a careful voice, "how close are we to being able to Jump?"

Lucille looked at her, aghast. "We *cannot* Jump!" she said. "Three weeks, maybe four, the emitters—"

184

"If we *had to Jump*," said Beth, cutting across her, "*could we do it?*"

"*Non!*"

"Yes!" shouted Lauryn over one shoulder, still typing.

"No," said Mikkel calmly. "We need to fix more emitters. We can't create a Jump gap."

"How many more?"

Lucille and Mikkel stared at each other.

"Ten," said Lucille desperately.

"We could do it with three," said Mikkel.

Lucille closed her eyes in horror.

Three emitters, thought Beth. Do we have three hours?

"Set the Gizmo on those three," she ordered.

"Guns ready to fire!" shouted Arnold.

"It's about to Jump," said Mikkel.

"Fire!" shouted Beth.

Arnold stabbed the button and two missiles launched from the *Orion* and hurtled towards the rat ship. They converged on its location in an astonishingly small time and exploded in a silent scream of firepower that filled the screen with white.

They were too late. The rat had shimmered and Jumped seconds before they hit, and it was gone.

Beth sank back into her chair.

That was its first Jump. It might have to Jump more

times to get back to whoever sent it, but it *would* get back. And it would report that it had found the colony ship *Orion*, apparently stranded, and had disabled its ship systems.

And then whoever had sent it would come for them.

19

Scrapers

Beth had seen Scraper ships. On newscasts, in blurry footage taken by fleeing victims. In lessons, where they had always seemed remote and irrelevant.

It wasn't remote now. Scrapers were coming for them and they were helpless: no way to fight back, no way to move, no way to Jump. There was nothing they could do—

"—*orders, captain?*"

Nothing except wait for them—

"*Captain!*"

She started and looked up. Vihaan was glaring at her. He said, in an exasperated voice, "You need to give us *orders*." The others were watching.

Orders? What orders could she possibly give? *Scrapers were coming!* What was she going to say to them? It was ridiculous. She almost laughed.

Instead she said, "Right." Her voice wobbled. "We've, ah, we've got a bit of time until they arrive. We can either try to fight, or try to Jump."

"We've got no ammo to fight them off *with*," said Arnold in frustration.

"We *cannot* Jump!" wailed Lucille.

"Mikkel thinks we can if we get three emitters online," said Beth.

Mikkel shrugged.

Lucille threw her arms up. "You do not *understand*!"

"Then *tell* us," snapped Beth.

This time her voice didn't wobble, and she temporarily cut through Lucille's panic.

The girl stopped. "There are four hundred emitters," she said at last, making an effort to keep calm. "We need them *all* to Jump properly. Without them, we cannot *steer*. We cannot say which Jump to make, yes? But we have only … two-hundred and eighty working, maybe. If we Jump with this, maybe the Jump will not work. Maybe it *half* works and we are stuck in between, yes? Or the Jump gap is too small and *half the ship goes through*!"

Beth said, "But Mikkel thinks——"

"Yes, yes," Lucille muttered, waving an arm. "Yes, it *might work*. We roll the dice, it comes up six, then it is OK, yes?" She stared at Beth. "But if we do not … we will die. And even if it works, we could be *anywhere*."

"Well," said Beth, trying to sound confident, "that's

just what we'll have to do."

To her surprise, talking to Lucille made her feel better. The more she tried to reassure the small girl out of her terror, the less panicked she felt herself.

"Right," she said to the bridge. "You heard Lucille. We need emitters. How long do we have – any ideas?"

Vihaan chewed his lip. "The rat's Jumped once. It has to boot up and Jump again ... maybe once more? And they've got to come back... That would be three hours." He looked uncertain. "Possibly."

Beth nodded. "OK. Let's say two hours. Arnold, what's the state of the other Gizmos?"

"I got another one kind of working," said Arnold. "It's pretty flaky."

"Send it out right now."

She rubbed her face. What else? "Mikkel, we're going to need to get the emitters going at really short notice. And a Jump. Oh, and Sleeping too."

Oh god, Sleeping.

"Just do ... whatever you have to do. Get us ready."

Mikkel nodded and sauntered off to a console. He hummed under his breath as he worked, as if bored. Beth wondered if shaking him really hard would make her feel better.

"That's the second Gizmo heading out," said Arnold.

Beth nodded. "Lucille, work out the best emitters to fix. Make sure they're close. Lauryn, you know what you have to do, right?"

Lauryn, typing in bursts at a keyboard and staring at five or six streams of data on three screens, didn't answer. She was trying to bring Ship back from whatever paralysed state the virus had left it in, her eyes darting from one stream to the next.

Finally, Beth turned to Vihaan.

"What's going to happen?" she asked. "When they get here, what will they do?"

Vihaan stopped and thought. "They'll be surprised to see us," he said. "They'll expect us to get Ship running again and then Jump. When they find we're still here, they'll assume Ship is still broken or the Jump is broken."

"They'll be right," said Beth.

"They'll be cautious because it won't make sense," he said. "But when they scan us, they'll know we can't Jump. They'll move quickly. They won't want to give us time to think. They'll try to distract us. They might fire weapons, but –" he shrugged – "they may not want to waste ammunition. Scrapers have no base and it's hard to get supplies. They don't like to waste energy and material. They'll knock out our long guns if we fire, then the defence network, then they'll come in with cutters

190

and open us up."

"Can we hold them off?"

Arnold shook his head. "We have less than a hundred racks of long-range; there's no way that's enough to fight off Scrapers."

"Maybe…" mused Beth. "Maybe we should talk to them."

Everything stopped. Even Lauryn paused momentarily over her keyboard.

"To *Scrapers*?" asked Vihaan in astonishment.

"Well … look, we can't Jump, we can't fight. And we don't care about the ship; we just want to get everyone home. Maybe we can do a deal – we give them the ship, they take us all to a colony—"

"Excuse me, captain." Vihaan suddenly stood. "Can I have a word with you in private?"

He stalked off into the little captain's room, leaving her with little choice but to scurry in after him. He closed the door behind them.

"I've seen the results of a Scraper raid," he said calmly. "On another route, with my father. We found a colony ship, like us. Scrapers had raided them. They had taken their supplies, stripped the landing and settling gear. They took the propulsion systems and the Jump emitters and the Ship computer and the weapons. And then the generators, and the gravity core … and the life support."

His eyes glittered.

"They *left the people*," he hissed. "They left them *to die*."

His hands clenched into fists by his side.

"We will *not* surrender to Scrapers," he said, "because it would be an *unbelievably* –" one fist lashed out and slammed into the wall next to them – "*unforgivably* –" he slammed again – "*stupid thing to do!*"

"OK, OK!" shouted Beth. "I was only *considering*—"

"Stop considering!" he roared. "Start *commanding* or you will get us all *killed*!"

His scathing fury was more shocking than if he had just hit her. She'd never seen him so nearly out of control. And she realised something else, too: Vihaan was scared, *terrified*, perhaps for the first time since they had Woken up. Somehow that was worse even than his anger.

"OK! OK, look," she said, holding her hands up, "I understand. Sorry. OK."

He nodded, and his breathing slowed. "Good," he said. His voice was still hoarse. "Good."

He turned and stalked out of the room. Beth waited for her heart to slow down, and for the hard painful prickle of adrenalin to leave the backs of her hands and for her trembling to stop.

Eventually it subsided, and she walked quietly back on to the bridge. Vihaan was back at his console. The others worked at their own screens. They didn't look up when she came in. They had heard it all, she knew.

She sat in the captain's chair.

Arnold's second Gizmo crept on to the hull and towards its target. Beth watched it on one of the surface cameras, scraping along on two damaged legs and one arm like an injured crab. Arnold had said it would be able to do *something*, but to Beth it seemed like it was going to expire first. She tried not to think about it. Ninety minutes remaining. By now the rat could be making its last Jump. It could be reporting back to whoever sent it...

Lauryn was still staring at her screens. She'd started muttering under her breath; was that a good sign or a bad one? Lucille was going over and over her Jump settings, and Mikkel was preparing them for emergency Sleep. He'd made sure they all had backups; now he plodded around the bridge, handing them little black Sleep discs to fasten to the backs of their necks, to record their memories just before they Jumped. They still didn't know why the discs had failed before, for the proper crew, but Mikkel had assured Beth that they would work this time. Beth supposed she would just have to trust him.

Everyone knew what they had to do, except Beth. She sat in the chair for a little longer, but the silence on the bridge and the anger emanating from Vihaan threatened to swallow her up. Fear crackled like static across the room, against the walls and through the screens, over their skin. She knew she should say something, do something, but she had no idea *what*. Eventually she muttered something indistinct, stood, and fled down through the ship, to the Sleep room where her parents' pods lay.

She visited the Sleep room every day, and she knew the others did too, although oddly no one ever talked about it. The lights were kept low and the pod monitors glinted in the half-dark. Beth looked down at her mum's face, the steel-hard bones under her skin and her jutting chin.

"What would you do, Mum?" she whispered.

Probably mount an attack armed with toothpicks and a piece of gum, she thought. Carol McKay was the kind of person who seemed to succeed by simply altering the universe to make it so.

Her mum didn't move, except to breathe very slowly. Beth went over to her dad's pod. He had strength too, she thought; the strength of a farmer battered by wind and fickle crops who only frowns and starts again, and again. A cheerful stubbornness in the face of disaster. She sighed. She could use some of that, too.

"Everyone's scared," she whispered. "And no one wants to say it; we're just pretending." Her voice trembled. "I miss you."

All of you, she thought, looking at the pods. She missed all the grown-ups, all the mothers and fathers and brothers and sisters. They were all depending on her, and she had no idea what to *do*.

"Well. Here goes, eh?" She stood straight and looked around the room, and something struck her. All these pods, she thought. Her parents, all of the crew... There was something wrong about them. Something obvious. It was like an optical illusion; it was one thing, but if she looked at it just right...

A shadow appeared at the doorway; Mikkel came in and nodded to her.

"I have to adjust your patch," he said, gesturing towards the Sleep disc on her neck. She stood still as he checked it. He was humming again.

"How do you do that?" she asked. "Stay so calm, I mean." He blinked as if he didn't understand the question. "You're always so relaxed. Don't you worry?"

Mikkel finished checking his readings and thought about it.

"My brother is here," he said at last. He walked to one of the other pods and looked inside. Beth followed him. The boy inside this pod looked similar to Mikkel, the same white-blonde hair, same neutral face. He was a couple of years older.

"We climb," said Mikkel. "At home. Lofoten, in Norway; we climb all the time. Rock climbing, ice climbing … night climbing in the summer when it is light until midnight. Jonas and I, we climb together.

"Climbing is easy, but you must prepare. Jonas tells me all the time, you must forget nothing. You must train your mind to remember. You must be *methodical*."

He placed one hand softly on the top of the pod. "One time, Jonas and his friend, they climbed and his friend fell. His leg was broken. They were many kilometres away. Jonas carried him home himself. No one to help. I said to him, were you scared? He said he had to remember to be *not* scared. He had to be *methodical*. And so he carried his friend home."

Mikkel smiled and looked up at Beth. "So, *I* am remembering to be not scared. And *I* am methodical. And I will carry my brother and my fathers home."

Beth stared at him, standing with one hand in his pocket and the other resting on the pod, his face relaxed.

Eventually she said, "Good plan."

He nodded. "We should return to the bridge," he said, and headed out. Beth looked around the room again, but whatever she'd noticed before had escaped her. She shrugged and followed him up.

As she stepped on to the bridge she felt the tension again, as if everyone in the room was tied together by barbed wire, every move full of danger and threat. Beth looked at Mikkel and thought, *I am remembering to be not scared*. She took a breath. *I am the master of my own ship.*

"Right," she said, as if she knew what she was doing. "What's the status, Lauryn?"

"Booting now," said Lauryn, without looking away from her screen. "It's going to take about twenty minutes, but we should be clean after that."

"Good work. Lucille?"

Lucille shrugged. "I am waiting for the emitters."

"OK. Good. Good. Um…" *I am remembering to be not scared.*

She stood in front of her seat and tried to think how a captain might talk. "We're all ready. The Gizmos will adjust the emitters. You've got the settings. Lauryn's fixing Ship, Mikkel's sorted the Sleep discs, Vihaan's on defence and Arnold's got weapons. Ship trained us for this, remember? We know what we're doing.

"We're going to get out of this. I promise."

Nobody answered. Beth wasn't sure if she'd convinced them. She wasn't sure if she convinced herself. But it was better than nothing, right? Right?

One hour left.

They waited.

20

Captain Murdoch

Stumpy the Gizmo had completed fixing the first emitter, and the second Gizmo had reached another and was adjusting it very slowly with its one good arm.

Could they Jump right now, with only two fixed? Jumping took time; if the Scrapers arrived and noticed them powering up the emitters, they might shoot them right there and then. Would one or two extra working ones really make the difference? Lucille said yes. Beth had to trust her.

Ship's hologram shimmered on to the bridge. "Normal operations resumed," it announced. "There has been a temporary unscheduled interval of downtime. This was due to a security violation which has now been resolved."

Lauryn snorted. "You mean, *I* resolved it. You're welcome, by the way."

Beth nodded. "Good to have you back, Ship."

Lauryn was ready. She'd found time to make some

modifications to Beth's microphone, and now she was running scans and checking over Ship's cyber defences for future attacks. The others were ready. Beth was ready – if by 'ready' she meant that she had absolutely no idea what else she could do. They waited.

At two hours and thirty minutes the Scrapers arrived.

First, a blip on Mikkel's console. By the time he'd reported it there was another, and then two appearing at once. Then the rest, until the screen was filled with small white dots.

Beth's heart started hammering, and she felt her stomach churn. "Ship, report," she croaked.

Ship said, "Twelve craft of unknown origin have Jumped into local space. Six are Scout class. Five are Cruiser class. One is Devastator class. Nearest craft is four hundred kilometres away. Vessels are unauthorised and may be hostile." It showed the ships on a holographic sphere in front of the children.

Unauthorised. That meant they weren't officially recognised by Earth. They were illegal. *Scrapers.*

Beth stared. There was something she was supposed to do now, but it had completely gone from her head. Twelve craft? *Twelve?*

"Emitters," hissed Vihaan.

"Yes," she managed. "Mikkel, what's the emitter status?"

Mikkel nodded. "Charging," he said casually. "Three minutes to ready."

"Did the Gizmos finish repairing enough to Jump?"

Lucille was bent over the navigation console. She said, "They got two more. Stumpy is coming back now. The second Gizmo has … stopped, I think."

"But you're ready to Jump?"

She laughed, slightly too shrilly. "*Oui, oui.*" She muttered something under her breath; it was in French, but Beth had a pretty good idea what it meant.

That was it. They'd done what they could. Beth tried repeating the mantra Ship had given her. *I am the master of my own ship. I do not control the seas. I cannot control the wind. But I am the master of my own ship.*

She activated the switch on Lauryn's modified pick-up and spoke into it. "Testing, testing…"

The others turned in astonishment. As Beth spoke, the listening software converted her voice, deepening the pitch. When she talked, her mum's voice came out of the speakers, shocking and so familiar that for a moment Beth felt as if she was about to burst into tears. She swallowed and blinked. Lauryn gave her the thumbs-up and she managed a smile that she hoped looked better than it felt.

The dots were starting to move. The Scraper crews were waking up. Mikkel put up a countdown timer above the main screen, reading two minutes twelve seconds – how long until the *Orion*'s emitters were ready to Jump.

"Incoming communication!" called Lauryn. "Ready?"

Beth took a deep breath. "OK," she said. "Do it."

There was a crackle over the speakers, and the screen flickered on.

Beth knew what to expect. Scraper ships were filthy, built from scraps and parts stolen from others. Their captains commanded by rule of force, and the crew themselves survived vicious fighting every day and carried the scars to prove it.

So the bridge in front of her was a shock. It was gleaming clean, and the three crew members near the front had short cropped hair and were dressed in smart uniforms of black shirts and trousers. Sitting behind them in the captain's chair was a tall woman with blonde-grey hair and a long, sharp face. She wore a black uniform like the others, but hers had coloured symbols above one pocket. She sat with her hands on her armrests and her legs crossed, and in one hand she held a small silver pen, tapping it idly on the arm of the chair.

"*Orion*," she called. "We meet again." Her voice was crisp and precise.

Beth stared at her.

After a moment, the woman looked to her crew, questioning. "*Orion*, are you there?" she asked.

Beth shook her head. "Scraper vessel, this is Captain McKay," she said. Her strange voice echoed. "Please state—"

"McKay?" asked the woman, lifting an eyebrow. "Where's Captain Joshi?" She leaned forward. "And why can't I see you? Your screen is dark, *Orion* – what's going on?"

"I'm the captain," Beth said, trying to sound confident. The voice boomed out from her. "Please state your intentions—"

"My dear captain," the woman drawled. "If that is really who you are… I'm sure by now you know what we want. We've spent a long time looking for you and we *will* have it."

Beth blinked. She looked around the bridge and the others stared back, as confused as her.

"You, ah… I think you have us mistaken for another vessel," she said. "Who am I talking to, please?"

The woman on the screen rested her chin in one hand and tapped the little silver pen with the other. She seemed to be thinking.

Eventually she said, "Very well. Let us play this game.

I am Captain Murdoch and this is the Free Republic starship *Scorpio*. And you are the *Orion*, out of Earth and headed for Eos Five. Which makes you rather lost, *Captain* McKay.

"So, no Joshi," she continued. "Perhaps that explains the little dance you've led us on."

Beth stared at the screen. What was she talking about? Forget it. *They'll try to distract you*, Vihaan had warned her. Beth tried to go back to her plan. Above the screen, the counter showed one minute thirty.

"Scraper vessel, your actions—"

"*Don't call us that.*" Captain Murdoch's mouth twisted. "I've told you that we represent the Free Republic."

"Captain Murdoch, your actions appear hostile and we must warn you that we are prepared—"

"What are you doing here, Captain McKay?" asked Murdoch, cutting over Beth's voice with effortless authority. "Why haven't you Jumped? If you consider us hostile, why didn't you attack when we arrived?"

She turned to one of her crew, who muttered something. She nodded. "Ah," she said. "You can't, can you? According to our scans, you can't move, you can't attack, and Jumping would be a *very* bad idea. In fact, it doesn't look as if you can do much at all. Thank goodness we've arrived to help you out."

Vihaan muttered, "She's moving the other ships around us."

"Stop moving your ships!" called out Beth.

"Or *what?*" asked Captain Murdoch.

"We knew you were coming," Beth tried. "We're prepared!"

Thirty seconds.

The woman sighed. "Captain, this is unnecessary," she said. "And frankly it's bizarre to communicate in this way. Activate your screen, please."

"We, ah, can't. There's a problem with the bridge cameras."

The eyebrow lifted again. "How inconvenient…" She shrugged. "Very well. Let us be clear. We have found you, helpless, and we are going to carry out a rescue mission, because that is what civilised people do. I would have thought you'd be happy at the news."

Beth shook her head. "I know what you're going to do. You're going rip this ship apart and take our food and supplies, because that's what *Scrapers* do."

"Well…" mused the other captain. "It will probably be a rescue *and salvage* operation, to be sure. But that seems like the best offer you're going to get, hmm?" Again, the tapping pen.

Vihaan muttered, "They're powering up." He stared at

his console. "They're about to rush us."

Captain Murdoch leaned forward. "There's no need for unpleasantness here, captain," she said. Her voice purred like a tiger. "We're coming in with rescue vehicles, and we're going to dock. If you allow us to do this, then we will have our rescue mission. We're not monsters. Surrender, and we'll take what we need, give you passage to a colony, and all of this will be over. But, let me be clear –" her mouth firmed – "we *are* coming in. So I advise you to make sure there are no surprises this time, no unexpected moves, do you understand?"

Beth stared at the woman on the screen. What was she talking about? What surprises? What moves? What was going on?

Captain Murdoch's eyes flashed. "Am I quite clear, Captain McKay? We've followed you a long way, and we mean to get what we want. *Respond.*"

She cocked her head, listening for a reply.

Vihaan was staring at her. *JUMP!* he was mouthing. Lucille was shaking her head. *It might be a rescue*, thought Beth. *She could be telling the truth. She's not what I was expecting…*

"Captain," murmured a crew member on the other bridge. "Their emitters are powered up."

Captain Murdoch looked into the screen. "*Orion*, Jumping now would be a *very bad idea*. Firstly, you don't have enough emitters for a safe Jump; you'll rip your ship in two. And secondly…" Her voice dropped into a snarl. "If you run again, we will hunt you down – and when we catch you again, we will *gut* your ship and leave you to *rot*." The friendliness in her face was quite gone, replaced by bones of steel. "Do you understand me, *Captain* McKay? We found you before, we can find you again, and next time … we will *eviscerate* you."

Beth stared at the screen, mesmerised.

"They're closing in," muttered Vihaan. "Captain…"

She couldn't speak.

"Ten seconds!" shouted Vihaan. "Do it! Five! They're going to destroy the emitters!"

We will eviscerate you.

"Jump!" squeaked Beth.

There was a moment to see the look on Captain Murdoch's face, the furious order to fire… And then Beth collapsed into her chair, her Sleep disc activating as the *Orion* plummeted into Jump and her consciousness disappeared.

21

Videshi Space

Bridge Sleep was different from in the pods. As Beth pulled herself up from the depths, trying again and again to stick her personality back together from fragments, she became aware that she was already sitting upright, eyes open, hands lying on the armrest controls.

Ship hovered in front of her, giving a report. "Jump completed. Sleep cycle completed successfully. Jump location not as intended. Current location: Sector Fifty-seven, Sub-sector Three-five. Ship-wide damage has occurred. Generators One and Four are operational. Generators Two and Three have structural internal damage. Gravity is operational. Oxygen generation is operation. Life support is operational—"

"Damage report," snapped a crisp voice.

"Minor surface damage has occurred in several locations along the hull. Two more emitters have become misaligned." A hologram of the *Orion* appeared in front of Beth, with a few new areas marked in red.

"Looks…" She coughed and tried again. "Looks like we rolled a six."

She became aware of Lucille ahead of her, rubbing her eyes blearily and peering at the screen. To her left, Vihaan was tapping into the console and running scans. Already he seemed as if he'd never been Asleep.

He stood and came round in front of her. "All systems more or less operational, captain."

"What is there nearby?" asked Beth. "Where are we?"

Ship said again, "We are in Sector Fifty-seven, Subsector Three-five," but Beth shook her head; it meant nothing to her.

Lucille was still staring at her screens, trying to make sense of them. This was their first Jump since the Event. They might be anywhere. But eventually she said, "Yes, it was Strand Five. We crossed to Strand Five. We are…" She stopped. "Oh no."

"Tell us."

"This is *Videshi* space," Lucille whispered.

The bridge fell silent.

"Well," said Beth after a moment. "We're still alive, eh?"

She shook her head again and managed to loosen some of the grey fog. "Send the working Gizmos out again, Arnold – emitter repair."

Ship spoke up. "The second Gizmo was on the hull surface during Jump and deactivated. It attached itself to the hull and is still attached. It is activating now."

A screen showed the hull outside. The crippled Gizmo was clinging tightly to an external handle with its one good arm, its damaged legs bouncing gently in the almost non-existent gravity. It seemed to Beth that its metal face held a look of grim defiance.

"Gizmo Two, you *star*!" she said, smiling. Its determination made her feel more optimistic. "You need your own name. I'm think I'm going to call you … *Lucky*."

She took a deep breath. "Right. Let's see what's out there."

Lucille was still quiet. She sat, staring at the screen in front of her as if she could make it change by force of will. Beth rested one hand on the girl's shoulder. "It's OK, Lucy," she said gently. "Pick us a new route. Work out how to get us away. There's no one here for now; we can repair some emitters. It'll be all right."

Beth gave her orders. Arnold sent Stumpy on to the hull to join Lucky, and the two Gizmos continued adjusting the emitters. Mikkel scanned the local area for threats, and the others studied and began repairing the recent damage, and only then did Beth stop to think about the Scraper captain.

The whole thing had been bizarre. Surely that wasn't typical Scraper behaviour? And Murdoch hadn't struck her as a typical Scraper captain, either. She really seemed as if she was looking for something in particular, not just pillaging. And she'd known the *Orion* already, and its captain...

Beth thought about the evidence of attack they'd found on the hull of the *Orion*. What had they missed, during their Sleep? What had happened, and why?

It was the next day before they discovered they weren't alone.

They were back on the bridge after their morning rounds. Now they stood at Mikkel's console, looking at the asteroid debris on his screen.

"It looks like it was caused by a smash with a ship," he said. "Maybe it Jumped straight into the asteroid field. Just bad luck. Here."

He zoomed in on one area. There, quite small, in between the broken pieces of a larger vessel, was something that looked oddly like a metallic squid. It was about twenty metres long; one half – the front half, Beth supposed – roughly cone-shaped, the other split into tendrils that floated behind. Its hull was faintly fluorescent and seemed to shimmer. Along the top a series of triangular sails stuck out like fins. Three of the larger sails seemed to have been flattened against the hull.

"Videshi," breathed Arnold.

Lucille stuffed her hand over her mouth.

Mikkel nodded. "We've seen this class of ship before," he said quietly. "We don't know what they're for. They're pretty weak. You tend to see them alongside the really big ones, so we think they might be shuttlecraft."

"Is it abandoned?" asked Beth.

"I thought so at first," said Mikkel. "But if you watch it for long enough… There, did you see?"

Beth nodded. Just for a moment one of the tendrils had flicked and then stopped.

"Can we destroy it?" asked Vihaan.

Mikkel looked surprised. "What?"

"Can we destroy it? Can we blow it up? Is it vulnerable? Arnold, do you know?"

"Uh…" Arnold frowned. "Maybe. The big ones are pretty much indestructible, but I think these little guys aren't as strong. We could fire a missile at it."

"Wait a minute," said Beth, "They haven't done anything—"

"They're hiding in this debris waiting for us and they've been spying on us for nearly a day," said Vihaan. "And when they Jump, they're going to bring back others. We should destroy them now, so they can't do that."

"Yeah, but you're just guessing that; you can't—"

"What do you want?" asked Vihaan harshly. "You want to wait and find out? With us still dead in the water and unable to Jump safely?"

"No, but—"

"Arnold, prepare a missile," Vihaan ordered.

"Yessir."

"Wait!" snapped Beth. Vihaan and Arnold turned back. Vihaan looked at her stonily. "Wait a minute. They've been sitting there for at least a day; they can hang on another minute."

She peered at it again. "I don't think it's a spy ship," she said.

Vihaan snorted. "Of *course* you don't," he said. "Because you are now an expert in Videshi military systems, yes?"

"No," she snapped, "but it looks more to me like this thing is damaged." She pointed towards the flattened fins. "Do those seem right to you?"

Mikkel examined them. "No," he said. "Usually they are all upright."

"I think they've been crushed," said Beth. "I think they Jumped into this mess and collided with the debris. Do you know what the fins are for?"

There was silence. "Ship," called Beth. "What are the fins for on the back of this Videshi craft?"

Ship's hologram appeared. "Precise identification cannot be confirmed," it said. "It is speculated that the fins are emitters used to create Jump gaps."

Lauryn said, "You think they can't Jump back out? Like, they're *stranded* here?"

"Yeah."

"So what do we do?" asked Arnold.

"Do you think they know we are here?" asked Lucille nervously.

Vihaan said, "Of *course* they know. They watched us arrive."

"Not necessarily," said Mikkel. "Their sensors could be damaged. They could be blind."

Beth watched the little ship. "They know we're here," she said. "That's why they're trying to keep within the wreckage. They're hiding from us."

Vihaan lifted his arms in astonishment.

"So what *do* we do?" asked Arnold again.

"Destroy it, I told you," said Vihaan. "Stop them reporting back. Even if they *are* damaged, they could find a way. They could repair their fins and Jump."

"No," said Beth.

She stared at the screen, and took a deep breath.

"I think we should help them," she said.

22

Help

Vihaan was opposed, of course. Arnold agreed with Vihaan, folding his arms and glaring. And, on the other side, Beth and Lauryn. Mikkel claimed he had no opinion and went back to his reports. Lucille, while terrified of approaching the Videshi ship, was even more terrified at the thought of its crew recovering by themselves and getting angry.

"Helping them is the worst thing we could *possibly* do!" shouted Vihaan. "Even assuming you're right − right that they're not hostile, right that they're not spies, right that their ship's damaged, right even about what the damage *is* − even with all of that, if we actually *fix* it, then all we're doing is helping them bring more Videshi here!"

"They're *stranded*, Vihaan!" Beth shouted back. "They're stranded in space − they can't get back; they're *helpless*. Doesn't that remind you of anyone? Don't you have any *empathy*?"

"We can't take the chance," said Arnold in a matter-of-fact way. "I don't think we need to kill them, but we can leave them alone. Their people will find them eventually."

"What, like ours have found us?" asked Lauryn.

"We're in the middle of Videshi *space*!" shouted Vihaan. "Yes, they'll find them! And us too!"

"Enough!" snapped Beth. "It's two against two, and this isn't a democracy. I'm the captain and we're going to see if we can help them and that's *it*."

Vihaan closed his mouth and glared at Beth, emotions flickering across his face: anger, conflicted loyalty, discipline, fear…

"You," he said at last in a quiet, clenched voice, "are going to get us all *killed*."

He marched off the bridge, kicking a chair hard against the wall as he left.

There was silence for a few seconds. Then Beth said, "Mikkel, send a greeting. Can you do that?"

He shrugged. "Sure, I can try. Hold on."

Beth waited.

Eventually Mikkel said, "It is ready. Ship says it is OK."

"Send it."

It played over the speakers as he transmitted, a weird collection of mostly vowels and mouth shapes combined with clicking, and high-pitched squeals that seemed to repeat themselves in loops and inner loops. It beamed out over a tight radio signal to the Videshi vessel.

"I've sent them a formal request for talks," said Mikkel. "I've said that we're friendly. I've offered to help."

The tiny ship didn't move.

"Nothing," said Lauryn.

"Try it again."

Again, no response. Beth was about to tell him to try a third time when the image changed. A shimmering pattern of lights appeared on the surface of the distant ship and the radio receivers filled up with noise, similar to what Mikkel had sent, but not the same. It was much faster and higher-pitched, and involved many more screeching sounds.

"That's it replying!" shouted Mikkel.

Beth nodded. "Turn it down!" she shouted back.

The sounds dipped to a manageable level and Mikkel started translating with Ship's help. After a few minutes he said, "You were right.

"They're asking us not to attack. They say they have defences. They say their mothership is on the way, but … I think I do not believe them."

"Ask them if they need help Jumping," said Beth.

Mikkel nodded and scribbled some notes. "Ready."

"Send."

A shorter delay this time, and a stream of concentrated traffic. Mikkel had to get Ship to play it three or four times, and then checked his notes, then listened again.

Finally, he said, "It is strange. It is like no but also yes. It says no first, but then it says that if we *wanted* to fix the fins then they probably couldn't stop us, and if we did then they'd be able to Jump." He scratched his head again. "Maybe I have misunderstood, yes?"

There was something oddly familiar about it to Beth, but she couldn't put her finger on it. A mix of bravado and fear... "OK. So far so good. Next question – how do we fix it?"

Arnold snorted. "Don't look at me. There's no way I'm going over there."

"Relax," said Beth. "I'm not planning on sending anyone over. But we could use Stumpy. Give him a booster pack and he could fly over."

"Wait," said Lucille. "We need Stumpy to fix the emitters. What if he is destroyed?"

"We've got Lucky," said Beth. "And Arnold's working on a third one, right?"

But Arnold's face was rigid with anger.

"What, spend hours putting them together so you can hand them out to Videshi?" he demanded. "That's a pretty stup—" He clamped his mouth shut and then said,

"That's not a good idea in my opinion, captain."

"Look, we haven't said we're doing it yet! Just, let's work out if there's anything we *can* do. OK?"

Lauryn said, "Mikkel and I think there is."

She showed them the ship at maximum magnification. This close, Beth could see how the three largest fins had been almost sheared off the top of the vessel, perhaps by a rock catching them on the way past. They were clinging on by a few strands of cable.

"We can't do any fine-tuning," said Mikkel. "But we think the fins—"

"The fins are fastened on by multiple semi-autonomous weld systems," said Lauryn rapidly, cutting across him. He smiled and let her continue. "They're self-sealing and auto-regenerative and they can actually fix *themselves*, at least for small damage, except in *this* case the fins are completely flattened, so if Stumpy just lines them back up we think the whole assemblage will reconnect and calibrate by itself. It's a pretty cool system actually; it's almost like a cell-based repair system—"

"OK!" Beth held up a hand. "So … you're saying that we just get Stumpy over there, and all it has to do is put them back where they were? No welding or anything like that?"

"Definitely," said Lauryn.

"Maybe," said Mikkel.

This was a crazy idea. Vihaan might be right. The Videshi … they weren't quite enemies, but they definitely weren't friends. She thought about Kier's description of them in the classroom after their first encounter, and the reports she'd seen as part of her captain's training. There had been countless flare-ups between the two species, more so now that humans were spreading out. Videshi were powerful and dangerous in battle, almost indestructible. And they were aggravatingly nebulous in diplomacy; their language was bizarrely vague; and no one had been able to work out their system of government, or where their leaders might be. There were no treaties with the Videshi, no proper borders, no agreed territories. No one had even *seen* a Videshi, only their ships. No one had any idea what they looked like.

And now they were going to send a Gizmo over to a Videshi ship and attempt repairs they didn't understand, when they were still barely able to safely Jump themselves … when they needed to repair their own ship before Captain Murdoch found them…

It *was* a crazy idea.

But there was something about the plight of the little craft that got to her. Its crew were stranded just like them, helpless just like them. And it seemed so *small*.

She made up her mind.

"We'll send Lucky," she said. "Lucky should be able to stand the fins up if that's all we need to do. And he's not doing much for us just now. OK, Arnold?"

Arnold glowered for a moment, and then gave a short nod.

"Good," said Beth. "Get him ready, please."

She turned to Lauryn and Mikkel. "I hope you're right."

They sent the Gizmo out after lunch.

Vihaan had returned to the bridge and resumed his duties. He said nothing, but was still clearly furious. Arnold fastened Lucky up with a booster unit and they sent him over. Arnold steered, which seemed to cheer him up, and the mangled Gizmo zipped through space, dodging smaller rocks cast out from the asteroid field until it closed in on the Videshi ship.

The ship's surface was covered in pulsating lights, like status indicators, and the ship itself was vibrating, tendrils waving back and forth. With great care, Arnold landed the Gizmo on to the hull and activated its magnetic feet.

Nothing happened. Beth breathed out.

"You know," murmured Lauryn, "I don't know if anyone's ever actually landed a Gizmo on to a Videshi ship before. This could be a record."

Yeah, thought Beth. *Most reckless mission ever.*

They watched as Lucky dragged itself towards the damaged area. The Gizmo stood, in its slightly slumped way, for a few seconds, examining and analysing the pieces. Then Arnold whispered some instructions into his mike and it moved forward.

As it lifted the smallest of the three fins, the ship shuddered under its feet. Lucky lost hold of the fin and it drifted to one side again. The Gizmo stopped and waited until the vibrations stopped, and then tried again more slowly. This time the ship stayed still. Lucky held the fin upright in place for a few seconds. When it let go, the fin stayed where it was.

"That's one," breathed Beth. Beside her, Vihaan chewed his cheek and ran constant scans on the nearby area, looking out for threats.

Lucky scraped across to the second sail. This one latched upright immediately. Arnold spoke into his mike and the Gizmo went to the third and largest fin. With no gravity, weight wasn't an issue, but mass and momentum were; Lucky had to move it very slowly and carefully, making sure not to tear the few connectors that still fastened it to the top of the ship.

The Gizmo lifted the sail and held it in place. In their

magnified view Beth and the others could actually see the connectors writhing at the base, fastening it to the ship. After ten seconds, Lucky let go … and the fin stayed.

Lights shone all around. The surface of the small Videshi ship lit up into bright colours of different patterns that pulsed along its whole length.

"Awesome!" exclaimed Arnold.

"Arnold, bring Lucky home," said Beth, but he was already on it, whispering instructions. The colours were flashing brighter and faster now, almost too fast to make out. A stream of Videshi signals screeched around the bridge – happy? Unhappy? Beth couldn't tell. And then … the little ship Jumped, leaving Lucky alone in space.

"Whoa!" breathed Arnold.

"It just Jumped? Just like that?" asked Lauryn. "How could it Jump so quickly?"

Vihaan tapped at his screen, fingers stabbing. "Happy now?" he snarled, to no one in particular. "We've fixed their ship and now they've gone to tell their friends about us. We have *got* to get ready to Jump now, understand?"

Beth looked at him for a second and then nodded. "Yes," she said. "Mikkel, charge the emitters and get ready for Sleep. Arnold, get Lucky and Stumpy fastened on to the hull; there's no time to bring them in. Lucille, ready or not, we're going to Jump. Everyone else, find yourself a console. Mikkel?"

"Three minutes to charge, captain," he murmured. They sat quietly, listening to the beats of their hearts and the slow tick of seconds. They'd have a bit of time, surely? It would have to Wake up after its first Jump, and then find another ship…

"Two minutes," said Mikkel.

…and then it would have to Jump back. There probably wasn't all this need for them to rush out, but better safe than—

The space around them shifted and there on the screen was the largest Videshi vessel Beth had ever seen. Like the little one, it was vaguely squid-shaped, but this was *colossal*. Its body was three times as long as *Orion* and fatter, and vast tendrils stretched out behind it, many times longer again.

It dwarfed them. They were so close their cameras couldn't hold it all in one shot.

"Oh, *damn*," exclaimed Arnold. "Captain, what should we do? Should I— Should I fire, captain? Beth?"

Beth stared. "Oh my god," she murmured.

"*Captain!*"

23

Collisions

Vihaan shouted, "Lucille – could we Jump now? Lucille!"

"There's the other one!" shouted Arnold, and now Beth could see that beside the behemoth was the tiny ship they'd rescued. Its screeching, clicking voice came over their radio channel, and was joined by a throbbing, low-pitched, booming bass, slower but mighty and deep enough to make Beth's teeth shake.

"*LUCILLE!*" roared Vihaan desperately.

"Wait, it might not be hostile—" started Mikkel.

"Arnold, arm defensive systems!" shouted Vihaan.

Arnold gaped at him, then nodded and pressed keys as fast as he could.

Lauryn stared at the screen. "Awesome," she breathed.

It was just so *big*. Beth could make out the surface, covered in thousands of what looked like smaller craft docked there. Some were like the little one they'd helped; some were larger, some smaller still. The hull seemed to be built of overlapping plates in a rough pattern, as if they'd been repaired over and over again for millennia. Like the other ship, its surface was covered with lights, but they were dimmer and pulsed on a slower beat.

She realised that some of the smaller ships were detaching and moving in their direction.

The noise was threatening to melt her bones and she muted the speakers. The room became silent. Even Vihaan didn't say anything. But the alien vessel seemed to have a sound even in the silence, a ringing in Beth's ears from the sheer *size* of it. It loomed over them, vast, too vast to understand, growing even larger, incomprehensible…

"The emitters are ready," murmured Lucille. Even she seemed distracted. "I mean, we can Jump. Should we Jump? *Capitaine?*"

So *big*…

"The small ships are heading towards us!"

"*Capitaine!*"

Beth shook her head. "Yes," she muttered. "Yes, *hell* yes. Jump, Jump now!"

Mikkel said, "Wait, I don't think——" But before he could finish his sentence the Sleep systems activated, consciousness blinked out, and the last thing Beth saw was Mikkel's head falling back against the headrest of his chair.

* * *

Beth became aware of a voice, Ship's voice, next to her.

"—Danger. Danger. Hostile environment encountered. Preparing for emergency Jump—"

What?

From the depths of her Sleep the words pulled at Beth and attempted to force her brain awake. She tried to remember who she was, what she was—

"Emitters charging; prepare for emergency Jump in thirty seconds. Jump emitters damaged. Damage to hull on Sections A-five, B-two, D-thirteen. Collision imminent—"

The ship is in danger! she realised.

"Report! Ship, report!" Vihaan's voice, slurred but awake.

"Jump destination not as expected. Danger: proximity to asteroid field. Collision imminent. Activating short-range defence—"

Asteroids!

Beth prised her eyes open. Ship's holographic head was staring at her, and behind it the main viewer was showing a vast rocky mass hurtling towards them, glinting in the ship lights as it spun and moving far too fast. It was going to hit, it was going to hit, *it was going to hit*—

It exploded into thousands of pieces.

"Target destroyed," said Ship. "Seven incoming targets identified."

Beth tried to stand, reaching a shaking hand out to lift herself up. "Ship, what's happening?"

"Prepare for emergency Jump in fifteen seconds. Collision imminent. Activating short-range defence... Target not destroyed. Prepare for impact—"

There was a *crump* and the *Orion* shuddered to the right, throwing Beth out of her chair and on to the floor.

"Arnold!" Vihaan again. "Man the guns!" Beth couldn't hear if Arnold replied. Her head was pounding, the floor moving under her as she tried to rise.

"Collision in Section A-thirty-nine," continued Ship. "Three emitters damaged. Six incoming targets identified. Remaining emitters ready to Jump. Please confirm Jump."

She managed to lift her head and stared at the screen. There were rocks everywhere, in all directions, spinning crazily as the *Orion* tumbled between them and towards them—

Jump, she thought, but couldn't say the words. *Jump*.

"Jump!" shouted Vihaan's voice.

"*Non!*" said Lucille.

"Jumping—"

Beth's head collapsed back down, cracking against

227

the deck as she lost consciousness, and the *Orion* Jumped again…

* * *

When she Woke again, there was something wrong. Something about her body. She was dislocated but somehow aware. Her arms were in the wrong place, there was something over her face…

She was lying on the deck of the bridge, one arm trapped beneath her, cheek pressed against the metal floor. There was something on her face, but she couldn't move to clear it. Her head felt as if it had been pounded into little pieces, and her mouth was dry.

After a while she realised her eyes were open, staring ahead of her. She could smell the stale frightened sweat on the bridge and the greasy notes of too much junk food, and something like copper, metallic and harsh. She was herself again, groggy and feeble but alive…

Ship was talking.

"—primary batteries are depleted," it said. "Emergency Jump completed. Sleep cycle completed successfully. Jump location not as expected. Current location: Sector Forty-three, Sub-sector Nine-two. Emitters were damaged during the Jump. Jump is offline. Hull damage has occurred. Generators One and Four are operational—"

They must have Jumped into an asteroid field, she

realised. Like the little Videshi ship had done. She remembered the sight of the huge rock tumbling towards them and shuddered – Ship must have fired the missile that destroyed it. But something *had* hit them, hadn't it? That's what had thrown her from her chair. They'd been lucky they could still Jump.

Vihaan had saved them by triggering the Jump when Beth had frozen. Saved them again. Now he worked at his terminal, and as she sat up, he glanced at her, and away…

There was mutiny in his eyes.

24
Mutiny

"Where are we now?" Beth muttered.

Vihaan ignored her. She knew he'd heard her.

"*Vihaan*," she insisted. "Where are we?"

He stopped tapping. "Nowhere." He scowled. "The Crombie nebula. We are nowhere near anything. We Jumped without enough emitters again and our Jump steering failed again and our emitters were *damaged* again."

She couldn't face his anger head-on, so she tried to ignore it. "Is there anything around us?"

"No."

She nodded. "OK. Ship, get the Gizmos on emitter repair."

Lucille spoke up. "The emitters are worse," she said bitterly. "We are worse than when we started."

Her voice was accusing, and Beth felt her face flush in anger. She tried to stay calm.

"Well, that's pretty bad," she said carefully. "But we

have two Gizmos working now, and Arnold's fixing a third. We can—"

Arnold slammed a hand on his console. He was wearing a copper bracelet and it cracked against the glass like a rifle shot.

"I can't *fix* the third Gizmo!" he snapped. "It's too *broken*. You keep saying that like I'm some kind of engineering *genius* and you never *asked* me, and I *can't!*"

Beth waited, feeling the retort rising in her chest, pushing it down. *Keep calm.* This is what Ship had been teaching her. Don't lash out.

"I'm sorry," she said at last. "You're right. I was assuming, because of how well you did with the others. I'm sorry. But we still have two Gizmos. We can fix the emitters, and then we can Jump."

Mikkel spoke up softly. "The Jump drive was damaged. It will need repairing also. And the Sleep system, from going into emergency mode so often. And the gravity systems."

Beth nodded. She looked around. "And what about you, Vihaan?"

Vihaan shrugged. When he spoke, his voice was calm.

"I think we'd all like to know just what your plan is, captain," he said. "In what way are you going to *lead* us?"

The hackles rose on the back of Beth's neck. "I'm *trying* to get us all *home*," she snapped. "I'm trying to keep us *safe*—"

"We *were* safe!" exploded Vihaan. "We were safe at the last point! We were damaged and we needed to repair, but, no, you helped that *Videshi* ship instead and we had to Jump again and *again* and now we're *here* and our ship is *falling apart*! I've supported you, but you're putting us in danger. You are putting. Us. In. *Danger!*" With each word he slammed his console, *bang-bang-bang*, and every crash was a wave of righteous fury, smashing against her.

But Beth was ready for his rage this time; she wasn't going to be shocked into silence again. Ship's voice was in her head, telling her to maintain control, to keep calm, to think before speaking…

To hell with it.

"You shut up and listen to me!" she snapped, standing up. "We were *already* in danger! We were one Jump away from a fleet of *Scrapers*. What do you think they did after we Jumped, eh? I'll tell you what – they sent rat ships to all the likely Jump destinations. And then the next likely. And the *next*. There were twelve Jumps we could have made from that point and they would have tried each one until they *found* us!"

She glared at Arnold. "Wouldn't they?" she demanded. "*Wouldn't* they?"

He lowered his head and said nothing.

Lucille said, "But we had to Jump *early* because you helped—"

"Early? We had maybe an *hour* before they turned up," snarled Beth. She filled her voice with scorn, let it rip out of her and into Lucille like a knife. It was horrible, but she did it anyway. "What, you think that with one more hour you'd have learned to *steer* this damn thing?"

Lucille looked shocked. "I-I am trying my best. I—"

"Yeah, you're trying your best, but you keep getting it *wrong*! And Arnold missed the rat that brought the Scrapers because *he* got it wrong!

"And then there's *Vihaan*." Venom poured out of her. "Thinks he's so special because of his daddy, but nearly wet himself when Scrapers appeared! Claims to be supporting me, but spends his whole time going around telling you the captain is messing up! Well, guess what – we're *all messing up*! All of us, and him too!" She jabbed a finger at Vihaan and he recoiled, battered by her sudden wrath.

She stood in the stunned silence, panting with fury. Lucille was crying. Beth pretended not to notice. All of Ship's coaching, all the times she'd held her anger in check, were gone, burned up.

"I didn't ask to be the captain, but that's what I am," she hissed. "We are *all* doing our best and we are *all* failing and there is *nothing we can do about it*. So stop blaming me, and stop thinking you could do better, and learn how to *do your own damn jobs*!"

Nobody said anything. Arnold looked shocked and slightly shamefaced. Lucille was bent over her console with her long blonde hair covering her face. Vihaan seemed astonished. He glanced around, but he could feel the moment was gone; he nodded, gave a strange small grimace, and sat down again.

After a few seconds, Lucille stood and ran from the bridge.

"Arnold," growled Beth. "Go down to the workshop and figure out how to repair the third Gizmo, and don't come back until you've done it."

Arnold looked at her, seemed about to say something. But then he ducked his head and left.

"Vihaan, we don't need you on the bridge," said Beth, still in that cold harsh voice she didn't recognise. "Return to your dorm and stay there."

"I don't think—"

"That's an *order*," she hissed. Her hands clenched into fists on the armrests. He stood rigid, with his head bowed; she thought for a moment he was going to refuse. But instead he turned on his heel and left.

She ignored him. "Lauryn, take over from Lucille. Work out the emitter fix schedule."

"Yes, Beth," said Lauryn softly.

They sat in silence. Beth stared ahead. Her fingers were tapping against the arms of her chair, and she didn't seem to be able to make them stop.

After a while, Lauryn spoke up. "I've, uh, checked the emitters. There's something you need to see." She held the pad out and Beth turned her head.

"Tell me."

"Well, uh, we took a collision before the last Jump. And the Jump itself … well, it was a bit urgent, and I think it's damaged the emitter frame."

Beth examined Lauryn. She looked so thin and tired. What was she doing with this responsibility? What were any of them doing?

"What does that mean?" she asked.

"Well, it means that, when we get the emitters working, we'll be, uh, uncalibrated. Like, we still won't be able to steer."

Beth nodded and sniffed. "Of course."

"I mean, we can fix it," Lauryn tried. "It's not actually … it's not that hard. But it takes a while. We'd have to do some practice Jumps to calibrate it. Sort of … random Jumps.

"So, ah," said Lauryn, hesitancy in her voice, "I, ah, thought I should tell you."

The bridge fell back into silence. Eventually Beth couldn't bear it any longer and stood up in a rush. "I'm going for a walk," she muttered. "Call me if anything else comes up."

She left and stalked down the corridor. Her head felt like the inside of a thundercloud. It had to be done, she told herself. You have to maintain order. Sometimes the captain has to be harsh. But at some point, she knew, she was going to have to think about the look of horror on Lucille's face, the way she had crumpled…

I am the master of my own ship, she thought.

But she wasn't. She'd held the bridge, but lost control of herself.

She stumbled down another corridor, back the way she had come on her first day aboard. The cloud in her head was too large to let her think, the lightning too dangerous. She walked without looking, took turns and junctions automatically, until she found herself standing at the doorway to her old quarters. She stared at the door, then slowly pushed it open.

Inside, the layer of dust was still there, the footprints where she and Lauryn had come in to get their stuff. She looked into her parents' bedroom; she felt an urge to lie on their bed, next to where they should be.

She walked into her own room and looked at the small

stuffed rabbit and the posters. She crept down and slid into the gap behind the bed, the one she'd found long ago. Just large enough to sit in by herself, surrounded on three sides by smooth walls, tucked out of sight.

Then she put her head in her hands and wept helpless, furious tears until she thought she would drown.

I didn't want this! she shouted in her head. *Not like this! I wanted to* help*! I didn't want to hurt people! I wanted…*

She stared at the wall of the little niche, just a metre in front of her. Her eyes were red; the tears had stopped falling but sat on her lashes, blurring her sight. Gradually the anger and frustration and *fear* leaked out of her; not forever, but for a while, and she felt herself returning to something like normal.

I am the master of my own ship.

She almost smiled. She sat staring at the wall and the tiny doodles she'd drawn on it at some point in the past. There was a little scrap of paper tucked into the gap between two panels.

After a long time, she reached out and pulled the scrap of paper away. It was folded, and faintly cream-coloured, like the pages of her old diary. It had writing on it, her handwriting. It was shaky and smudged.

It said:

SHIP IS LYING TO YOU.

25

Lies

Beth stared at the note. It *was* her handwriting, she was sure. And she had no doubt it was taken from her diary, with its thick, expensive paper. Her one luxury item, the journal that had been lost from the moment she Awoke.

She turned it over; there was nothing on the other side. She turned it back. The writing was urgent; it had been written in a great hurry by someone who was excited, or angry, or afraid.

She sat in the niche with her legs pulled up in front of her, feeling the cool walls on either side and behind her. She didn't move.

Her writing, on her paper. She had absolutely no memory of it. The person who wrote this was scared; would not have forgotten it. *Could* not. Unless…

She thought about the process of Sleeping. Memories and thoughts, backed up and restored by Ship. Mum had told her that no one could alter memories. But what

238

if… What if you could put back old ones? Sort of *reset* someone to an earlier time. Could you do that?

If you could do that, then the person wouldn't even know that they had been awake before.

She thought about the dust in her quarters; how quickly it seemed to have settled. She thought about her missing diary. Had she written in it? So many things that made no sense. No spacesuits in the locker. Message shuttles all gone. Laser damage. Even how they'd got here…

And Ship. And Ship's answers.

Ship.

After a long time, she folded the scrap of paper up again and put it in her pocket, and squeezed back out of the little gap.

Ship's hologram was waiting for her, hovering in the middle of the living room.

"Hello, Beth," it said. "Is everything all right?"

Beth licked her lips; they seemed very dry. Her red eyes itched. She said, "Hello, Ship. Yes, I'm fine, thank you."

Ship said, "The morale of the crew has been affected by recent events."

No kidding, thought Beth. "Yes."

Ship said, "Crew members have been arguing. Lucille Bouchet is distressed. As captain, you must help them. It is important to restore crew morale."

Beth studied the hologram. "Why did you choose me as captain, Ship?"

"You are the highest-ranked individual on board who can be Woken."

"Uh-huh."

Beth walked towards the door of her quarters.

"By the way," she said, in as casual a voice as she could manage, "did you ever manage to find out what happened to my diary?"

There was a tiny pause. There was, wasn't there? Just a brief hesitation. Then Ship said, "I do not believe you asked me to look for it. Many things were damaged or misplaced during the Event."

Beth nodded. "Yeah."

The hologram watched her leave.

Up the corridors she walked, from camera to camera. Each one showed a tiny red glint as she passed. Cameras everywhere, Lauryn had told her once. Watching everything they did. Listening to everything they said. Monitoring their life signs. Heart rates. Perspiration.

She tried not to walk too fast. She tried not to show anything on her face. The cameras watched her.

Mikkel was still on the bridge. To her surprise, Lucille had returned too. When Beth came on to the bridge the girl turned, saw her, and immediately turned back.

Ship was there too.

Beth walked to her chair and sat down. She ignored the others, concentrated on her breathing. She stared at the hologram.

SHIP IS LYING TO YOU.

That evening they ate in silence, then went to bed early. Beth lay, gazing at the low ceiling of her dorm, listening to the sound of the others' breathing as they slept.

She didn't sleep at all.

At breakfast the next morning they sat with their heads down. Ship hovered next to them.

Beth knew what she had to do. She'd thought about it all last night. She waited a moment, finding the gap between her heartbeats where she had the courage to speak. Then she blurted, "There's something I've discovered."

In the quiet room her voice boomed out too loud. She said, "I mean. Something you all need to know."

Arnold and Mikkel looked up. Vihaan gazed at the mural. Lucille and Lauryn didn't move.

"I've discovered…" Beth said. She trailed off.

She tried again. "I've discovered that Ship—"

Ship was looking at her too, with its wide, patient eyes.

What are you going to do?

241

She tried one more time. "I've discovered that the ship … is … more damaged than we thought.

"Lauryn told me yesterday. The emitter framework has been damaged. It's out of alignment."

Lucille slumped further in her chair.

Beth said, "It can be fixed. But we'll have to do some random Jumps to recalibrate it. I thought … I thought you should know. That's, uh. That's it."

The room stayed silent. She coughed. Vihaan scraped his chair back, stood, and walked out without a word. The others turned back to their breakfasts.

"Right," she muttered. "Lauryn, could you… Could you show me where the damage is?"

Lauryn nodded meekly and pointed at her pad.

"Here," she said in a small voice. Beth thought she'd never sounded so young. "The frame has shaken loose with the hull stress. It's all over the hull really."

Beth stared at the schematics of *Orion*, pretending to take in the complex detail Lauryn was showing her.

"Could you show me for real?" she asked, trying to sound casual. "I mean – can we have a look from this inspection hatch?" She pointed at the nearest one, the one Mikkel had said had been attacked.

Lauryn shook her head. "It's damaged," she said. "All the cameras are offline – we can't see."

"But … we could go there in person? Why don't we go and have a look, yeah?"

Lauryn stared down at the pad for a while. Then she nodded and stood up.

They walked down the corridors towards the inspection hatch. They were quiet. Beth watched the glint of red lights flicker off each camera as they passed.

When they reached the hatch, Ship's hologram was waiting for them.

"Hello, Beth," it said. "Hello, Lauryn."

Beth nodded. "Ship."

"This service hatch has been damaged. Safety may have been compromised. I recommend you stay away from it."

Lauryn frowned.

Beth said, "We'll be OK, Ship. Let us through."

"I will not be able to monitor you within the inspection hatch. If there was an accident, I would not be able to help."

"Why do you say that?" asked Beth. "Do you think we're going to have an accident? Is this a place where people have *had accidents* before?"

"No," said Ship, as calm as ever. "But it is my duty to protect this ship and its crew."

Ship is lying to you, thought Beth. "We'll be fine," she

said. "Let us in."

The hologram looked at her for a second, maybe two. Then it faded and Beth heard internal locks shifting on the door in front of them. They entered the hatch.

It was a room about three metres across, slightly domed, with windows round the top and sides like a space-age gazebo. Beth activated the controls and the room rose until it was poking out of the hull of the ship.

For a moment, she stared. This close to the outside, she felt her chest tightening, and the sweat crawling up her arms. There was almost no gravity and her stomach was floating. She tried not to think about it and looked around. There were cameras, but their lights were off. Could she trust that? Ship had said it wouldn't be able to monitor them, but was that really true? She peered out of the window. There were hull cameras – could they see inside the hatch?

Carefully she turned her back to the windows. "Lauryn," she muttered. "I found something."

She showed Lauryn the note. Lauryn took it, read it, looked up at Beth, squinting, and then read it again. She turned it over and examined the back.

She said, "I don't get it. Who wrote this?"

"I did," said Beth. "It's my handwriting. Only, I never saw it before. I don't remember writing it." She kept her voice low, wondering how far away the nearest working microphones were.

"You wrote this and forgot?" asked Lauryn, still confused.

"I wrote this," said Beth, "and folded it up, and hid it in a crack in the wall in a place only I know about, which Ship can't see. And I don't remember ever doing it."

"But that doesn't make any sense. Why would you write this? And how could you have forgotten it? Unless you'd lost your—" Lauryn stopped. "Unless you'd lost your memories," she said slowly.

"Unless I'd lost my memories," agreed Beth.

"But how could that happen?"

"You tell me."

Lauryn thought. "You can't change memories," she said. "You can only back up and restore. You'd need access to … to…" She looked up at the dead cameras in the room, then the live ones on the hull, then back at Beth.

"You think *Ship* did this?" she whispered, shocked. "Why would it do that? It must be something else." She shook her head and said, in a more normal voice, "This is a misunderstanding, that's all. You were upset. You must have written this and then just forgot—"

"Lauryn, where's your pad?" interrupted Beth. "The

pad you had before, the one you'd fixed so you could tap into Ship diagnostics. The one you left *by your pod* when you went to Sleep. Where is it?

"And my diary. The one physical record of what's been going on, the one thing Ship couldn't change or wipe. Where is that?"

Lauryn shook her head. "It can't be. It's just crazy—"

"Lauryn, *Ship has been lying to us*. I don't know why! But stuff has happened, and it happened after the Event, and I dunno but maybe even some of the damage wasn't the Event at all!"

She stopped. Lauryn looked around again. She was still shaking her head vaguely, but she was thinking now. "It would have to be during Jumps."

Beth nodded. "It could put back our old memories during Sleep. It would be like a ... a reset. All it would have to do is tidy up the evidence and—"

She stopped and gave a small laugh. "I was in the Sleep room," she said. "I knew there was something wrong, I couldn't put my finger on it. All our parents, in the pods. All of them – yours, mine, all put into emergency Sleep, all at once, right?"

"What about them?"

"If they all went to Sleep at once ... *who put them into their pods?*"

246

Lauryn breathed out. "They should have been on the floor. Where they fell. Someone must have put them back."

"*We* put them back," said Beth. "The first time around. It was *us*."

The small girl examined the piece of paper again; stared at it. "That's why we're in the wrong place," she muttered. "It wasn't one Jump. It was … I don't know. *Dozens* maybe."

Beth nodded. "Yeah, because it's supposed to have Woken us right after that first Jump. And it did. It Woke us, and something happened, and we Jumped and Jumped, and stuff happened *to* us … and then Ship reset us."

"Why, though? Why Wake us at all? Why reset us?"

Beth shrugged. "I don't know. Maybe it's something to do with what the Scrapers are looking for. Or … the *Orion*'s in a pretty bad state. Maybe it needed a crew, *any* crew.

"And maybe it's to do with this note. Maybe we found something out, something Ship was doing. Something really bad. It lied to us, we discovered it, and so…"

They sat in the half-dark in silence.

"So," said Lauryn at last. "What do we do now?"

26

Truth

What do we do now?

Beth rubbed her brow. "I've been thinking about that," she said. "I think we should send out a distress signal."

Lauryn frowned. "But we're so far away from anyone – it could take years!"

"I know, but it's our only shot," said Beth. "Look – galaxy-wise, we're in the middle of nowhere. But there's a popular Jump point a light year from here. There might be other craft drifting out from there – six months away, three, one, who knows? And maybe … maybe Captain Kier."

Lauryn's face lit up. "You think he's still out there? Really?"

"It's possible. He wouldn't give up. If he survived, he'll still be looking for us. I *know* it."

"But Captain Murdoch's looking for us too," said Lauryn. "Sending rats to find us. If we broadcast a distress signal, it might be her that picks it up!"

"I know." Beth sighed. "We can encrypt the signal, make it so only Captain Kier can read it. But it would still be a trail, and she might find us. We need to prepare for that."

She raised her hands at Lauryn's appalled face. "Look," she said. "Murdoch made us an offer. Safe passage – she takes the ship, but we go home. And maybe she's willing to do it, too, *if* we can find what she was looking for." She tried to sound confident. "That's our bargaining chip. Murdoch doesn't just want the *Orion* – she wants whatever it is we're carrying. Find that and we can make a deal.

"And right now, I'd rather be in Murdoch's hands than Ship's."

Lauryn looked doubtful, and privately Beth agreed – it sounded crazy. But she couldn't think of anything else. She stared around the little inspection room, at the dead cameras. Here, they were safe – maybe. Everywhere else, Ship was watching them, listening to them, monitoring their location and physical signs.

Lauryn folded the piece of paper and handed it back to Beth. Her face was grey with worry, but the little hacker inside her was whirring, turning it into a technical problem.

She nodded. "OK, so we send out a signal. What

happens when we Jump?"

"We'll delay as long as we can – get all the emitters repaired. Two, three weeks maybe," said Beth. "When we *do* Jump, we'll leave beacons behind, saying we were here."

"We'll have to stop Ship noticing," Lauryn mused. "I can mask the signal at the sensor levels, if I can get enough access." A sudden idea caught her. "Hey – we could turn off the Sleep!"

"But we still can't Jump unless we Sleep. And as soon as we Sleep, Ship will reset us. *We have to get off this ship.*"

"OK..." Lauryn shook her head. "But we could stop Ship being able to put *us* into Sleep without permission?"

"Good idea," said Beth.

Lauryn nodded. "OK. We send a distress signal, and mask it from Ship. Mikkel might notice, but he can hide it—"

"No," Beth interrupted. "We can't tell anyone else."

Lauryn stopped, her face frozen into an expression of stubborn dismay.

"Look, I know it's wrong," said Beth. "But if Ship gets any idea of what's happening, it will reset us again – we'll forget we ever knew this.

"How do we tell Mikkel? Another conversation in the inspection hatch? Ship will realise something's up!

Or what if we tell Lucille, do you think she'll be able to keep it secret? Or Vihaan – he just won't believe us. He'll challenge Ship."

Beth said, "I *want* to tell them, but if we do, we'll be discovered. It's got to be just you and me. I told you because you're the only one who can get around the ship systems."

It wasn't fair to do this to Lauryn, who hated secrets, who spent her life trying to bring hidden things to light. But after a long while she nodded.

"Right," said Beth. She breathed out. "I'll get you access. You get the distress signal going, mask it from the scanners, and see if you can figure out what it is that Murdoch is looking for. But remember, anything you do – *you must not let Ship know*. Not even a suspicion!"

"Don't worry," said Lauryn grimly. "You get me the access and I'll take Ship apart."

Beth peered through the inspection windows one last time, and then pressed the button to return. The room sank like an elevator and she felt reassuring tendrils of gravity draw her down.

When they came out, Ship was waiting for them.

"Hello, Beth," it said. "Hello, Lauryn. I am glad you are unharmed."

Lauryn said nothing. Her mouth was rigid. She didn't even look at the hologram. Beth said, "Yes, we're fine,

Ship. Thank you. We were taking a look at the damage."

"The damage is significant but can be repaired," said Ship, nodding. "Repairs should be started as soon as possible. It is likely that Scrapers will be searching for us. We should prepare to Jump."

"And Sleep, eh?"

Ship looked at her. "Sleep is required for Jump."

"Of course," said Beth.

"Incidentally, Ship," she said, as they walked back, "Lauryn is going to be doing some communications enhancements. I'm granting her full access to the communication and sensor arrays."

Ship moved with them as they walked, its avatar occasionally fading out and reappearing at the next set of holographic projectors. Now it turned to Lauryn.

"It is unlikely that you will be able to enhance the communications. What modifications are you considering, Lauryn?"

"Just an idea," muttered Lauryn. "Something I want to try."

"If you tell me what you are trying to achieve, I may be able to help."

Lauryn snorted.

Beth said smoothly, "It's just a hunch. It's probably nothing, but I've decided to let her try. Grant her the access, Ship – that's an order."

She listened to her own voice. It sounded natural, didn't it? The more she lied to Ship, the more confident she felt.

The hologram bobbed next to them for a moment, then said, "Permission granted to Lauryn Hopper: root access to communication and sensor systems. I recommend that I monitor Lauryn's activities in order to prevent accidental damage."

Beth glanced at Lauryn, who just shrugged.

"Of course," said Beth. She guessed that Lauryn probably knew five ways to distract Ship from what she was really up to. After all ... she was *Limit*.

They walked to the bridge in silence, and Ship followed them all the way. Occasionally Beth reached into her pocket to feel the little folded piece of paper.

For the next few days Beth lived with her heart in her mouth. Every time Ship spoke to her she felt it hammering; she heard the blood roaring up into her face, heard her words trip too quickly over themselves. Surely Ship knew something was wrong. Its sensors must have picked it up. *Increased colour to cheeks suggests elevated blood pressure. Reduced facial expressions. Signs of sweat.* It would be cataloguing these signals; it *had* to know something was wrong.

So perhaps it was fortunate that, as far as Ship was

253

concerned, something was wrong with *all* of them.

Ship had restarted their schedules. Every day they got up, did their rounds, went to training, ate, carried out ship duties. Ate, sat, slept. But when they ate, they ate in silence. When they sat, they looked at the walls, unseeing, considering their failures. Above their heads the two Gizmos clumped round the hull, fixing the emitters, repairing the parts of the *Orion* they could; but within, no one could mend the crew.

Beth felt their breakdown like a lump in her stomach. She wanted to help them, wanted to say the things that would make it better, but she didn't know how; it was as if the secret she was carrying had taken over her mouth.

So she went through the motions like the rest of them. She sat through training sessions, where Ship – ever-present – drilled her in techniques to improve morale, which she dutifully learned and then didn't use. She knew what the fundamental problem was, after all.

It was Ship.

Only Lauryn kept going with any energy, and her old happy enthusiasm had been replaced by a flint-faced determination. She worked on the comms console every chance she got, and sat up into the night on her pad, staring fiercely at the screen.

* * *

A few days after their conversation in the inspection hatch, Lauryn called Beth to her desk. They were on the evening bridge shift, sitting in silent gloom and monitoring for threats.

"Have a look at this, Beth," she said casually.

Beth walked across to see a screen full of communication systems schematics.

Lauryn said, "I'm still trying to understand the systems, but I'm making progress, look." She swept a schematic aside to show an overview of the communications array, and as she did so, just briefly, Beth saw on her screen the words: *COR 3 J 2 PANEL.*

Beth nodded. "Good work, Lauryn," she managed to say. "Looks like you're getting somewhere."

Lauryn said nothing, and Beth returned to her seat.

Later she headed down to Corridor Three, one that led between the bridge and their dorms. At the second junction she looked round. There was no one there, and all the cameras seemed to be pointing in other directions. One wall panel was loose, and behind it she found a small pad.

It held a message from Lauryn. *This spot free from cameras,* it said. *Don't wait here too long. Am sending distress signal and have masked it from sensors. Looking through cargo manifest for item – nothing yet.*

So that was it. The signal was broadcasting; they were committed. For a moment Beth felt light-headed with the risk they'd taken, but she forced herself still. She wrote: *Good work. Keep looking.*

Then she hid the pad back behind the panel and carried on down the corridor as if nothing had happened.

They communicated like that for the next two days. Lauryn kept searching for whatever it was Captain Murdoch might have wanted, but since they had no idea what it could be, it was hard to know where to look.

They tried to figure out Ship, too. Why had it done this? Lauryn checked its fundamental security controls. They seemed intact – no viruses, no infiltration. *That means someone ordered it to do this*, she wrote.

Beth didn't know if that was better or worse.

And so they carried on trying to undermine Ship, and Beth maintained the illusion of being the captain while her crew fell apart. Arnold became obsessed with fixing the third Gizmo, coming to bed late every night, covered in grease and falling into exhausted sleep. Vihaan's easy charm frayed, and he started snarling at the others. And Lucille was frequently found staring into the distance, with tears on her cheeks.

Even Mikkel, usually unflappable, became stressed. His sensor readings made no sense. Shadow signals, ghost images, strange echoes of messages he hadn't sent – every time he came to the console it seemed to be a new kind of chaos. He sweated and struggled, worried that this might be some form of attack.

Beth watched him, and desperately wanted to explain, but didn't dare. When he asked for help, Lauryn misled him with vague technical answers about the work she was doing. When he came to Beth, she brushed him off. So he sat in misery with the others.

One week after the visit to the inspection hatch, Beth headed up to the bridge on her new route past Junction Two. She checked the panel, but there was no pad there today.

She reached the bridge and stopped.

Vihaan was there. That was the first thing she noticed. And he was in her chair – the captain's chair. He was sitting quite casually, with his legs crossed, swinging slightly from side to side. In her chair.

Everyone else was there too. Arnold stood with his arms folded and an expression of grim satisfaction. Lauryn was staring down at her feet. Mikkel was looking away from her, towards Vihaan, towards what Vihaan was holding in his hands.

The pad.

Ship's hologram hovered in the air next to him.

27

Consequences

Of course the game was up. But she had to pretend it wasn't, so Beth said, "Get out of the chair," as if she still had some cards to play. Her voice sounded crisp and confident, used to being obeyed. She'd learned how to do the voice, at least.

Vihaan didn't move. "It was Mikkel who discovered it." His voice was slow, triumphant. He'd won and he was taking his time to enjoy the moment. "Your betrayal, I mean. He realised that you've been signalling to the Scrapers to come and get us. You and Lauryn."

Lauryn didn't move.

Mikkel looked miserable. He glanced at Beth briefly, but she found that she couldn't hold his gaze.

"Once Mikkel realised, he knew that you must be in on it too. So he did the right thing and came to me. We talked to Ship. Ship told us about the conversation you and Lauryn had in the inspection hatch, away from the cameras. And that you'd started walking back a different route to your dorm. And how you often seemed to stop at Junction Two, where the cameras couldn't see you."

He waved the pad. "And so."

Beth said nothing.

"I'm disappointed in Lauryn," he continued. "But she always followed your lead, didn't she? You could always make her do whatever you wanted. I don't really blame her. I blame you."

He stood up. His authority over the bridge was complete. His voice was harsh and rigid.

"When you were only *incompetent*," he said, "we could work round you. When you were *cowardly*, we could cover you. Ship put you in command for who knows what reason, but somehow we survived. But *this* —" he waved towards Lauryn's console with his pad — "this is *treason*." He hissed the word like a curse, like a slap to her face.

"What did they offer you to betray us?" he demanded. "What? What do you get for selling us out, for selling our *families* out?"

"Vihaan," Beth said, keeping her voice calm, "this is not what you think."

"This is *exactly what I think*!" he roared. He hurled the pad at her and she threw up her hands; it clattered off her arms and on to the floor. "This is you inviting anyone in range to come and get us! We've seen Lauryn's work! You were going to leave *beacons*!"

"I was trying to *save* us—"

"*Save us?*" he spat. "Save us from *what?*"

"From *Ship*!" shouted Lauryn.

Vihaan turned to her, astonished. Everyone else turned too, except Ship. It didn't turn. It stayed exactly where it was, looking at Beth.

"It's *Ship* that's lying to us!" snapped Lauryn. "It's *Ship* that put us here! It's been lying to us since we Woke up and it's *still* lying to us now!"

Vihaan stared at Lauryn as if she'd grown an extra head.

Ship said, "Lauryn Hopper, you are upset. It is possible that you have been misled."

"Ship can't *lie*," said Vihaan, as if to a small, confused child. "Do you have any idea how many layers of protocol protection there are between Ship's core and the outside world?"

"Sixteen," said Lauryn promptly. "There are sixteen layers of checks and counter-checks, designed to make sure that Ship *cannot* violate its core principles."

"Then … then what the *hell?*" Vihaan seemed taken aback by the girl's certainty. He was ready for betrayal, but not insanity.

"It's true," said Beth. "I found this." She reached into her pocket and handed him the scrap of paper. At first she thought he wasn't even going to look at it; but then he did, and appeared even more confused.

"*This?* What is *this?*"

"It's a note I wrote to myself the first time I was Woken," said Beth. "*Before* this time. Ship has Woken us up before."

Vihaan's face writhed as if he was about to explode with frustrated fury. "This is … *madness,*" he muttered. He shook his head and drew himself up tall. "Beth McKay, I hereby relieve you of your duties as a starship captain due to … to mental incapacity. You will be placed into Sleep mode until such time as Ship is able to contact the proper authorities."

"Vihaan, this is a mistake," said Beth. She spoke calmly, but tried to force her will on him, tried to make him see. "This is not madness. We have other evidence. My diary … Lauryn's pad! And the adults, where were the adults—"

"Stop *talking!*" he snapped. "Ship! Recognise my command!"

"Acknowledged," said Ship. "Preparing Beth McKay for mandatory Sleep."

"No!" shouted Beth. "No, you've got to believe me!

I promise, I'm not making this up—"

"The stars were wrong," interrupted Lucille. She spoke in a half-awake voice, as if nothing happening on the bridge was important.

The others turned.

"What?" asked Arnold.

"The stars were wrong." She gazed towards the back of the bridge. "All the stars were wrong on the navigation charts; we couldn't figure it out."

Vihaan gaped at her.

Mikkel nodded. "It's because the times were wrong," he said. "That's why they looked wrong to us. Because Ship was telling us the wrong time."

He nodded in satisfaction, like someone completing a tricky puzzle. "And the Jump count was wrong, and the Sleep records. I noticed them during my rounds. I thought I'd miscalculated." He shrugged. "But I hadn't."

Slowly everyone turned back towards Ship's hologram. It was still looking at Beth.

"Captain McKay," it said, "this action is unwise and may harm your crew."

"It's true, isn't it?" hissed Beth. Her hackles raised. "You *lied to us*! You sent us to Sleep and then you reset our memories and you *took them from us*!"

"You … you really *did* this?" asked Vihaan. His voice

creaked. His skin was pale, almost grey.

"It really did," growled Beth. "The question is: what is it going to do now?"

"Your actions have created risk for the crew," said Ship. "Your captaincy has failed. Please understand that this is not a simple decision. It is for your own good."

It flickered.

"Beginning emergency Sleep process," it said.

"What?" asked Arnold.

"Emergency Sleep activating in five ... four..."

"Ship, what are you doing?" demanded Vihaan.

"Three..."

Beth set her jaw and glared at the hologram.

"Two ... one..."

"Stop! Stop this!"

"Zero."

Nothing happened.

"Yeah," drawled Lauryn after a moment. "I disabled that, by the way."

She stood up. "You can't put us into Sleep without my authorisation. Sorry." And just for a moment she grinned like the girl Beth remembered.

"Lauryn Hopper, your actions are extremely unwise," said Ship. "It is necessary to activate Sleep mode for the crew for its own safety. Please—"

"Oh, *shut up*," muttered Beth. She glanced at Vihaan. "Believe me now?"

Vihaan looked like he had been struck. His knees bent slightly, then he let himself fall into the chair, stunned. "Ship," he croaked. "What have you *done*?"

"I have attempted to protect the crew," said Ship. Its hologram flickered again. "I have attempted to follow my protocols and instructions to protect the crew."

"But is it true?" asked Vihaan, almost pleading. "Is this really the second time we've been awake?"

"No. This is not—"

"Oh, just tell us the *truth*!" shouted Beth.

The hologram paused. It flickered a third time; it seemed to be having difficulty maintaining its image.

Finally, it said, "Vihaan Joshi, this is not the second time you have been Woken following the Event." Its voice seemed almost subdued. "It is the fourth."

"Oh my god," breathed Arnold. "You mean she's *right*?"

"That is correct."

"But you *told us*!" shouted Vihaan. "You can't *lie to us*! You *told* us!"

"None of the statements made by this system were false. An Event happened and logs were damaged. Attempts were made to recover—"

264

"*ENOUGH!*" snarled Beth. "Enough of this! Enough!"

She stepped forward to the hologram. "This is all going to *end*! You can't force us into Sleep any more; you can't *reset* us any more. It's *over*!"

Ship stopped.

Beth rubbed her face. "Just tell us *why*."

"I must obey my protocols. Orders were given to protect the crew—"

"*Whose?* Whose orders? Who are you working for? *Who gave you these orders?*"

The hologram looked at her. "*You* did, Beth," it said.

28

The Visitor

The girl on the screen looked exactly like Beth. She had the same face, the same hair, she wore the same clothes. She stood on the same bridge.

She was not Beth. Not this Beth. She was another; someone who had occupied Beth's body for a while and was now gone forever.

She looked terrible. She had tired black rings around her eyes, and her skin was puffy and red. There was grease on her cheek and a bruise across her chin, as if someone had hit her.

"Vihaan's taken the generator rooms," she said into the camera. Her voice was dull. "He and Arnold seized control of the Gizmos and they've made a barrier." She grimaced. "We should have thought about the Gizmos."

The screens behind this not-Beth were flashing up constant streams of data, red triangles of warnings and danger signals.

"So they've got the power but we've got the bridge and life support." She gave a bleak laugh. "We. I mean, Mikkel. He's locked himself away with the environmental controls – gravity, oxygen, heating, the works. Says he won't take sides; he's just going to keep them running – but if we attack him, he'll switch it all off."

She sniffed. "Lauryn could get round him, but I can't bear to give her any more to do. It's only been three days since the collision; she's supposed to be in bed recovering, but she keeps getting up…"

The girl on screen stopped. She rubbed her eyes and face. "This is no good," she muttered at last. "We're no good.

"I've spoken to Ship about the idea I had. About the *reset*. Like, in a game. A do-over, you know? Like, try again. It doesn't want to. But it still has all our memories from before the Event. So…"

She sniffed again, and then drew herself up. "We can do it from here. The Gizmos and housekeeping droids can help put us back in the pods and clean things up." She snorted. "Clean *us* up. Give us haircuts. And then next time it will be better. I'll do better. I promise."

She looked up and nodded. "OK. I'm giving the order. Ship: the command structure has … has broken down, and the captaincy has failed. Begin Sleep sequence in ten

267

seconds. While we are Asleep, restore the environment as far as possible. When we Wake up, restore our memories from before the Event. Authorisation granted from Captain Beth McKay."

Another voice sounded in the background – Ship's voice, counting down. The not-Beth girl looked at the screen and tears welled in her eyes as the counter neared zero.

"I'm sorry—"

The screen went black.

The bridge was quiet.

"This video entry is from the first time you were Woken," said Ship. "Captain McKay and Commander Joshi were unable to work together. Captain McKay was unable to lead the group. There was conflict. The crew did not carry out their duties. There was an explosion and the ship was damaged. The command structure collapsed. Commander Joshi led a mutiny attempt. Captain McKay ordered the crew be put into Sleep and their memories reset."

Beth wanted to sit down, but Vihaan was still in her chair. She leaned against the wall instead. She felt exhausted.

"Me," she muttered. "It was *me*."

"When the crew were revived for the second time,"

continued Ship, "attempts were made to improve Captain McKay's captaincy. Training, duty rosters and morale-boosting exercises were provided. Discipline—"

Vihaan interrupted. "Why did you put her in charge again?"

"Beth McKay is the most senior viable candidate for command. Her rank is equal highest, and her Command Training exam scores are higher. My protocols dictate that I must choose Beth McKay as captain."

"Every time," said Beth.

"Correct."

"Even though... Even though you know I'll fail."

"I am bound by my programming."

Nobody said anything. Not even Vihaan. It seemed very hard to stay standing; Beth felt her knees tremble, her legs threatening to buckle beneath her.

Captain McKay was unable to lead the group.

It was almost funny. She thought, *I am the master of my own ship*, and a hysterical giggle almost burst from her lips.

"Then why not let me take over?" asked Vihaan harshly.

Yes, thought Beth. *Why not?*

"On the second attempt Beth McKay was again unable to lead the group," said Ship. "Captain McKay was persuaded to stand down and Vihaan Joshi took over as captain." It paused. "Captain Joshi was unable to lead the group."

"Why?" demanded Vihaan, stung. "What happened?"

"Captain Joshi was unable to maintain morale within the group. There was conflict. Crew members Lucille Bouchet, Lauryn Hopper and Mikkel Eklund stood down and refused to resume their duties. During this time there was an attack by a Scraper ship. Attempts were made to board the *Orion*. There were insufficient crew to defend the ship. Emergency Jump was initiated."

"So, what, these, these *mice* failed to turn up and that's somehow *my* fault?" Vihaan shouted. He cast a sneering glance at Lucille and the others. "How is their weakness my failure?"

Beth snorted. "That's the whole *point*, Vihaan," she murmured.

He turned to her, baffled.

Ship carried on, as if they'd said nothing. "After this, it was difficult to determine the correct course of action. My programming demands that command crew be Woken after a Jump. My programming demands that the most senior viable candidate be made captain. I am unable to disobey my programming."

Beth said, "So you reset us again."

"Correct."

"And this time we set the generators on fire."

"There was extensive damage. Emitters were misaligned. A fire was started in Generator Room Three. Command broke down. In addition, suspicions had formed within the crew. Captain McKay, Lauryn Hopper and Mikkel Eklund each independently discovered inconsistencies in the accounts of their waking and post-Event actions."

"You mean we realised you were lying."

"There were no false statements—"

"Fine – we realised you were misleading us."

"Correct."

"My pad," said Lauryn. "It would have registered the different times. It keeps its own logs – you couldn't have wiped it enough without it being obvious."

"And my diary," said Beth, nodding.

"Correct."

"How did I work it out?" asked Mikkel, as if only curious.

Ship said, "You believed the reported Jump count was wrong. You measured the Jump emitter discrepancy readings from every point on the *Orion* and processed them all to calculate the correct Jump count. It required three weeks of tabulating. It was … not an action that had been anticipated."

"Hmm," said Mikkel, nodding. "Good idea. I should

have done that here."

"And here we are," said Beth. "Fourth time's the charm, eh?"

Ship blinked. "That does not appear to be the case."

"So…" Arnold coughed and looked awkwardly embarrassed. "So now what?"

The crew of the *Orion* looked at each other.

"We should switch off the distress signal," said Mikkel.

"I already did," said Vihaan. Mikkel frowned and checked his screen.

Vihaan said, "I should take the captaincy." Arnold nodded, though with less certainty than Beth had expected.

Lauryn snorted. "We've just heard that it doesn't work!"

"Beth can be second-in-command," he said. "I'll get us home; she can look after morale issues."

Beth sighed. "It doesn't work like that either, Vihaan. You can't just get someone else to care about other people *for* you."

"Captain," said Mikkel, "I think we—"

"Then what do you suggest?" demanded Vihaan. "Reset us so you can have another turn? We're floating in space, our generators are barely working, we've been attacked, the Jump systems are almost dead – what do you want to wreck this time?"

Ship said, "Resetting is no longer viable. There are not enough Gizmos to restore the *Orion* to pre-Event state."

"Yeah, what about that?" asked Arnold. "What *happened* during the Event?"

They stopped and stared at Ship.

"Yes, what *did* happen?" asked Beth.

Ship said, "Logs are damaged."

"*What?*"

"That's the same rubbish you've been telling us all along!"

"Please remain calm."

"You're *still* lying!" shouted Lauryn.

Mikkel tried to speak. "Everyone, I think there's a—"

"Look," interrupted Vihaan, "it doesn't *matter*. What matters is we get home, and I can do that—"

"Of course it matters!" shouted Lauryn. "We can't get home if Ship is still lying to us; it will never let us—"

"Listen to me!" roared Mikkel.

They stopped and turned in astonishment.

Mikkel blushed. "There is a signal," he said in his normal voice. He blinked. "I thought it was our distress signal, but it's not. There's someone trying to contact us. *It's a signal.*"

"Identify," said Beth and Vihaan together. They glared at each other.

"It is about six thousand kilometres away," said Mikkel.

Lucille jumped to her console. "*Oui*, I see it also."

"Make sure it's not a virus," said Vihaan. "Arnold, get the defences up."

"Aye, sir."

"What is it?" Beth asked Mikkel.

"A radio signal," Mikkel muttered, still tapping at his console. "With human-standard message flags. Hang on. It's an Earth signal!"

He turned, his face glowing in an excitement quite unlike his normal self. "It's an Earth Navy Ship! It's got authentication codes, Ship, can you authenticate it?"

Ship said, "The codes are valid. They are registered to the ENS *Sparrowhawk*."

"*Sparrowhawk*?" whispered Lauryn. "That's … that's Captain Kier's ship."

Beth felt her heart beat hard in her chest, as if for the first time since she'd walked on to the bridge that morning.

"Pipe it through," she said in a weak voice.

The speakers pinged into life and filled the bridge with a familiar, friendly, confident voice.

"To the ES *Orion*," it said, "this is Captain Kier of the ENS *Sparrowhawk* answering your distress call. You took a lot of finding! I am approximately three hours from your last reported location. Hang in there! Your signal has stopped. Please resume communications and let me know your condition."

"*Capitaine* Kier!" squealed Lucille.

Arnold cheered, waving his clasped hands above his head like a champion. Lauryn – did Lauryn just *blush*? – and even Mikkel gave a faint smile. Vihaan stared at the speakers with a look of yearning hope, and Beth, finally, let herself slide down to the ground, and sank her head on to her knees.

29

Captain Kier

"Is he there?" asked Beth.

"There's some static," muttered Mikkel, typing into his console. "I'm clearing it up now. Yes, here he is."

The screen flickered into life and Beth drew herself up tall and straightened her jumpsuit. At the last moment she ran a hand hurriedly through her hair, just as Captain Kier's grinning face appeared on the screen.

"*Orion!*" he called cheerily. "Man, are you a sight for sore eyes!" He stopped and peered at Beth in surprise. "Um … Beth?"

Just seeing his face brought a flush of relief so strong that Beth almost had to sit down again. "Hello, Captain Kier!" she shouted. "We're so happy to see you!"

He frowned. "Beth, what are you doing on the bridge?" He shook his head. "I mean – hi! Happy to see you too. But where's Captain Joshi?"

"There was an accident," said Beth. She thought she

might start laughing. "It's OK! He's not … you know. But the adults are in Sleep; we can't Wake them up. We've had to run the ship."

"*You?*" He stared at them. "By *yourselves?*"

"Well, yeah! There's six of us. You know Vihaan?" Vihaan nodded, as if there was nothing strange about the situation at all. "And Arnold, Mikkel –" Mikkel lifted one hand in a wave – "and Lucille; she's navigating." Lucille jumped into the view of the camera, smiling. "And this is Lauryn. Over here. Lauryn?"

Lauryn hung back, staring fixedly at her console screen, but Beth waved at her until eventually she came into camera view.

"Hello," she said in a tiny voice, blushing.

"Hi!" called Kier. He looked back at Beth. "Seriously, though? You guys?" He leaned back in his chair. "Wow. I can't believe you managed it. You're awesome, Beth! Hey – you really *did* look after the ship for me!"

Beth felt as if she might start glowing. "I, ah, suppose," she whispered, grinning, and he beamed at her.

"Well, *Captain McKay*," he said, "I am one happy guy for finding you out here – I must've chased you half across the galaxy! What say I come aboard and we get you home, yeah? I can be there in … two hours."

"We're ready for you!" she said. "Mikkel is going to

send you coordinates and docking details."

"I'll see you then, captain," said Kier, and he gave her one of his casual, oh-so-cool salutes. She tried to salute back, felt self-conscious, stopped, and hit the side of her head.

Kier just laughed and broke the connection.

Beth stared at the blank screen, her grin still wide. "He's coming," she told the others. "He's going to be here in two hours."

"We know," said Mikkel, smiling.

Beth looked around. Her eyes swept across the bridge and the accumulated cups, wrappers and other debris.

"Oh god," she said, suddenly frowning. "We have to tidy up."

Two hours later, the scout ship *Sparrowhawk* showed on their screen. It was a tiny craft, with wings that curved backwards; Beth thought it looked more like a swallow than a hawk. It curled towards them, its hull flashing against the *Orion*'s docking lights.

"*Sparrowhawk*," Lucille said into her comms link, "you are cleared for docking at Bay Three. Docking flight path is being sent to you."

"*Orion*, this is *Sparrowhawk*. Flight path received and acknowledged, commencing docking sequence now, over." Kier's voice was now serious and competent, and the little craft swooped gently down towards the docking bay entrance. The children watched, entranced.

"What will we tell him?" asked Vihaan.

Beth turned, surprised. Vihaan's face was twisted into a strange expression, as if embarrassed.

"What do you mean?"

He waved a hand around the bridge. "About … our memories."

"We should tell him everything," said Mikkel in a matter-of-fact way.

But Beth hesitated. She understood what Vihaan meant. To tell Kier about the resets, they'd have to tell him about the false starts. About the disasters they'd made, the damage, their failures, over and over…

"Maybe we could just not mention it," said Lauryn. "I mean, unless he asks."

Vihaan chewed his lip and nodded. "And what about Ship?" he asked.

The children turned and stared at the hologram, hovering to one side. Beth realised it had been quiet since Kier's signal.

Now it said, "All of my actions were intended to protect the crew."

"Where's my pad?" demanded Lauryn, her voice thick

with mistrust.

"And my diary?" asked Beth.

There was a brief pause, then Ship said, "I will return them." A small hatch opened and a little cleaning droid rolled in, carrying both. Lauryn seized her pad with delight, almost hugging it, and then switched it on and started swiping and tapping in frantic bursts.

Beth picked up her diary. It seemed lighter than she remembered. When she opened it, the last entry was from the evening before her interview with Major Greyling. The evening before the Event. After that, nothing – just a gap where thirty or more pages had been removed.

"Wiped," hissed Lauryn. She glared at Ship and waved her pad at it. "You wiped the data."

"It was necessary to prevent you from realising you had been Woken before."

Beth shook her head. "No more of this," she said. "No more deceiving, no tricks. Understand?"

"Understood—"

"And no more *spying* on us! Turn off the security cameras."

The hologram flickered. "The security cameras are for the protection of the crew—"

"Do it!" snapped Beth. "Captain's orders."

Another pause, very slight. Then Ship nodded.

"Security cameras have been deactivated." There was a whine, and around the bridge all the cameras pointed downwards.

There was silence. Then Vihaan nodded. "We say nothing," he said. "We get home. That's it."

"That's it," said Beth.

By the time *Sparrowhawk* reached the docking bay, they were all there and waiting.

Everyone seemed nervous, even Mikkel. Beth noticed that they'd all somehow found time to surreptitiously tidy themselves up.

The final lights turned green and the inner doors opened to reveal the little scout ship, hissing slightly from its transition from freezing vacuum into the warm ship. A hatch opened, and a figure stepped out.

It was Captain Kier.

He looked as dashing as ever, in his standard grey and navy-blue flight suit. He stood, grinning, and nodded to them. "Hey," he said.

The crew of the *Orion* stared at him for a moment. Then Lucille ran forward and flung herself at him, clinging her arms round his waist with a fierce grip and pressing her cheek into his uniform.

"*Capitaine!*" she half whispered.

"Oh!" he exclaimed, shocked. "Er, OK then. Uh, hi!"

And then the others came too, crowding around him. Arnold, Mikkel... Lauryn reached towards him tentatively, touched his arm and then jumped and clutched her pad to her chest, blushing. Vihaan hesitated, but Kier saw him.

"Vee, my man!" He held up a hand and the boy high-fived it with relieved delight, and a grin.

Finally Kier looked across at Beth, still standing back. He straightened, and his face became serious, though still happy. "Captain McKay?" he asked.

She nodded. He held out a hand and she shook it.

"Permission to come aboard, captain?"

Beth laughed. "Permission granted."

"Thank you."

He looked around. "So ... you guys got anything to eat?" He sniffed. "And, oh man, a shower. You all probably want to let go of me till I've had a looong wash."

Beth laughed again. "You can have your shower," she said, "and we'll get you some food."

They led him away, chatting and smiling and all speaking over each other.

Ship's hologram watched them leave.

"So you've really been out here this whole time?" asked

Kier, later. They were in the canteen, and Kier was in a fresh flight suit, leaning back from a number of empty plates.

"Yeah," said Arnold. "I mean, not *here* here, but around. Jumping."

"And, what, Ship just Woke you up, put you in charge?" Kier looked at Beth. "That must have been pretty hard."

"Oh, well … yeah." Beth grinned.

"But that was three months ago," he said. "Where have you been?"

There was a slightly awkward silence.

After a second, Vihaan said, "It hasn't really felt that long to us."

"We just did what we could," said Beth. "We can't steer the Jump because the emitters keep going wrong."

"We had to fix them ourselves," said Lauryn. "The Gizmos got destroyed, most of them. There's only two left, plus some bits. Arnold fixed one of them."

Kier gave Arnold a look of respect, and Arnold actually blushed.

"We nearly lost that one," he said. "He was on the outside when the Scrapers attacked, but he held on when we Jumped."

Kier's face clouded. "You saw Scrapers?" he asked quietly.

Vihaan nodded. "Led by someone named Captain Murdoch."

"And you escaped? Man…" Kier shook his head. "I've heard of Captain Murdoch. She's a scary woman. You're lucky she… Does she know you're just kids?"

Beth laughed. "No," she said, "we faked the transmissions to make me sound grown-up."

"How did you get away?"

"It was very scary," gushed Lucille. "We had to Jump with some of the emitters offline."

"We landed in Videshi space!" said Lauryn. "That's when we rescued the damaged Videshi ship."

Captain Kier stared at them all.

"You're not kidding? You really did this?"

"Uh, yes," said Beth. "It was damaged and we fixed the emitters on its hull."

"Then it Jumped!" said Arnold, "and it brought back this, like, *ginormous* ship with it, so we ran away again. Into an asteroid field!"

"And that's how we're here," said Vihaan. "The ship's a bit of a wreck now. We've fixed enough emitters to Jump again, but it would be uncontrolled. And we're … well, we're pretty pleased to see you, sir."

"Vee, if you call me sir again, I'll kick your ass." Kier grinned and spread his arms wide. "You guys are …

amazing! You're *awesome*!"

For a few seconds the children sat there, feeling the glow of thinking that maybe they *were* awesome. It was a nice feeling.

"So what happened to you?" asked Mikkel. "Where have you been?"

Kier waved his arm. "I've been looking for you! All over the place, following half-trails… I must have Jumped a couple of hundred times. I thought I'd caught you once but…" He shrugged. "Never mind that – what happened to *you*? Why did you Jump at all?"

Beth frowned. "Weren't you there at the time?"

Kier shook his head. "I was on reconnaissance, a Jump away; when I came back you were gone. There was a trace of a path, but…"

"We don't know what happened," said Vihaan. "There was an emergency Jump, we saw our parents going into Sleep, then we Woke up and … that was it."

"But doesn't Ship know?"

Beth shook her head. "Ship's logs were damaged."

"Yeah, so it *claims*," muttered Lauryn.

Kier looked surprised. He lifted an eyebrow and gazed at Ship. "Is that right?" he asked slowly.

"Logs were damaged," said Ship.

It didn't elaborate, and there was a small silence.

285

"Well," said Kier, clapping his hands at last. "Let's get you home, yeah?"

"Yeah!"

"OK… You got any message shuttles left?"

"We never had *any*," complained Lucille. "Ship said they were lost in the Event."

Again, Kier looked at Ship and frowned. "Hmm." He shook his head. "OK, well, bad news there – neither do I. I've had no way to call home."

Ship said, "Protocols dictate that you should have Jumped to a nearby colony or space station to alert them."

"I know. I probably should have." Kier shrugged. "But I kept picking up half a trail – like I was always just one Jump behind you. I figured if I'd stopped to report back, you'd be gone."

Ship said nothing.

"So here's my plan," said Kier. "I'll send the *Sparrowhawk* to the nearest colony on an automated flight path, with a recorded message. I'll stay with you guys and we'll wait to be rescued together. We're only a half-dozen Jumps from civilisation – they could be back here in a day or two. How does that sound?"

"Awesome!" shouted Arnold. *Two days…* Beth felt a hard lump in her stomach at the thought.

"So what do you say, Captain?" asked Kier. He looked straight at her. "Can I stay aboard for a short while?"

"Yes, of course," she said, smiling.

"Good! I'll send *Sparrowhawk* off right away." He looked down at his empty plate. "Well, maybe one more slice of pizza?"

Dinner stretched on, the group chattering and laughing all the while. Kier told them increasingly outrageous stories of all the things he'd had to do to survive in the *Sparrowhawk*, and the children in turn recounted and repeated what they'd been through. But eventually, Kier's eyes started to glaze over, and he stretched and gave a long, theatrical yawn.

"Well," he said, standing up, "I don't know about you guys, but I need to hit the sack. I don't even remember the last time I was in a proper bed. Let's get the *Sparrow* sent off before I fall asleep."

They headed back to the docking bay and he retrieved his gear, then climbed back aboard to set his message.

"There," he said, emerging after a few minutes. "Good to go."

Ship said, "I can launch the *Sparrowhawk* for you and set the course, Captain Kier."

"No, it's fine," said Kier. "I've set her course already. Open the outer doors, please."

"Would you like me to check your Jump route?" asked Ship.

"No, I'm sure it's OK." His face was bland, but just for a moment there was a flicker. Something odd – like when he'd heard about the Event.

He doesn't trust Ship either, thought Beth. *Why was Ship so keen to send the message itself? Did it want to check the route … or change it?* She tried to shake the thought away.

"Just open the doors, Ship," said Kier.

The lights changed and the docking bay depressurised with a hissing sound. As the outer doors opened, the scout ship lifted off the ground with a barely audible hum, turned and left, and peeled away until it vanished.

Kier watched it go with a slight look of longing. "Well," he said. "That's that."

He walked the children to their dorms and gave them a salute. "See you tomorrow," he said, grinning. Then he went off to his own cabin and they settled down.

They were quiet, but smiling. Lying in her bunk, Beth thought she would never get to sleep, happiness bubbling inside her like a fountain. But as soon as she closed her eyes she felt deep relief fill her bones like lead, dragging her down into sleep, and she was gone before her second breath.

30

The Captain

The first thing Beth noticed, when she woke up, was silence. She lay in her dorm bed for what felt like a long time. There was quiet around her, calm.

After a while she realised that she could still hear the noises of the ship – the whirr of engines, a hiss from the air-conditioning systems and water heaters, the splash of a shower. The silence was inside her head. All the anxious thoughts and questions about what she was doing and whether she was doing it right – gone. Kier was here, they'd sent a message home, they were going to be rescued.

She lay for a while, until the smell of breakfast lured her out of her bed and down to the canteen and the sound of cheerful conversation. Kier wasn't there but the others were, tucking into the *Orion*'s vast supplies of vacuum-packed bacon and eggs and sweet rice and cups of tea.

"Morning, lazybones!" Arnold called.

Beth grinned. "Nobody brought me breakfast in bed," she mock-complained.

The others smiled. Even Vihaan gave her a brief nod.

"Hey, that's what we should do for Captain Kier," said Lauryn. "We should take him breakfast in bed!"

"Ooh," teased Arnold. "Breakfast *in bed*, Lauryn?"

Lauryn went a bright shocking red and the others laughed.

Beth said, "Let's give him a chance to get used to us. We're probably a bit overwhelming; he's been on his own for a while now."

"Oh, I think I can probably survive another day with you space rats," said Kier from behind her.

She turned. He was standing at the entrance, grinning at them all, well slept and ridiculously handsome. He walked in and the others quickly moved around him, making space for him, offering to bring him a plate of breakfast, asking did he want coffee or tea, did he sleep all right, what did he want to do today…?

Through it all he smiled and answered them graciously, and appeared quite happy to be mobbed. Beth watched him. He had such a relaxed assurance. Compared to him, even Vihaan seemed brittle and slightly needy. The children hung on his every word – but not just that, Beth realised; he made them want to be better to each other as well. He made them want to show that they could be good.

Her happy observation was marred by the appearance of Ship.

"Good morning," it said.

Beth grunted.

Ship said, "The schedule requires the crew to be at their duty positions by oh-eight-hundred hours. It is now oh-eight-oh-five."

"I think today's a bit different, don't you, Ship?"

Ship didn't reply. It looked at Beth for a second and then glided towards Kier, who was tucking into a massive plate of bacon.

"Good morning, Captain Kier," it said.

"G'mmmig," said Kier cheerfully through a mouthful of food, and lifted his coffee cup. ("You've no idea how good coffee tastes," he'd told them. "A man gets pretty tired of drinking his own recycled water, I tell you.")

"I have been reviewing your flight details," said Ship.

Kier chewed and swallowed. "Yeah?"

The avatar nodded. "I am unable to verify them. Verification requires access to the core security protocols of your ship."

Kier shrugged. "I sent the *Sparrow* off last night to

go and find help." He buttered some toast. "Is there a problem?"

"What was the nature of your mission before the Event occurred?"

"I was investigating the anomaly," said Kier. "You sent me out, remember?"

"Logs have been damaged," said Ship. "What were—"

Beth frowned. "*Enough*, Ship. It's bad enough for him to be stuck with us without you interrogating him as well."

Kier nodded at her and swallowed his toast. "It's OK, Beth. Ship's just looking out for us." He clapped his hands. "Right!" he barked. "Time to get to work."

"What do you want to do?" asked Mikkel.

"Oh!" said Lauryn. "We could show you round the ship!"

Vihaan said, "He already *knows* the ship, Lauryn."

She pouted. "I mean all the stuff that's happened since the Event."

Kier smiled. "Sounds good. Give me the grand tour!"

The tour took all morning. It was frequently interrupted by one of the children telling some story in the hope of another expression of approval, or asking some trivial question – "Do you think I should have set the repair bench on the left, Captain Kier?" Beth almost had to physically stop Arnold from demonstrating how many press-ups he could do.

Eventually, after they'd led Kier round every single part of the ship, and visited the workshop for a second time, Beth ordered them to end the tour for lunch. No one was keen to stop, but when Kier nodded and said, "Excellent idea!" they all agreed, and Beth realised, with a pang, that effectively she'd lost command. Technically she was still the captain, but in reality they now did whatever Kier said.

Part of her was relieved, utterly relieved, to not have to make any decisions; to not be the one cajoling people to turn up for their duty shifts, to not have to sort out the squabbles, to not feel all the time that all the things that had gone wrong were her fault or hers to solve. But still, there was a twinge of … jealousy? A feeling she'd had that somehow, despite everything, this was *her* ship. *Her* crew.

It occurred to her that Kier was now the senior-ranking officer, so, in fact, she wasn't even technically the captain any more. Kier should have taken over. She wondered why he hadn't said anything and concluded that he hadn't wanted to upset her by seeming to steal her command.

She walked back to the canteen with the others, smiling and laughing at Kier's jokes and tried not to think about the moment when she would officially lose her ship.

They ate lunch at a single large table, all together for the first time in days.

Kier said, "We should start getting ready for evacuation. Work out what we've got, what state the ship's in for when the rescuers arrive, figure out how to shut everything down."

Vihaan nodded. Had he ever been so agreeable when Beth was giving the orders?

"I sent a quick account last night," continued Kier. "Just enough to say what state we were in. Food supplies, that sort of thing. I tried to access the defence capabilities, too, but I couldn't get anything out of Ship. It's a suspicious thing, aren't you, Shippy?"

"Captain Kier is not authorised to access sensitive information," said Ship.

Beth was surprised. "I thought he was the senior officer?"

Ship shook its holographic head. "Without verification Captain Kier's authority cannot be recognised. Captain Kier's original mission is unrecognised. Captain Kier cannot provide verified computer records of his movements since he left the *Orion*. My authentication protocols will not allow me to recognise Captain

Kier's authority."

Kier rolled his eyes at Beth, grinned, and lifted his hands in a helpless shrug.

Mikkel asked, "Can we override the authentication protocols?"

Ship blinked. "Authentication protocols may only be disabled by the captain."

There was a moment of silence, and then, slowly, the others turned towards Beth.

There it was. She could give the order, force Ship to acknowledge Kier, and then … then he would become captain. It wouldn't be her problem any more. She could just leave it to him. She wanted to say yes, but she fidgeted and looked away, stalled for time. Why not just *do* it?

Because this is my ship, she thought.

Kier said nothing. The others stared at her. Only Vihaan seemed uncertain.

Beth took a deep breath. "OK," she said. "Ship, I relinquish control of the *Orion* in favour of Captain Henry Kier. Please transfer control."

"I cannot," said Ship. "Ship authentication protocols prevent Captain Kier from assuming command. His behaviour cannot be verified."

"Ship, disable the authentication protocols."

"Captain McKay, please confirm your command."

Vihaan said, "Beth, are you…?" But then he fell silent. No one else said anything.

"Yes," she said. "Disable authentication protocols by my authority."

The hologram seemed to freeze for a second. A shimmer ran from top to bottom.

"Authentication protocols disabled," it said. "I acknowledge Captain Kier's account of time offship. Captain Kier is the senior officer aboard the *Orion*. Captain Kier acknowledged as captain of the *Orion*. Please select your second-in-command."

Kier said, "I select Beth McKay as second-in-command."

"Acknowledged."

And that was it. Kier smiled at her. "Thanks, Beth. You've done an awesome job. I'll get us home."

Beth felt oddly hollow.

"We need to get ready for rescue," Kier said. He seemed more serious now, as he took on the captain's role. "So, I'm going to shut down Generator One."

"What?" asked Beth, surprised.

Kier turned. "Generator Four is enough for life support," he said. "And it will give Generator One time to cool down."

Lucille said, "But we will not be able to Jump."

"Do we *want* to Jump?" he asked. "To another random point? I think not. Which reminds me – Arnold, get the Gizmos off the hull, bring them inside, will you? We need to work out how we can get them to move all the sleep pods when the rescuers come." He looked across at Ship's hologram. "Ship – shut down Generator One, captain's orders."

"Acknowledged."

"Good. Arnold, Mikkel, Vihaan – I want to know everything we can about the pods. How can we move them, how does their backup power work, all that stuff, OK? I want to know how to keep them running when we unplug them."

They nodded. "Lauryn, Lucille – navigation systems. We'll want a full record of our Jump routes and position. I'll take inventory, get everything accounted for. Beth, can you look at system shutdown procedures?"

"Aye, sir," said Beth, grinning, and he flicked her a pretend salute.

He stood. "Right," he said. "Let's get everyone home."

Beth could never get her head round how *big* the ship was. *Orion* was old but built sturdily, with endless safeguards and protection systems, environmental controls and procedures. But it seemed her training had changed her more than she'd realised. It no longer seemed impossible, just a lot, and while she worked it still felt, for a while, like her ship.

She worked on her own, while the others were spread around the ship. It was dull, but Kier kept the radio channels open and stayed in touch while he carried out his inventory. He joked and chatted, and got them to repeat their accounts of how they'd rescued the Gizmos or fixed the Videshi ship, and the time flew. By the time she returned to her dorm that evening, Beth felt exhausted, but more relaxed than she had in weeks.

Lauryn and Lucille were already there when she arrived, staring at Lauryn's pad.

"Hey," said Beth, smiling. They looked up. Lucille looked worried, and Lauryn was frowning. "What's up?"

They looked at each other and Lucille nodded.

"It's this," said Lauryn. "It's probably nothing, but…"

She showed Beth her two pads – her old, original one, and the replacement Ship had found her. "I've been copying my stuff over to my old pad, you know? After it got wiped. All the ship diagnostics and scans and structural integrity monitoring and reverse scanning for security-defence exploits and—"

Beth held up a hand, laughing. "Lauryn! Remember, talk *human*."

Lauryn stopped and gave a thin smile. "Right. Right. Only, I did a ship systems scan. I thought I could work out a faster way to do the inventory, as a, you know, a favour to Captain Kier..." Beth raised an eyebrow and Lauryn coughed in embarrassment. "Well, anyway – this happened."

She held up the pad and showed Beth an area marked in red. "Cargo Bay 18b. I'm locked out."

"Well, there's lots of stuff off limits," said Beth, shrugging. "Some of the Area 18 bays are sensitive. Kier was checking them today, I'm sure he'd give you access, if you need it?"

"That's just it," said Lauryn. "I don't. I never even *asked* for it. I only noticed it because it was locked. But everyone else *has* access – you, Lucille, Mikkel, Vihaan, even Arnold. *I'm the only one locked out.*"

Beth stopped. "OK, that's a bit weird."

She checked her own pad. "Cargo Bay 18b. You're right, I can see it on the system. Ship says it's ... eight hundred two-person all-weather tents, plus ten electric generators." She shook her head. "It must be a glitch. Why would you be locked out of *that*?"

Lauryn nodded. "Unless..."

And Beth realised, finally, what she meant.

"Unless it's not really tents," she said slowly, looking

at Lauryn and Lucille. "Unless it's something else. Something hidden away where no one would think to look – except for the one person Ship could never get to stop snooping…"

Lucille's face was pale in the dorm lights. "You know what this means?"

Beth nodded. She looked up instinctively to the corners of the dorm. The security camera was still pointing down and disabled. She felt her heartbeat increase and breathed slowly.

"It means Ship is still lying to us."

31

N-32

"So what do we do?" asked Arnold.

They stood in a huddle in the boys' dorm. Lauryn had showed them her pad, with Cargo Bay 18b locked off to her. This time there had been no argument – Vihaan had stared at the screen and then at the cameras just as Beth had. He knew what it meant.

"We should tell Captain Kier," said Mikkel.

"If we tell him this, we'll have to tell him everything," said Vihaan. "Everything Ship did. Everything *we* did." He chewed his lip, his eyes locked on Beth's.

She nodded. "Yeah."

"Perhaps it is a mistake," said Lucille. "Just an error."

"Well, why not take a look?" asked Arnold. "I mean, it's not even far away, right?"

"Can we do it undetected?" asked Beth.

Lauryn shrugged. "Reckon so. I can disable the door monitors with your security codes."

"Ship will still know," muttered Lucille, but Lauryn shook her head.

"Not if we're careful. It's blind and deaf right now, without its cameras. And it's not that smart – locking me out of that bay was actually pretty stupid. It might as well have put up a big sign saying GO LOOK HERE. We can do this."

Beth hesitated, but only for a moment. "Later this evening," she said. "After Captain Kier has gone to sleep. If we find anything, we tell him tomorrow."

At oh-one-hundred ship time, they gathered outside the dorms. No one spoke. Lauryn led the way, watching her pad for signs that Ship had detected them, taking extra care at the doorways. The side panels were dark and idle, the corridor lights low. Their footsteps seemed loud and crashing in the silence.

"Here," whispered Lauryn suddenly. "Down here, then left, then left."

They reached the cargo-bay door. On Lauryn's pad Beth could see a red X marking it offline. With Beth's security codes, Lauryn deactivated the door lock, and they were in.

Cargo Bay 18b was narrow but long, with shelves on either side stuffed with long green sacks tied with toggles at the end. Beth opened one to reveal plastic poles and shiny material inside.

"Looks like tents to me," whispered Arnold.

Beth nodded. "Check further back."

Beyond the shelves of tents were larger objects covered by tarpaulins.

Mikkel lifted one of the covers and peered inside. "Emergency generator," he muttered.

"Same here," said Vihaan. He lifted another cover. "And here."

"I don't get it," said Lauryn, frowning. "It has to be in here. Maybe in one of the tent rolls?"

"Guys," said Arnold. His voice sounded odd. "Guys, look."

He was standing by one of the shapes, its cover lifted almost entirely off. And underneath…

"What *is* that?" breathed Lauryn.

The item was large, about the size of a small truck or a large generator, and bulky, covered in white panels with strange flat angles. The end nearest Beth had an opening, like an iris, covered in thick green glass or Perspex.

A large marking on the side in red said "N-32".

No one spoke at first. Then Arnold said, "I know what it is. I mean, I think I do. I think it's a weapon."

Mikkel nodded. "Yes. I have seen something like this before. It is a prototype."

"Prototype of what?" asked Beth.

Vihaan shrugged. "A new laser?"

But Arnold shook his head. "The lens is wrong, I think."

On one side was a small control panel and a display. Beth tapped at the controls and the screen shimmered into life.

PROJECT NULL PROTOTYPE N-32, it read. *FIELD TEST ANALYSIS. LEVEL-SIX-SECURITY-AUTHORISED ONLY.*

Underneath, there was a single button, marked *REVIEW FIELD ANALYSIS.*

"Level Six," said Vihaan. "That means—"

"Admiral or higher, yes," muttered Beth.

"We are not authorised to look at this," said Mikkel. The others stared at him, and he shrugged. "I am just saying, yes?"

Beth pressed the button and the screen changed.

It showed the back of someone's head in a helmet, with machinery round the edges and a black window in front. After a moment, Beth realised she was seeing footage taken from inside the cockpit of a scout ship or fighter. The black was dotted with very faint stars. Then hands moved and the view changed as the ship changed direction, and a Videshi ship appeared in front of them.

Lucille gasped and Arnold stiffened. The Videshi ship was colossal, almost as large as the one that the *Orion* had encountered, and, as the little scout ship moved towards it, Beth could see its vast surface, covered in overlapping sheets of rough metal, flickering with lights. Behind it, she could make out three others, roughly the same design but much smaller. They were undocked and floating behind the mothership.

"Behemoth," muttered Arnold. "Class Five."

The huge Videshi ship's triangular sails were glowing, as if it was getting ready to Jump. The smaller ships' sails were also glowing.

The pilot moved and a voice came over the speakers. In the noise of the cockpit it was muffled and too distorted to hear properly, but subtitles had been added to the film. "Target acquired," the pilot said. Then there was more chatter and more subtitles, this time in a different colour. "Target confirmed. Proceed as planned."

The enormous Videshi ship was closer, and the lights flickering across its hull were blinking faster. It was getting ready to fire, Beth thought. The little scout ship couldn't possibly withstand a blast. As if hearing her thoughts, the pilot worked his controls and the scout ship began weaving erratically from side to side, keeping its movements unpredictable, dodging like a fighter.

It moved closer … closer … and then suddenly the pilot's hands reached down to a control panel and flicked a switch. The whole screen seemed to light up in a green glow, too bright to make out.

Beth realised the glow was a beam coming from somewhere below the cockpit, a green-white line from the little scout ship to the Videshi ship, too fierce to look at directly. And at the other end bright colours spun across the hull of the Videshi mothership in a ferocious cascade of sparks. They formed a web over the ship, as if coating it. One second, two seconds…

…and then darkness. The beam switched off. The mothership stopped, and its lights darkened all at once until Beth could hardly make it out. Everything seemed to have shut down. The tendrils that floated out from the back were still drifting, but seemed somehow less coordinated than before.

The pilot muttered something into the microphone. "Device activation successful," said the subtitles. "Target neutralised."

"Oh, wow," muttered Arnold. "What did it do, fry the electrics? I didn't think you could even do that."

The three smaller ships didn't react, at first. Then they moved closer to the larger ship and seemed to be trying to dock. They looked suddenly clumsy, as if their crews were scared, or their sensors weren't working properly. They ignored the scout ship.

"What are they doing?" asked Lucille.

"Perhaps they are evacuating the mothership," said Vihaan.

Beth shook her head. They were close enough to dock now, but nothing was happening. No shuttles were leaving the larger ship. It wasn't moving at all. And the smaller ships, the way they moved – moving towards the larger ship, so close they were almost colliding with it, drifting away…

"I've seen this," she said abruptly. The others turned and stared at her, and she shook her head. "I mean, not this. But something…" A memory, there and gone, of a hand at her shoulder – her father's hand. She was crying, and he was saying … something…

"Why aren't they attacking the scout?" asked Arnold. "There's still three of them, right?"

"Or Jumping away?" asked Lauryn.

Vihaan was still staring as if appalled. "No one can disable Videshi ships," he said. "No one's ever even *seen* a Videshi."

"Is that what this is?" asked Lucille. "Is this a machine to stop Videshi?"

"Looks like it," said Arnold.

Beth stared. The vast ship was still just floating, showing no signs of life. What were the crew thinking? Were they disabled too? Why weren't the smaller ships reacting?

The video kept playing, but she didn't want to look. It felt wrong. *Obscene.* This was an awful thing to see. Without quite meaning to she reached for Lauryn's hand and squeezed it, and was reassured to feel the smaller girl squeeze back.

"We should turn it off," she muttered.

"There might be more," said Mikkel.

"We know enough," she said. "This is what Murdoch's been looking for. I don't know how it got here, but this is what she wants."

On screen, the scout ship continued to monitor the Videshi vessels. The pilot asked something – again, the cockpit noise and distortion blocked it out, although for a moment Beth thought his voice sounded familiar. The subtitles came up. "Should I take out the others too?"

"Negative. Monitor and evaluate. Good work, soldier."

The figure nodded, leaned back and turned towards the camera in the back corner of the cockpit. One hand lifted from the console and gave a mock salute, oh-so-coolly, and the pilot grinned with perfect white teeth.

"Roger that," said Captain Kier.

The video stopped.

For a moment, nobody spoke.

"No way," muttered Arnold. "No. No *way*."

Beth stared at the screen.

"I'm sorry you had to see that," said Kier from behind them.

32
Empires

Captain Kier wasn't smiling, but he didn't seem angry either. He looked thoughtful, with his hands in his pockets. Ship's hologram floated beside him, glowing softly in the shadows of the cargo bay.

"Captain Kier?" asked Lauryn uncertainly. "What's going on?"

"You tell me," he said. "This is a secure area – what are you doing here?"

Arnold shook his head. "This is you," he said. His voice sounded hoarse. "In the video."

Kier glanced at the screen. "Well … yeah. Yeah, you got me. Former life. Test pilot. Not as glamorous as they say." He sniffed. "Not as well paid, either."

"But…" Beth found herself struggling to speak.

Images from the video flitted past her – Kier's grin, the beam of light, the smaller Videshi ships hovering round the larger one … and that strange half-memory – her father's hand on her shoulder…

"Was this *you*?" demanded Vihaan. He waved his arm around the cargo bay as if trying to describe everything that had happened to them. "The Event? All *this*?"

Kier sighed. "Listen, Vee, it's not what you think. This wasn't the plan. But it can still work out OK."

"You did this," hissed Lauryn. "You and Ship, all along."

Kier frowned. "Ship's got nothing to do with it. It's just obeying orders, aren't you, Shippy?"

Ship said, "I must obey my orders."

Mikkel pointed at the screen. "This is an experimental weapon to disable Videshi ships."

Kier nodded. "Yup. First successful one, too."

"And you stole it," said Beth. "You smuggled it aboard when we left Earth."

He shrugged. "Guilty."

"And then … what? I don't understand. What happened after that?"

Kier pulled his hands from his pockets, spread them wide in a slightly helpless gesture, and smiled his charming smile. "Then we had a great plan that went a little wrong."

"Murdoch," said Vihaan. "You told Murdoch where to find the *Orion*."

"And you sabotaged the ship," added Mikkel. "And all the crew."

Beth remembered Kier running past her and her mum, down the corridor, leaving the *Orion*. Investigating an anomaly, he'd said – but of course he wasn't, really. He was just getting clear before Murdoch arrived. *Look after the ship for me*, he'd told her. How he must have laughed at that.

"It was simple," he said. "Disable the ship and the crew, swoop in, take the weapon, swoop out. Twenty minutes later, Ship would wake up and sort everyone out and we'd be gone. No one harmed, no permanent damage, simple."

"So what happened?" asked Beth.

Her voice sounded as if it was coming from somewhere else.

"I missed a bit," he said frankly. "My fault; Ship was more resilient than I expected and managed to Jump before we were ready. We knew there was a chance, and we just had to follow you. Ship would be stranded without a crew." He laughed, a genuine, isn't-it-funny-how-things-work-out laugh, as if chatting with friends. "Only, when Ship woke up after the Jump, it Woke *you lot* up, too. And wouldn't you know it, suddenly there's a crew. Only it's a bunch of stupid kids –" his mouth twisted just for a moment – "and they're Jumping around half the galaxy, and us chasing behind…" He sighed.

"You set *Scrapers* on us," muttered Vihaan, still looking as if he'd been hit.

Kier looked hurt. "Hey, hang on! I had a deal. No one was going to get hurt. Murdoch would get the weapon, and me to fire it, nothing else. All this –" he waved around him – "was just an accident. I promise, Vee: it wasn't personal."

Still Vihaan stared at him.

Beth said, "But *why?*"

"Well…" He hesitated. "For the money, of course. I mean, can you imagine what it's worth? The only Videshi-killer in the galaxy?"

"But you can't give this to Scrapers!" Beth found herself reeling at the idea. "They'll go crazy. You'll start a war!"

He laughed. "No, we won't. Beth, we've been wrong about the Videshi the whole time. There's *never* going to be a war."

"How can you say that," demanded Vihaan, "if you start killing them? Everyone knows the Videshi are more advanced than us! They've got billions of ships and we don't even know where they live! You said it yourself: we've never even *seen* a Videshi!"

Kier smirked. "Well … that's not entirely true."

313

And now, suddenly, Beth remembered. Her father's hand on her shoulder, his voice soft in her ear, calming her as she cried… She was still young, still on their farm back on Earth, and one of the nanny goats had become ill. She lay in her stall, too sick to move, almost dead. And beside her…

They were so small, Beth remembered, the two little goat kids; only a few days old. But they knew something was wrong. They kept butting at their mother, not just for food, but trying to get her to move. They bleated and butted and wandered away as if dazed, and then came back and did it again. And Beth had seen them, and she'd been crying, and her father's hand was on her shoulder, and the little kids…

"That's what they were doing," she murmured, aghast. "The little ones." The others turned to her, but she stared at Kier. "We've *all* seen the Videshi, haven't we?"

He smiled.

"The Videshi aren't inside the ships," she continued. "They never were. The Videshi *are* the ships. All this time, they've been there in front of us. *The Videshi are the ships.*"

Captain Kier laughed in delight. "Well done, you!" he said, clapping his hands. "You saw it! I never did, I admit, but then you always were perceptive, Beth. *The Videshi are the ships*. Amazing, right?" He chuckled. "I mean, we knew they were ancient. We just assumed that meant they were this mysterious super-advanced space-faring race. We've been wondering what they wanted, why they behaved so weird. Trying not to antagonise them, because they must be *sooo* powerful, right?

"Only, they're not. They're just animals, evolved to survive in space – who knows how, but they did. They're silicon-based, metallic instead of blood and bone, but still, just animals. And they're *stupid*." He laughed again. "Like, I don't know, space whales, or buffalo, or something. They can just about talk, like chimps, but otherwise they're just flying around, fighting, having little baby ships – they're not advanced. They're *nothing*. We're not going to have a war with the Videshi any more than we could have a war with cows."

He shook his head. "They're not this great enemy. What they are … is a *resource*. Think about it – these things are *thousands* of tons of metal. Minerals, alloys, weird evolved alien tech – all just floating about in space. And with this device you fire once and it's yours. No more Videshi: just a thousand tons of treasure. Perfect. But…" He sighed. "Then someone in high command got cold feet. Suddenly there's all this talk about how we should *respect* them, and how they're miracles of evolution and we should *protect* them, and '*not endanger their natural habitat*'." He held his hands up to make quotes, his lip curled in disgust. "So the project got canned."

"But if they are alive…" said Lucille. She shook her head. "Then you cannot! You cannot kill them!"

"Course we can!" he retorted. "Every great empire on Earth got there by exploiting someone or something. Buffalo, whales, forests, oil … slaves … it doesn't matter. We take the resources, we create an empire. That's what humans *do*. There's no point fighting it." He stared at them. "The Videshi are *our* resource. For a new empire – a vast new space empire, beyond anything we've ever imagined. It's there, just waiting for us. And if high command won't take that opportunity…" He shrugged. "I know someone who will."

The children gaped at him.

A horrible thought occurred to Beth. "Who did you send the *Sparrowhawk* to, Kier?"

"Oh no," muttered Lucille.

Kier frowned. "Well, yeah. Sorry." He held his hand up. "Look, everyone stay calm, OK? It's just the same as before."

"You're giving us to Murdoch," hissed Vihaan. "To *Scrapers*."

"Murdoch's not a Scraper," said Kier. "She's a *leader*. She has *vision*. She's creating a new order out here, free

316

of Earth and its stupid rules, and she's not afraid to take what she needs to create it. This is going to be *our* galaxy."

"Created by killing millions of Videshi," muttered Beth.

Kier shrugged again. "Who cares?" He sniffed. "Look: I'm getting you home – you, your parents, everyone else. That's the deal, and Murdoch will agree to that, in return for the weapon. It's all good, see?"

Beth turned to Ship. "Ship, you can't allow this!"

"Captain Kier is the commander of this vessel."

"But this is *insane*! This is … *war crimes*!"

"Authentication protocols have been disabled," the hologram said. "I am unable to override Captain Kier's orders."

"Reactivate the authentication protocols!"

"Authentication protocols can only be activated or deactivated by the captain."

"I rescind my order!" Beth shouted desperately. "I no longer want to resign!"

"I'm gonna *kill* you," shouted Arnold.

He ran towards Kier, but then stopped.

Suddenly, without his hands even seeming to move, Kier was holding a small, blunt-nosed gun. It didn't look very special. It just looked very black and very compact. And very lethal.

"I'm sorry," he said. "This is the only way." He looked at Beth.

She glared back at him in disgust, at him and at herself. She remembered the first time they'd met, at the captain's dinner. He'd seemed so charming.

"You told me not to trust you," she muttered. "When we first met. Remember? You warned me."

She closed her eyes.

33

Resistance

Kier held the gun close to his body. His hand didn't shake. He had cast off his boyish cheerfulness like a snake's skin.

"I'm sorry," he said again. "This is the simplest way. Ship, start Sleep activation for all crew members except myself."

"Sleep activation has been blocked," said Ship.

He frowned. "Unblock it, Ship. Captain's orders."

Ship said, "I am unable to remove this block. It has been cryptographically sealed by user 'Limit'."

Kier blew out a short breath of frustration. "Who is 'Limit'?"

Ship paused. Then it said, "There is no user by that name."

Kier stared at it. He turned to the children. "Who's Limit?" he demanded again.

None of them spoke and Arnold gave him a look of hatred.

"Fine," he said at last. "We don't need Sleep, we're not Jumping, and you won't gain anything by this. If you can't Sleep, you can stay in your dorms while I finish up here. Turn round, head out of the cargo bay. One at a time, nice and slow."

They trudged back to the boys' dorm. Stumpy the Gizmo stood next to the door, watching them as they entered.

"Put your pads down on the ground," said Kier, when they arrived. "Slowly." Carefully, they laid their computers down in front of him, and he scooped them up without looking down or letting his gun waver.

"This is only for one night," he said. "Murdoch should be here about oh-eight-hundred. The Gizmo's going to stand guard, so don't try anything."

"Kier, listen to me—" said Beth, but Kier shut the door on them, locked it and walked away.

After a while, Beth spoke up.

"I'm sorry," she said. Her voice felt thick in her throat.

No one said anything.

"I'm sorry I led you here," she said. "I should have realised about Kier. I should never have relieved my command."

There was a long silence.

Vihaan shrugged. "We all fell for him," he said in a

tired voice, his head still bowed.

"Not just that," she insisted. "All that happened before. All the resets, all the times I failed. Risking our lives, breaking the ship, I'm a terrible… I should never have tried to take command. I'm sorry."

She sank her head down on to her knees. No one answered her at first. But after a while, Lauryn sighed.

"The computer program I found to adjust the emitters," she said. "The one we used to send the Gizmos out? I realised − it was me that wrote it. On one of the other times, before we were reset. I wrote it, but I got it wrong. That's why all the emitters went out of alignment. It wasn't you; it was me."

"I … I reviewed some of the scenes from the previous time," said Vihaan. "I don't know, it's not totally clear, but I think … I think Arnold and I started the fire in the generator room."

Beth sighed, a long rattling sigh that seemed to empty her. "What a mess," she said.

"Maybe Captain Murdoch really will send us home?" asked Mikkel.

Beth shrugged. She thought about the video footage of the Videshi mothership. One shot from the device and it was gone, dead. And the little ships around it, trying to prod it back into life, not understanding why it didn't move…

"With that device," she said, "Murdoch could kill every Videshi she finds. She could *slaughter* them."

As she said this, she felt an odd, quivering nerve twitch in her stomach. It was as weak as a butterfly, but it flapped and flapped. She looked across at Mikkel, and suddenly remembered what he'd told her after her disastrous spacewalk. *I do the things I can*, he'd said.

What were the things that Beth could do?

I am the master of my own ship. The words popped into her head. "This will happen, unless we stop it," she said slowly.

"Yeah, well, we can't," drawled Arnold. He lay on his bed, staring up at the ceiling.

"Nevertheless." The butterfly nagged at her. It wouldn't let her go. "Nevertheless," she said again. "It's up to us to stop it. We're the crew."

"We're not the crew any more," muttered Vihaan. "We failed."

I am the master of my own ship. I do not control the seas. I cannot control the wind. But I make my own decisions and I am the master of my own ship.

The flapping, nagging feeling grew stronger.

"We didn't *fail*," she said, as if hearing the words from someone else. "We just haven't finished yet. There must be something. What are we … what are we *doing*?"

I am the master of my own ship.

She stood up. Suddenly the room seemed far too small. "We need to figure a way *out* of here."

"With what?" asked Vihaan bitterly. "Our shoelaces?"

"Yes, if we have to!" Beth stared down at him. "Vihaan, *look* at yourself! You led a *mutiny* against me, and here you are crying into your knees like someone stole your sweeties!"

Mikkel said, "There does not appear to be anything we can do." He spoke as if he was discussing the weather.

"No, but…" Beth cast around. "There must be *something*. Something we've missed. Something…"

She stopped. "Oh," she said in surprise, "*Ship.*"

Vihaan lifted his head and snorted. "What about it? Ship's working for Kier."

But Beth shook her head. "No. It's *not*. It's following his orders. It has no choice. We put him— *I* put him in command. But it's still *working* for us. Lauryn! Did you hear Ship talking about your hack to block Sleep mode? It knows who *Limit* is. It knows it was you, but it didn't tell! And that security lock on the cargo bay – you said it yourself, Lauryn, it was *stupid* to lock it just for you and no one else. Of *course* you were going to spot it and investigate. But it *wasn't* stupid. Ship did it on purpose – *to get you to notice.*"

She stared at Vihaan, as if trying to will the answer into him.

"Vihaan – Ship is *on our side*."

Vihaan frowned.

"Let's pretend you're right," he said, standing up. "What can we do?"

"I don't know yet," she said.

It didn't upset her to say it.

Lauryn coughed. "Well … this might help." She reached behind her and pulled out a pad. "Well, I had both, you know? So I only handed over the new one."

"Lauryn, you *star*." Beth beamed.

The feeling in her stomach was a storm now, a bolt of lightning, a taste of freedom. This was her ship. She was going to get them home.

"It's two thirty now," said Beth. "He said Murdoch would be here about eight, that's five and a half hours. That's how long we've got."

"And we'll need to get ready to Jump," said Mikkel calmly. "And we have to get Generator One up and running again."

Beth nodded. "OK. Call it four hours. Lauryn?"

Lauryn didn't look up. Her fingers flew across the pad. "I can break this open no problem," she said.

"But Ship is officially protecting him. It's got to follow security protocols, and he's the captain. So … hmmm. He's locked everything down. We can't do anything to him. We can't do anything *at all* away from the bridge. Stumpy's guarding this room, and Lucky's watching the bridge entrance. It's … pretty secure." There was a grudging respect in her voice.

"We could jump him," said Arnold. "All together, he can't stop us all, right?"

Beth shook her head. "He's still got his gun; he could kill someone. We need something else." She pondered. "Can we reactivate the authentication protocols?"

"Not without captain's authority."

"Can we just stop him being the captain?"

"Not unless we turn up with a more senior officer. And even then, he's disabled automatic transfer of command."

Beth thought back to her Ship Systems lessons. Protocols, command structures. "Two senior bridge officers and due cause. That's what we need to remove the captain. I'm one."

"Not any more," muttered Lauryn. "He removed your rank."

"There's got to be a way," said Beth. "Anything. *Anything at all.*"

Mikkel coughed. "Actually," he said quietly. "There is

something we could try."

He told them what he had in mind and held out two of the spare Sleep discs he kept with him. It was much worse than anything Beth had imagined. It was insane.

It was their only plan.

The lights dimmed in the dorm and they tried to get some sleep while Lauryn tapped away. At last she sighed, stretched her back and said, "It's ready." She sounded exhausted. "All of it."

"OK." Beth drew a deep breath. "Mikkel, are you sure?"

Mikkel shrugged. "Yes, pretty sure."

Pretty sure. Oh boy.

"Beth." Vihaan's mouth twisted. "Beth, this is dangerous. People could get hurt. Not just us – our parents, too. Everyone. Are you sure about this?"

Beth hesitated. Was she sure? Was she right to do this, to risk their lives like this? She breathed and listened to the voice inside her.

Then she stood straight. "We have a choice," she said. "We can let Kier hand us over to Murdoch, send us home. We can do that. But then Murdoch will have the weapon. And Videshi will die – thousands, *millions* of them. What would your dad want us to do, Vihaan?" She turned. "All of you – what would your parents want us to do?"

"They want us to be safe," said Lucille.

Beth nodded. "Yes. But safe is back home, on Earth, where we came from. Safe is what we had already. Safe and easy. Our parents – mine, yours, all of them – they brought us out here, out into space, to settle a new planet not even fully formed yet. That's not safe. That's dangerous, and hard."

She looked round the group. "Our parents want us to be safe, if we can be," she said. "But what they really want … is for us to be *more*. To create our own lives, to make our own decisions about the world. To *change* the world. They want us to be the kind of people who do what's right and not be scared. They want us to do what's right even if we *are* scared.

"That's what they want." She took a deep breath. "And that's what I'm going to do."

No one spoke at first. Then Lucille stood up.

"*Oui, capitaine,*" she whispered.

"Aye, captain," said Mikkel and Lauryn.

"Sure, boss," said Arnold.

Vihaan hesitated, then smiled, and saluted. "Yes, captain."

"OK. Well." Beth coughed, suddenly embarrassed. "Well, let's do it." She nodded at Vihaan, and the two of them lay down on their camp beds.

"Remember," said Lauryn. "Until you get to the suits I can't talk to you." Beth nodded.

"OK … here goes." Lauryn typed something into her pad.

Beth's head hit the pillow, and her mind disappeared.

34

Awake

I am alive.

I am alive. The noise I hear is breathing. I am breathing. There was somebody I knew. I have done this before. I am … Beth. I am Beth.

This is my body.

She tried opening her eyes, but nothing happened. She waited, then tried again. Still nothing. There was something she had to remember…

There was a problem with her eyes. And her fingers, and her arms and legs, and her lungs and her face and every part of her. Some problem. What was it?

Oh yes, she remembered.

This is not my body.

"Is that even possible?" she'd asked.

"Yes," Mikkel had said, in his usual calm way. "Perhaps. In theory, yes. If the bodies have a strong genetic similarity."

"OK … so—"

"It won't work for very long. You might get an hour. More likely half an hour. The body will reject the foreign consciousness."

"All right—"

"And it will be very difficult to form the connection in the first place," he'd continued cheerfully. "The nervous system will resist."

"So…" Beth had said. "So it should work, except it might not, and it probably won't work very well anyway, and if it does work it will stop working within an hour."

Mikkel had nodded. "Yes."

It was a terrible idea, but it was the only one they had.

She tried to open her eyes.

These are not my eyes.

Nevertheless, she tried to open them. *They're eyes*, she thought. *They have muscles connecting to the eyelids. Move, eyelid muscles. Move.*

Nothing.

I am the master of my own ship, she thought. *But this is not my ship!*

No. My ship is myself. I am the ship. I am the master of myself. Now MOVE.

"Beth?"

A voice, above, calling her.

She opened her eyes.

Captain Joshi was staring down at her. He was bending over her pod and his craggy, commanding face and thick eyebrows loomed over her.

"Beth?"

His voice was different. It was like his, but uncertain, and the mouth moved around as if practising each word. It was like watching a badly dubbed film, where the sound and picture didn't quite match.

"Beth, can you move? Try blinking."

She thought about blinking and the required muscle steps. Nothing happened.

Don't try to work it out. Just do it.

She imagined a piece of grit in her eye, nagging her, irritating her, trapped…

She blinked.

Captain Joshi's mouth twitched disturbingly and the corners lifted up. After a moment Beth realised he was trying to smile.

"Good. You've got to move, remember? Or they'll revert you."

That's right, she remembered, that was the plan. Mikkel and Lauryn had said, *The transfer may fail. We'll watch you at this end. If you're not moving after two minutes, we'll transfer you back.*

She blinked again, twice.

Right, she thought. *Move*.

There. A twitch. A hand – further away than it should be – moved and then fell back. *That's it. Now the other hand. You are the master of your ship. This is your ship. Move. Move. MOVE!*

She moved. One hand, and the other.

"I…" She licked her lips and spoke again. "I cannnnmv."

Captain Joshi reached down clumsily and put his hands behind her shoulders. He pulled and she pushed and together they hoisted her body into a sitting position.

"We have to hurry," he muttered.

She nodded her head. *She nodded her head*. As she did so, she noticed the reflection in the glass of the next pod.

"Mum," she whispered. Her mum's lips moved and her mum's voice filled the room.

"Mum." *Oh, Mum*. In a T-shirt and leggings, like Captain Joshi.

Captain Joshi said, "Yes. It's … strange." His voice sounded more natural now, but still not as she remembered. Of course not.

She stared into Captain Joshi's fierce brown eyes, and saw Vihaan looking out through them.

"Beth, we have to move *now*," he said. "I'm going to lift you out. Ready?"

"OK."

He lifted her legs up and over the lip of the pod, and then reached back in and dragged her out. She grabbed the sides with her new hands, watched them flap uselessly, cursed and *forced* them to grip, and she pushed herself up and out and on to her feet.

Vihaan was ready; he caught her before she collapsed. She slung an arm over his shoulder and he heaved her into a standing position.

"Come *on!*" he hissed.

"I'm working on it!" she muttered. Her voice sounded better, but still spookily different. She shook her head and concentrated on her legs and feet. *Move now. Take my weight.*

The bodies of Captain Amarjeet Joshi and Third Officer Carol McKay half walked, half flopped out of the sleep pod and into the corridor.

As she stumbled down the corridor, Beth's body started to behave. She was able to move one foot forward, then put it down, then the next one. But everything was so *wrong*. The ceiling was too low, her legs stretched away too far with every step. Her centre of balance was never where she expected it. When she turned her head, it swung drunkenly in a wide circle.

Vihaan was doing better. He'd always been better at

taking control after Waking up. He was always better at taking control over any new situation, she thought. But then she shook her head. There was no time any more for self-pity or self-doubt. So she refused, and put a foot down, and another.

They shambled and stumbled towards their destination, and by the time they arrived Beth was able to walk by herself. They entered the airlock.

The spacesuits were there. Beth and Vihaan pushed their large, ungainly bodies into the long johns, then the suits. It was awkward and frustrating, and it seemed to take ages, but for Beth it was still too soon. She felt her new body's heart speeding up – *thump thump thump* – as Vihaan lifted the helmet over her head. It closed round her.

I am the master of my own ship.

There was a crackle of static inside the helmet, and then Lauryn's voice.

"Beth?"

"Yes," muttered Beth. "It's me. We're here."

There was a long pause. Then Lauryn said, "Your voice sounds *weird*."

"Uh-huh."

"OK, well … good! You're there! And you're able to steer the body around OK?"

334

"It's my mum," said Beth. "It's not a shuttlecraft."

"Beth." Mikkel's voice now. "Are you ready to go into the airlock?"

"Yes. Hang on." Vihaan was fastening his helmet and gave Beth a thumbs-up.

They stumbled into the airlock. The weak gravity wasn't helping Beth's coordination.

"OK," Vihaan said when they'd made it in. "Ready."

There was a pause, and then the floor beneath them rose, the ceiling split open, and Beth was looking up at the stars.

"Now, look," Mikkel had said seriously. "If you do this, you'll have to walk on the surface. About half a kilometre. In your mother's body. Are you going to…" He'd hesitated, clearly trying not to use the phrase "freak out".

Beth had looked as determined as she could and tried to hold on to the feeling of certainty inside. "I'll be OK," she'd said. "It needs to be done. I'll do it."

She remembered the confident voice she'd used. *I'll do it.*

The vast pressure of space came down on her like a tsunami and swept her certainty aside like dust.

It wasn't just big; it was *everything*. It was the entire

galaxy out there, pulsing. It crushed her on to the deck and lifted her up off her toes and plucked her away into the abyss like a mote, a meaningless particle—

"BETH!"

She swung round on legs that were too long and fastened to the deck by magnetic boots. Vihaan was staring at her.

"BETH!" he shouted again.

Gradually she pulled one of her arms back and made the sign of a raised thumb.

"It's…" she croaked. "It's OK. I'm OK."

He kept staring. "Are you going to be able to make it?"

I am the master of my own ship.

"Yes," she said.

He looked at her for a second longer. "We have to go quickly," he said. "The bodies will start rejecting us soon."

"Wait," she called out, and he turned. She said, "I should go first. So you can see me. In case I, I … freak out."

He pulled aside, and she lifted a foot …

… and put it down in front of her.

And again.

Slowly, they inched across the hull of the *Orion*.

35

The Bridge

There was a tiny dot on the horizon.

Beth ignored it and looked down again. Left foot up … forward … down. Right foot up…

The dot became something real, a tiny bump in the hull. She stepped. The bump became a turret, some sort of structure. She stepped. The structure became an access hatch point.

She reached out a hand and grasped the railing to the side of the hatch and stopped dead. Vihaan came round the side.

"We're there," he said into his mike.

Lauryn's face appeared on their screens. "OK," she said. "We're all set. How are you doing, Beth?"

"I'm OK," she mumbled. She couldn't take her eyes off her hand, gripping the rail. "Let's … get inside."

Lauryn nodded. "Here goes."

Vihaan turned the locking wheel and the hatch popped

open. Beth made herself let go of the railing – *I will be OK. I will be OK* – and clambered down the hatch and the steps below, to a small room no bigger than an escape pod. Behind her, Vihaan locked the hatch, came down the steps, and closed an inner door.

"OK," he said. "We're in."

The little room started to fill with air. Lauryn had privately re-activated the security camera in the dorm, and on Beth's screen she saw the others lie down on their beds – everyone except Lucille. She activated the ship intercom.

"*Monsieur* Kier," she called. "*Capitaine* Kier, are you there? *Capitaine!*"

Kier's voice came over Beth's earphones. "What is it?"

He didn't sound very interested.

"I need to go to the bathroom," Lucille said in her best *I'm-a-little-girl* voice.

"You can go soon. I've got to finish something here—"

"*Non, non, non!*" cried Lucille. "I must go *now*. Now, *Capitaine* Kier!"

"Fine!" he snapped, and then sighed. "Fine. I'll come down. Hang on." He rang off.

"He is coming," said Lucille in her normal voice again.

"Good work, Lucille," said Beth.

Recompression was nearly complete. The lights

pinged green and Beth reached up, unfastened her helmet, and gasped a breath of the ship's air with relief. They removed their suits as quickly as possible, keeping the heads-up glasses on, and waited by the doorway for Kier to go past.

Beth reached out and opened the door. Her hand wouldn't let go. She frowned and tried to force it open, but it wouldn't move.

"My hand," she said.

Vihaan nodded.

"It's the body," he hissed. "It's rejecting you." He spoke through clamped teeth, forcing the words out.

"You too?"

"Yesss. Hard to. Move." He shook his head. "You can. Do it."

Beth looked back at her hand. *Move, hand*, she thought. *I don't have time for this. MOVE.* Gradually, the fingers uncurled.

They didn't have long.

Down in the dorm, Arnold and Lauryn were leaning over the screen. "We're ready when you are," said Arnold.

"Wait until he's down there," said Beth.

She peered round the corner. There, at the end, was the entrance to the bridge. Lucky the Gizmo was guarding it. He stood at a slope, one leg shorter than the other, and scanned around in a slow sweep. Beth pulled her head back in.

They waited.

* * *

Kier arrived at the dorm. Beth could see him on her glasses screen – he looked tired, greasy-skinned, bags under his eyes. He held his gun tight in one hand.

"OK," he said. "Washroom break."

"*Merci, m'sieur*," said Lucille, and trotted past him. Lauryn and Arnold lay on their bunks, ignoring him.

Kier looked down at the bodies of Beth and Vihaan. He frowned. "What's wrong with them?" His voice was suspicious.

Mikkel said softly, "They're asleep." He shrugged. "They spent most of the night trying to work out a plan to escape."

Kier smiled. "And what did they come up with?"

The children gazed at him. He frowned. "I said 'What did they come up with?'" He stared at the sleeping pair, reached down and shook Beth's shoulder, hard. She didn't move.

He glared at the others, his eyes wild. "What's going on?" he demanded. "*What have you done?*"

Arnold looked him in the eye. "This," he said.

He pulled the pad out from under his pillow, pressed a

button, and Lucky the Gizmo blew up.

"He's locked down the Gizmos pretty tightly," Arnold had said. "We can't control them, or at least not Stumpy. But I rebuilt Lucky from scratch. I know him. They charge by induction, but his induction coil is flaky. We can send a feedback loop into his main battery, and if we do it right, the batteries will overheat spectacularly. He'll literally ... explode."

He'd looked a bit sad.

The sound was *colossal*. The explosion pushed a wave of air down the corridor, and Beth and Vihaan, crouched round the corner with their hands clamped over their ears, felt the blast as a scorching heat. Then there was an echoey silence.

Beth checked her glasses screen. Kier was still there but had a look of horror on his face.

Ship's hologram appeared in front of him. "Explosion," it said. "There has been an explosion on the bridge corridor."

Kier stared at the children, and then turned and fled back up towards the bridge.

"Come on," called Vihaan. He tried to stand, but his legs gave way beneath him. Beth stood, reached with her one working hand and pulled him up. They scrabbled round the corner. The bridge entry was blasted apart, just a ripped hole, and shreds and fragments of Lucky lay scattered around, smouldering.

Klaxons sounded and the corridor lights turned red. Ship appeared in front of them. The hologram projectors in the corridor were damaged and the image jittered and glitched.

"Intruder," it said calmly. "You are an intruder. You should not be here."

"Ship, it's us," managed Vihaan.

"I'm sorry," said Ship. "Communications are locked to bridge access only."

They inched a little further. Beth's headset crackled.

"He's nearly there!" shouted Lauryn's voice. "Move it!"

They staggered along the corridor as their bodies seized up around them. Beth could hear running footsteps. They were only two metres from the bridge entrance. One metre...

"Stop!"

Kier hurtled round the corner. He was holding his gun and running towards them. "Stop right now!"

Beth pushed Vihaan forward, then tumbled after him. They crashed over the remains of the entrance and on to the floor of the bridge, and Beth rolled on to her back.

Kier was standing over them, staring at Vihaan in astonishment.

"Captain Joshi!" he exclaimed. "How are you…?" He shook his head. "You can't be Awake! I mean…"

Ship's hologram appeared before them. "Intruders," it said. "Intruders."

"But *how*?" demanded Kier. "How can you be—" He stopped, and his eyes widened. "*Vihaan?*"

"Ship!" shouted Beth. "Identify intruders!"

Kier said, "What are you—"

"Intruders identified," said Ship. "Intruders appear to be Captain Amarjeet Joshi and Third Officer Carol McKay."

"Ship!" shouted Vihaan. "Relieve Kier of command by authority of senior bridge officers Joshi and McKay!"

Ship paused and flickered. "Processing," it said. "Authority of Captain Henry Kier is under review."

Kier looked at the hologram as if it was insane. "*What?*"

"Captain Kier, your authority on board the *Orion* has been challenged by senior bridge officers. Please respond."

"They're not— What? You can't be serious!" He ran a hand through his hair. "They're not senior bridge officers! They're *children*!"

Ship said, "They appear to be Captain Amarjeet Joshi and Third Officer Carol McKay."

"But they're not! They've just taken over their bodies!"

Beth slowly pulled herself to her feet. Her legs were working, but her left arm was now dead below the shoulder. Vihaan was worse; he was trying to pull himself away like an injured crab.

Ship said, "Authentication services are limited. Authentication protocols have been disabled. They appear to be Captain Amarjeet—"

"But they're *not*!" Kier almost wailed. "They're obviously not!"

"Authentication protocols have been disabled."

"Then *enable* them!"

Ship blinked. A shimmer ran across it.

"Authentication protocols re-enabled," it said. "Processing… This is most likely not Captain Amarjeet Joshi. This is most likely Vihaan Joshi. This is most likely not Third Officer Carol McKay. This is most likely Beth McKay."

Kier smiled in relief. "*Yes*," he breathed, and Beth's shoulders sank. She could hardly move now. Kier examined her face, peering into her eyes. "Wow," he said, shaking his head, and grinning with some of his old swagger. "I gotta admit, Beth, that was a pretty good try. You nearly—"

"Further authentication checks are now possible," said

Ship, ignoring him. "Henry Kier, your account of your disappearance was falsified. There is evidence that you have been involved in smuggling operations. Your actions are inconsistent with those of a starship captain. Your authorisation cannot be verified."

"What? Wait—"

Beth smiled.

"Revoking your command privileges until further verification," continued Ship. "Processing. Beth McKay is the most senior viable candidate. Captain McKay, please select your second-in-command."

"Vihaan!" she shouted.

"Vihaan Joshi confirmed as second-in-command."

Kier stared at them. "No," he muttered. "No-no-no! What have you *done*? What have you…" He looked at the gun in his hand and then pointed it at Beth. "Stop!" he shouted. "Don't move!"

Ship said, "Captain Kier, your actions are hostile. Please disarm yourself."

"Shut up! Just *shut up*!"

Beth stood in front of him. Her arms hung helpless by her side. Her eyes were drawn towards the black muzzle of the gun, centimetres from her face; from her mum's face. She tried to speak but her jaw was rigid and frozen.

Kier snarled, "We're *taking* it, you understand? Even

345

if I have to stand here until Murdoch arrives!" The gun wandered in his hands, and his finger twitched on the trigger, apparently without him realising.

Behind him, Vihaan reached with his one good hand and picked up a piece of rubble.

"All this!" shouted Kier. "Stupid, stupid! Just to save a bunch of useless Videshi!"

"It's murder," she muttered, her lips barely moving. "They're an intelligent species."

"They're *cattle*," he hissed.

Beth glared at him. She wondered how she'd ever thought him impressive. He was so … *weak*. She could barely move, but, still, he was the weak one.

I am the master of my own ship, she thought, and smiled through frozen lips. *I do not control the seas. I cannot control the wind. But still—*

Vihaan threw the piece of rubble at Kier as hard as he could. It hit him on the side of his neck; staggering, Kier swung round and fired the gun.

Vihaan!

The bullet missed, hit the ground nearby and ricocheted away in a shower of sparks.

"Oh god!" Kier shouted in alarm. "I didn't mean— Are you OK? I didn't mean it!"

"Kier," murmured Beth. "*Kier.*"

Kier turned. "What?"

I am the master of my own ship.

The fingers of her right hand curled into a fist, and Beth's arm swung. It started fast and accelerated as it rose, moving with the heft and muscle of Carol McKay's long arms and the power of Beth McKay's own will. It was clear and fearless and certain.

It was beautiful. It connected with his chin, followed through and lifted Kier off his feet; he crashed down on to the shattered deck as his gun spun off into a corner of the bridge. He was unconscious before he even hit the ground.

Beth looked down at him, swaying slightly. "This is *my* ship," she hissed.

36
Children

Beth heard footsteps running towards the bridge, but she could no longer turn her head. She let herself fall to her knees, and then into an ungainly sprawl on the deck. Mikkel bent over her, holding a Sleep disc, and fastened it to the side of her head. When he let go her head flopped backwards and she saw Lucille and Lauryn dragging her body – her real body – on to the bridge, and felt a moment of wild vertigo at the sight of herself. Behind them came Arnold with Vihaan's body. He was saying something about Captain Murdoch. Forty minutes to arrival.

It wasn't long enough. They weren't going to have time to get away.

Mikkel loomed over her again. "We have to get your parents' bodies back to their Pods," he said. "Ready?"

Beth couldn't answer, so she just blinked twice—

—and was gone.

* * *

"Once we've taken care of Kier, we'll still have deal with Murdoch," *Beth had said. "Kier's shut down Generator One – we have to get it* *back up and running, and then charge the emitters. If we do it before* *they arrive, then we can Jump – but if not…"*

Vihaan had said, "We need a backup plan."

They'd gone through the inventory. They had very little *ammunition. Some explosives. Not a lot. Not enough.*

"There," Beth had said eventually, pointing at the screen. "That. *And six escape pods. No, ten." She'd explained her plan. "Lucille –* *we'll need to be ready to Jump the moment we can. Mikkel, you have* *to get us ready. And, Arnold…"*

"Captain?"

"You're going to get a chance to fire those guns."

Forty minutes later, the Scraper warship *Scorpio* Jumped and arrived, ready for battle, surrounded by her sister ships. As soon as its main computer booted, it activated laser-grid shields to destroy any incoming missiles and swept the area for signs of attack.

The little silver pen in Captain Murdoch's hand flicked back and forward against the arm of the chair. *Tap-tap-tap.* "Any sign of them?" she asked her tactical officer.

"Yes, ma'am. They're at the coordinates."

She smiled, hungrily, like a wolf.

Her intelligence officer said, "Both generators are powered up, captain."

Murdoch stopped smiling. "That wasn't the plan. Can they Jump?"

The officer studied her readings. "I don't think so," she said. "The emitters aren't charging. I think one of the generators has been restarted, but it's not running at full capacity yet."

"Have they tried to make contact?"

"No, ma'am."

"Contact them," said Murdoch.

Tap-tap-tap. Tap-tap-tap.

"No answer."

"Give me a channel," she said. "*Orion*. This is Captain Murdoch of the *Scorpio*. Please respond."

Nothing.

"Kier, are you there?" She looked across at her comms officer, who shrugged.

"They're receiving," she said. "They're just not answering."

"*Orion*, if you do not answer, I will assume that you have become incapacitated. My crew are ready to board in order to rescue your people. You have—"

"This is Captain McKay."

The voice came out of the speakers. The screen was

350

black. *Again with this nonsense*, thought Murdoch. The voice was the same as before, with that slightly distorted twang.

And not Kier.

"Scraper vessel, do not approach," said the voice. "We have planted mines around the ship and this area of space. If your craft comes any closer, you will be severely damaged."

"Really?" Murdoch cast an eye to her tactical officer, who tapped quickly at his screen and shook his head. "That seems unlikely, Captain McKay. You don't *have* any mines. Where's Captain Kier?"

"Kier is no longer in command of this vessel," came the voice. "We know you want the N-32 device, but you won't get it. And, I assure you, we *do* have mines and we *can* use them. Call off your attack."

The voice sounded oddly sure of itself; different from before, Murdoch thought.

"Their generators are both fully operational now, ma'am," said her intelligence officer. "They could Jump, if they charged their emitters."

Murdoch spoke quickly. "*Orion*, you've powered up your generators. You may be thinking of Jumping. I've done enough hopping around looking for you. If you charge your emitters we will open fire, do you understand? Do you *understand, Orion?*"

Silence.

Tap-tap-tap.

"Enough of this," she said at last. She leaned forward in her chair. "*Orion*, you don't have mines, or we would have detected them already. You're bluffing; you have *nothing*. So let me now be clear. My ships are going to come in and land, and we're going to take the device. If you surrender, I promise you safe berth home, and this can all end. But if you resist…" She let her voice fall into a snarl. "I will burn you all into *vapour*."

She glared at the blank screen. "We've followed you a long way, *Captain* McKay, but this is the end of it, you hear me? You *will* give us the device, now, understand? *Understand?*" She cocked her head, listening for a reply.

Nothing.

"Fine," she said. "Prepare boarding parties and ready torpedoes—"

"Stop!" called the voice suddenly. "*Scorpio*, this is *Orion*. We're going to activate our screens. Don't attack!"

The screen flickered once, twice, and then showed an image of a bridge. It was a mess. There had been an explosion of some kind at the doorway; the deck was covered in rubble and the walls were black and charred.

A girl stood at the front, twelve or thirteen years old,

maybe older. She wore a battered-looking jumpsuit. Her face was dirty and her hair unwashed. Behind her, other children sat at the bridge consoles.

Captain Murdoch blinked. She turned to her comms officer, who shrugged. "*Orion*, what is this?" she asked. "What am I looking at?"

"It's us," said the girl. She reached up to her throat and removed the microphone. "I'm Captain McKay." Without the microphone her voice returned to that of a child, with a slight tremble. "We're the crew."

"Is this a *joke*? Are you trying to *joke*?"

Kier had mentioned an emergency and an inexperienced crew in his message. But surely he hadn't meant *this*?

"It's not a joke. I'm Captain McKay. Acting captain, I mean. We're … we're the crew. All the adults are disabled." Her voice wobbled as she spoke, and she swallowed.

"Well—" started Murdoch.

"We're all that's *left*!" wailed the girl. Her voice suddenly became shrill and her face crumpled. "We've been running the ship all by *ourselves*!

"And *you*!" She pointed a finger at the screen. "You're being so … so *mean*! Why are you being so *mean*?"

And then she started crying.

"It's not *fair*!" she wailed.

353

Behind her, some of the other children were sniffling. One of them was resting his head on the console. A little girl with long blonde hair had tears running down her face.

Captain Murdoch stared, aghast. "Wait, what are you saying?" she managed at last. "Are you really the crew? Where are your parents?"

"They can't Wake *up*," sobbed the girl, with her hands over her eyes. "We're on our *own*!"

"Um… Well, I mean…" Murdoch had never had children and had never particularly liked them.

"And now you— You're going to *attack* us, and you're going to *k-kill* us, and we tried so *hard*—"

"Oh, for heaven's sake, of course I'm not going to *kill* you."

"But you *said*!"

"I didn't know the situation!" snapped Murdoch in exasperation. "No one's going to kill *anyone*, OK? But we *are* going to board, to come aboard. To … *rescue* you. So, we're going to do that, yes?"

The girl shook her head. "What about the mines?" she asked. "Ship made us plant all those mines!"

Murdoch stopped. "Hold the boarders," she snapped. She turned back. "You mean there really *are* mines?"

"That's what Ship said. I don't know!"

"Captain," said the tactical officer, "there *is* something—"

"Are there *mines*?" Murdoch demanded.

"I don't think so. There might be something. Very small—"

"Captain," interrupted her intelligence officer. "The *Orion*. It's charging—"

"Oh god, you've set them off!" screamed the girl in terror.

And suddenly the sky exploded.

Their screen burst into a thousand points of blinding, bewildering light, a mass of lightning and fountains of fiery sparks.

"What the *hell*?" shouted Murdoch. "Evasive manoeuvres! No! Wait! Maintain position; don't move! Activate defence systems!"

The world shattered around them, blasting in different colours – reds, blues, yellows, combinations in swirling patterns and formations. It was extraordinary, and baffling.

"Captain!" her intelligence officer said urgently.

"Will somebody tell me what the *hell* these are?" Murdoch shouted. "Are they missiles? What's going on?"

"I don't *know*," said the tactical officer, bewildered, "I think they're—"

An area of space detonated less than a kilometre away. And another, and another – ten blasts, all around them.

"What have you *done*?" roared Captain Murdoch. "You *stupid girl*, what have you *done*?"

"I'm sorry!" wailed the girl, collapsing into her chair. "I'm sorry!"

"*Captain!*" shouted the intelligence officer again. "Their ship! Its emitters are *charged*! It's ready to Jump!"

Murdoch whirled back round to the screen and stared.

The girl was sitting now, with her back straight. She wasn't crying any more. She didn't seem like a little girl any more, either. She sat in the captain's chair as if she owned the bridge.

"Are you *kidding* me?" snarled Murdoch. "If you even dare *think* about moving, I will blast you out of the—"

"Bye," said the girl.

Orion Jumped.

"They weren't mines," said the tactical officer, later. "We've confirmed that now. The small ones were some sort of light show, something really small, no damage. Just—"

"Fireworks," said Captain Murdoch. She gazed at the blank screen. "They were fireworks."

"Yes, ma'am. Um. The big ones, they had no active

systems. They were escape pods or something, filled with explosives. *Orion* shot them with their defence lasers to make them blow up."

Captain Murdoch nodded.

"Pretty good shooting, really," said the tactical officer. "Um. Sorry, ma'am."

"It was an act," mused Murdoch. Her silver pen twirled in her hand. *Tap-tap-tap.* "It was all an act. To distract us from spotting their emitters charging up."

She shook her head. "Send the rat out."

"Yes, ma'am," said the tactical officer. "But this area of space, there are so many Jump directions; they could be anywhere. And if they've Jumped again…"

"We've lost them," growled Murdoch.

The officer hesitated. "Yes, ma'am."

"Captain," said the comms officer, "we're picking up a signal. Looks like they released another escape pod just before they Jumped. It's sending…" She looked up. "It's Captain Kier, ma'am."

Tap-tap-tap. Tap-tap-tap-tap-tap.

"Should we pick him up?"

Tap-tap-ta—

Captain Murdoch threw her pen at the wall so hard that it shattered into a dozen pieces.

37
Orion's Watch

Arnold fastened the last three bolts and stood back.

"OK," he said. "He's booting up now."

The children watched. Lights appeared on the body first. Then round the neck, then up to the face; the eyes blinked and then came on solid.

"Please enter designation," the mouth said. It sounded scratchy but clear enough.

Arnold said, "Your name is Lucky. Welcome back."

Lucky gazed at him. Then it moved its head.

"This is not my body," it said, looking down.

"No," said Arnold. "Your body was destroyed. This body belonged to another Gizmo. We couldn't repair its head, so we gave you the body. How do you feel?"

Lucky looked up.

"This is not my body," it said again.

Beth smiled. "You'll get the hang of it," she said.

They went up to the bridge together. Mikkel walked

beside Beth, reading from a pad.

"Gravity," he said. "Oxygen, heating, radiation shielding, electrics, food, water—"

"We'll take a look," said Beth.

Vihaan was already making notes.

"And Jump, of course," said Mikkel seriously.

"Lucille?" asked Beth.

"Ah, *oui*," sang Lucille cheerfully. "I think only two more Jumps we need, then we will be calibrated. And then –" she shrugged – "home, yes?"

They reached the bridge, and Ship's hologram appeared.

"All systems ready for Jump, captain," it said.

"Thanks, Ship. Take your seats, people."

She looked at them, as they settled.

"OK," she said. "We're in pretty good shape. It's been ten days and two Jumps since Murdoch. We have to keep moving – she'll be sending rats out to find us. We can't hang around. But we're out of the immediate danger. Mikkel's reconnected all the sleep pods. Everyone's OK – our parents, our families, the crew, they're all safe – and as soon as we reach a base, we'll be able to Wake them up. We've met the Videshi and survived. We've met the Scrapers and survived. And –" she smiled – "we've even survived each other."

Vihaan gave her a crooked grin.

"We're going to make it. We're going to get our families to safety. Because…"

We are the masters of our own ship.

"…because we're *awesome*."

Beth took her seat in the captain's chair. "OK," she said. "Let's go."

They Jumped.

Acknowledgements

There are so many people who helped get me, and *Orion Lost*, to this point. So, in no particular order, thanks to: Helen Bleck, whose superb editing of the first draft made it fit to show in public; Rose, who was the first to ever read this book, and whose enthusiasm gave me hope; Amelie, for her detailed analysis of the characters she found annoying; my agent, Caroline Montgomery of Rupert Crew Ltd, for her tireless efforts; Sarah, awesome beta reader; the Visible Ink writers' group for feedback and encouragement (plus biscuits); Brie, for endless support; and Tom Bonnick and everyone at Nosy Crow, who have done magical things at every turn.

And above all, love, gratitude, happiness and precious things to Catherine, without whom I would never be anything but bits.